Shenandoah

Shenandoah

Ally Blue

Samhain Publishing, Ltd.
577 Mulberry Street, Suite 1520
Macon, GA 31201
www.samhainpublishing.com

Shenandoah
Copyright © 2011 by Ally Blue
Print ISBN: 978-1-60928-179-3
Digital ISBN: 978-1-60928-166-3

Editing by Sasha Knight
Cover by Kanaxa

First Samhain Publishing, Ltd. electronic publication: August 2010
First Samhain Publishing, Ltd. print publication: July 2011

Dedication

This is for all the readers out there, over at the Fiction With Friction blog and elsewhere, who stepped up to the proverbial plate and helped me out every single time I showed up on the interwebs scratching my head over medicinal plants and various other aspects of life without modern conveniences. My idea of roughing it is staying at the Super 8 and my knowledge of plants pretty much consists of "plant" vs. "not plant", so your help has been absolutely invaluable with this butt-kicker of a book. Thank you. A million times, thank you.

Any inaccuracies in this text are the fault of yours truly and not the folks who so generously lent me their time and knowledge.

Chapter One

Dragon's knife opened the last grime-crusted belly from groin to rib cage. The fevered light died in the big man's eyes and he crumpled to the ground in a puddle of his own bloody intestines.

Bear eyed the five motionless bodies strewn among the weeds. "That's the last one, for now."

"You think there's more?"

"I know there are. Several times this number, most likely. They always move in groups." Large groups, generally, to counter the strength of the Packs that protected every tribe. Lifting his arm, Bear mopped sweat from his brow with a relatively clean patch of sleeve. "They scatter during the evening, capture who they can, then gather at some prearranged spot after dark for their fun. I think we were supposed to be part of the night's entertainment."

A muscle twitched in Dragon's jaw. He crouched to clean his gory knife on the back of the dead man's shirt. "The light'll be gone in another hour or so. We should find a safe place to spend the night."

Squatting beside the nearest corpse, Bear wiped the blood off his stone blade as best he could using the man's pants. The vest the dead man wore looked suspiciously like cured human skin, which did nothing to make Bear feel better about the area where he and Dragon now found themselves. He scanned the silent ruins looming like jagged black teeth against the red-orange of the sunset sky. "There's no safe place in this part of Char."

Dragon stood, raking a stray lock of his waist-length braid out of his eyes. "Then we need to find the most secure spot we can." He looked down at his blood-splattered clothes with a frown. "And we need to bathe, if we can find water. We'll draw every animal and nightfeeder for miles around if we don't."

"Yeah." Keeping his knife in a loose grip, Bear studied the pattern of crumbling buildings around him. It had been two years since he'd last walked through this section of Char, on the patrol where his Pack had lost Rabbit, but the area ought not to have changed much. "There used to be a cistern nearby where water collected when it rained. We can bathe there."

"It ought to be full after the storm we had last night." Something scuttled through the vines climbing the metal skeleton of what had once been a building a stone's throw away. Dragon tensed, knife whipping up. He relaxed when a rat emerged and raced off into the lengthening shadows. "Can you find it again?"

"I think so. There's several pretty intact buildings near it where we can spend the night and be as safe as it's possible to be around here." Bear eyed the sky. "Which is good, because we're running out of time."

Dragon glanced up. His expression didn't change, but Bear saw the apprehension behind the hardness in his eyes. They'd known each other less than three days, but Bear could already read Dragon better than he'd ever been able to read any of his Pack Brothers, with the possible exception of Lynx. If he tried hard enough, he sometimes felt like he could look straight into Dragon's mind. And he knew Dragon saw him just as clearly.

The knowledge left him feeling exposed in a way he never had before, a way he couldn't quite explain even to himself. It was terrifying and exhilarating, and he wouldn't have traded that feeling for all the wine in the Carwin Tribe Council's stores.

A quick sniff of the air told Bear the only creatures close by right now were rats, squirrels and a couple of wild cats crouching in the ruins. Throwing caution momentarily to the winds, he strode forward, curled a hand around the back of Dragon's neck and kissed him hard. Dragon grunted in surprise, but his mouth opened anyway to let Bear's tongue in. The hand not clutching his knife grabbed Bear's ass in a bruising grip.

Electricity jolted up Bear's spine. In spite of the constant danger he and Dragon now faced—danger he knew wouldn't let up until they were well clear of Char—he didn't regret leaving the Carwin Tribe and his Pack for Dragon. His heart and his gut told him he'd made the right decision.

"We'll be okay," Bear murmured when the kiss broke. "Come on."

The corners of Dragon's mouth quirked upward. He slipped out of Bear's embrace and they moved through the weeds together, Bear scanning for landmarks while Dragon kept an eye out for any signs of people. Carwin Tribe members never strayed this far from their walled city, not even the Pack unless they were on a special patrol. Therefore, any human beings other than the two of them were enemies.

Like the five men lying dead in the dirt behind them. Bear had encountered their type before. Bloodthirsty butchers who'd slice a man open just for the pleasure of watching him die, then skin him and clothe themselves in his flesh. String his teeth together for a necklace.

Bear preferred the nightfeeders. At least they only killed for food.

Not that these nomadic bands were above a little cannibalism. The bodies and bones they left behind showed tooth marks often as not.

The glint of light on water caught the corner of Bear's eye. He swiveled toward the gap in the buildings to his right at the same time as Dragon. "There. I see it."

Dragon nodded. "You smell anything?"

Bear sniffed the air. Greenery, damp earth, animal dung, charred wood. People had been here, but not in the last day or two. "Nothing to worry about. I'll go first. You watch my back."

They moved through the narrow space together, knives at the ready. The remnants of last night's rain pattered from the vines overhead onto Bear's shoulders. After the day's oppressive, muggy heat, the cool drizzle felt good.

A few seconds later they emerged from the shadows into a wide clearing surrounded by some of the tallest, best preserved structures in the ancient city. Not a breath of breeze stirred the soupy air. In the middle of the clearing, ringed by a tangle of wildflowers, tall grasses and young trees, sat a large, rectangular stone cistern full to its knee-high brim with water. The sunset reflected dazzling orange off the flat liquid expanse. Bear squinted against the glare.

"What's that thing in the middle?" Dragon asked as they approached the cistern. "It looks like a plant, but it isn't, is it?"

Bear eyed the piece of stone rising from the center of the water like an enormous petrified blossom. "No, it's not a plant." When they reached the edge of the cistern, he motioned to Dragon to skirt the perimeter in one direction while he did the same the other way. "It's part of the cistern. Made by the people of Char, before the Change. Other than that, I don't know. Nobody does."

Dragon turned away and began his circuit of the reservoir without another word, but not before Bear caught the spark of excitement in his eyes.

Bear waited until he'd put his back to Dragon to let the threatening grin tug up the corners of his mouth. He knew exactly what Dragon was thinking, because he was thinking the same thing. Knowing someone besides himself who could be catapulted into old-world daydreams by a mysterious hunk of stone gave him a strange, warm sensation in the pit of his stomach. He liked it.

They met on the far side. Rising on tiptoe, Dragon kissed the corner of Bear's mouth. "Everything still smell clear?"

Bear nodded. "No nightfeeders hiding nearby. No nomads, either. They'll be here, though, eventually."

Dragon's gaze darted sideways toward the blackened, stone-ringed circle in the grass a few paces away. "Theirs?"

"There's no way to tell for sure, but I think so. Carwin Tribe Pack doesn't camp in the open inside Char, and nightfeeders don't build fires."

"Maybe we should find another place to hole up for the night."

"There isn't anyplace as secure as the buildings in this area. Besides, we don't really have time to hunt for another spot."

Dragon's brow creased with a frown, but he nodded. "You're right. We'll just have to hope they won't sniff us out."

"We'll make sure they don't." Bear wormed his knife-free hand into the back of Dragon's pants, one finger sliding into the sweat-slick crease between his buttocks. "What about you? Did you see anything?" He'd learned the previous night—their first night in the Char ruins—that Dragon possessed incredibly keen vision. In fact, his night vision was nearly as good as Lynx's, and Bear had never known anyone who could see in the dark as well as his former Pack Brother.

Dragon shook his head. "I looked in between all the buildings. Nothing." He hissed and clutched at Bear's shoulder when Bear's finger pressed against his hole. "Great Mother, Bear. Here? Really?"

"No." Regretfully, Bear pulled his hand out of Dragon's pants. "But I wish we could. I want you."

Dragon peered up at Bear with a heat that turned his simmering desire into a sharp, aching need. Unable to help himself, he fisted his hand in Dragon's hair and took a deep, rough kiss. Even as their tongues curled around each other and Dragon moaned into his mouth, Bear's senses remained on high alert, and Dragon's body twitched in his grip, ready to jump at the slightest sign of danger.

After a few searing seconds, Dragon pushed him away. "Let's get clean and find a good spot to spend the night. Then I'll suck your cock until you forget your own name."

Bear's prick, already half-hard, jerked and swelled. He grinned. Dragon grinned back, gray eyes glittering, and Bear laughed out loud. "I'll get the soap."

Later, in the deepest part of the night, Dragon sat staring past their small fire into the yawning blackness while Bear slept. Dragon had only managed a couple of restless hours before the noises woke him. The sounds wound their way in from outside, along the clogged passageways he and Bear had navigated after their bath, down the steps, through the remains of the thick metal door and past the detritus of the centuries to the corner of the huge, high-ceilinged room they'd picked as their hiding place for the night. Yells, whoops, coarse laughter, songs with words Dragon was glad he couldn't make out.

When the screams started, he'd stopped trying to sleep through it and taken his turn at watch early. With food and water plentiful as they'd been so far, he could stay awake two days at a stretch easily enough. He'd sleep when they got free of this Mother-forsaken city.

He turned to study Bear, who lay curled naked on top of a thick blanket—they'd hung their wet clothes over a hunk of rusted metal near the fire to dry—with one arm folded beneath his head and his other hand curled around the handle of his knife. His face, hard and dangerous when waking, softened in sleep to the point where Dragon had to resist the urge to stroke his cheek. Though no one would ever mistake Bear for anything but a warrior, he looked young and almost sweet with his features slack and eyes closed.

Great Mother, those eyes. Dragon had never seen anything quite like them—amber-gold, with a gaze sharper than the best-honed blade. Sharp enough to cut a man to the bone.

Or make him come without being touched. Dragon smiled, remembering how a single heated look from Bear had him spilling his seed on the forest floor without a hand being laid on him not so long ago. And that look was definitely what had sent him over the edge. Not the big, muscular body, or the strong hands gripping Lynx's hips while they fucked, or even the cock so long and thick it was just this side of scary. No, the thing that did it for Dragon was those eyes that pierced him straight to his core.

After a lifetime of the twisted games it took to stay alive in the Ashe Tribe, honesty had become his greatest aphrodisiac. Bear radiated honesty like heat from a wildfire.

Something shuffled through the debris in the darkness on the far side of the room. A small, stealthy sound, barely audible through the muffled shrieks from outside. It came from the corner opposite the room's only exit. Dragon rose to his feet, every nerve on edge. He and Bear had made sure the room was empty and the door barricaded before settling in for the night, but complacency never got you anything but killed.

He picked up the makeshift torch Bear had prepared earlier in case they needed it and lit it in the flames. Moving with a silence born of long practice, he skirted the fire and paced toward the source of the noise, among the cluster of rusted, half-collapsed metal shelves against the far wall. He darted a glance around the periphery of the torchlight as he went. Nothing stirred in the stillness. Behind him, Bear's breathing remained deep and even.

That, more than anything else, eased some of the tension from Dragon's shoulders. Char and the surrounding area were Bear's territory. He'd been here with his Pack often enough to know its dangers well. If the noise Dragon had heard belonged to anything more threatening than a small animal, the sound and smell of it should have woken Bear instantly.

When he reached the edge of the shelves, Dragon heard the sound again. It was clearer this time—the soft skitter of tiny feet on a surface mired in centuries of decay. Keeping his knife at the ready, Dragon leaned around one of the more solid old shelves and peered into the narrow space between it and its neighbor. The firelight caught the frantic kick of pale little paws and the whip of a tail as a blur of dark fur bolted through a crack in the wall.

Dragon let out a near-silent laugh. A rat. Just a rat, scavenging for food. A few hours ago he would've wondered what self-respecting rat would look for food *here*, of all places, but no longer. The remains of campfires dotted the floor of this room and several others in this building. The newest was no more than ten or twelve days old. Evidently a lot of travelers used this place, though he and Bear had both been baffled as to *who* those travelers might be. Bear swore his Pack had only ever made camp in this building a few times, and not recently.

With no need to stay here, Dragon pivoted to go back to the fire. A pattern of black lines caught the tail of his eye from between the sagging metal racks. Curious, he walked around the corner of the last shelf and thrust the torch forward. Cobwebs draped the space between the shelf and the wall. A large black spider scurried up a piece of metal and out of sight into the shadows. Under the dust and dangling silk threads, the torchlight revealed crooked words scrawled in what looked like charcoal across a fair chunk of the wall.

Writing. Oh, Mother.

Dragon's pulse picked up. In the Ashe Tribe, only the tribal Mother and the council were allowed to read and write. Anyone else caught doing so got thirty lashes for their trouble. Dragon had almost got caught once himself, sneaking his single, precious book out of the Pack camp and into the forest to read in rare and blessed privacy. He'd hidden the book in its old spot beneath the cupboard in his parents' house that night. He hadn't held a book or seen a single written word since.

Heart pounding, Dragon paced closer. He swept the cobwebs out of the way and brushed the film of dust from the stone wall. His eyes watered as he traced the words with his fingertips, sounding them out in his head one by one. Scowling, he scrubbed the moisture from his cheeks. *Damn dust.*

Outside, a woman's wail cut off with an abruptness that spoke of a swiftly slit throat. An ominous silence descended. Dragon glanced in the direction of the door just in time to see Bear round the end of the shelves.

"That was the last one," Bear said unnecessarily. "They'll settle down and be quiet now, most likely. I'll take watch, if you want, so you can get some sleep." He frowned at the wall. "Is that writing?"

"Yes." Dragon turned his attention back to the smudged and untidy markings. "I'll stay on watch. I don't think I could sleep anyway. The more quiet they are up there, the more I'd lie awake waiting for them to come looking for some other way to entertain themselves. We're good, but we can't fight off all of them at once. There's too many."

Bear shuffled over, wrapped an arm around Dragon's waist from behind and squeezed. "They're done for the night. They'll butcher the bodies for whatever food they want and leave the

17

rest for the scavengers." Ducking his head, he planted a kiss behind Dragon's ear. "Come back to the fire. Sleep for a while. I'll keep watch."

The warmth of Bear's body and the low rumble of his voice made Dragon want things other than sleep. But he couldn't ignore the tale scribbled in charcoal on this ancient wall. It might've started with a dream—probably had—but that didn't change the fact that it had apparently ended with the same journey he and Bear had set for themselves. Ignoring it would be stupid, if only because of the possibility that they might be following the trail of one of Bear's tribe-mates.

Dragon tilted his head sideways, baring his neck for Bear's wandering kisses. "The night before last you told me you can't read, but your Brother Rabbit could. Are the Carwin Tribe members allowed to read and write, then? Or is it just the Pack?"

"No, anyone can. Most people just don't see the need." Bear nipped at the spot where Dragon's neck joined his shoulder, tearing a soft sound from him. "Mmmm. Come back to the fire, and let's fuck. I bet you'll sleep after that."

Dragon's knees nearly buckled when Bear's hand slipped between his naked thighs to cup his balls. "So. *Oh.* Are there many in Carwin like Rabbit?" He leaned back against Bear's big, solid body, legs planted apart, and rocked his swelling groin against Bear's palm. Great Mother, it felt good.

"Mother Rose. Most of the council. A few others." Taking his hand out from between Dragon's legs, Bear cupped his chin, tipped his head back and peered into his eyes. "Why are you asking all these questions? Is it because of that writing on the wall?"

Dragon nodded. "I was trying to figure out who might've put it there. And when. I thought someone from Carwin would be the most likely."

"Probably. Although no one comes into Char but Pack, and

we only ever patrolled this area a few times." Bear cast a thoughtful glance at the wall. "I don't think it could've been here more than a few weeks. The charcoal wouldn't've lasted much longer than that. What does it say?"

Resting his free hand over Bear's where it laid on his belly, Dragon read the words aloud. "las nite, The Grate Mother taked my speret on a jurny. we flied over char, way up over the beldins, then over the river an th big grass, an up in the mowtin far off, to an vally hided away. She say its name like Shenandoah, i rite the leters jus like it how She tell me. it wuz so buteful, an all th peepls wuz so happy. im goin ther just lik how The Mother show me. if you is redden this, you go to. north, at the mowtin. ever body ar hapy at Shenandoah."

In the quiet following the end of the strange passage, Dragon heard Bear's breath quicken. The arm around Dragon's waist cinched tighter. He twisted to look up at Bear. The sudden light in his eyes told Dragon his suspicions had been right.

He clutched Bear's wrist. "Bear?"

"The Great Mother took my Brother Raccoon on a spirit journey once, during a drought. Our main spring had dried up. The next day, he followed Her directions and led us straight to a new water source."

"So you think this story is real?"

Bear's eyebrows went up. "Don't you?"

Dragon didn't answer. He'd known too many people who'd used supposed "spirit journeys" to talk their way out of tight spots.

He shifted in Bear's embrace. "What about Shenandoah? What do you think it is?" He thought he knew, but he wanted to hear it anyway.

"That's the tribe I was telling you about. The northern tribe where anyone who wants to join is welcome, and the only law is that you can't harm another person." A tremor ran through the big body pressed against Dragon's back. "That's where we're going. Shenandoah. And now we know how to get there."

Chapter Two

That wasn't quite true. The words on the wall gave them only general directions toward Shenandoah. They really didn't know much more about how to get there than they had before. Bear knew it, and he knew Dragon knew it too. But at least they now had something a little more specific than just "north". It might not be much, but Bear decided it was reason enough for optimism. After all, they had to travel in *some* direction. It might as well be the one laid out by the unknown writer.

He didn't mention his dream from the night before. The one featuring a bright, lively city nestled in a green valley far away. It was just a dream, no matter how real it had seemed, or how well it meshed with the words on the wall. After all, this wasn't the first tale he'd heard of Shenandoah.

Wanting to see Dragon smile, he flashed the grin that always melted the wariness from Dragon's eyes and made the corners of his mouth quirk up.

Dragon's lips twitched. "Will we reach the river tomorrow?"

"Should get there by midafternoon."

"Okay." Shaking his head, Dragon drew out of Bear's arms. "Let's get back to the fire. I'll stay on watch, and you get some more sleep. I want you well-rested so you can get us across that river."

Bear nodded. "Don't worry. I'll get us across."

Dragon didn't answer. He turned and picked a path out of the debris-littered space between the shelf and the wall, the torch held high in front of him to light the way.

Bear followed him across the cavernous room back to their campfire. He knew Dragon wasn't entirely confident in Bear's ability to cross the river. Then again, Dragon clearly didn't quite believe in Shenandoah in the first place. He was obviously going along with this plan only because Bear believed it, and because neither of them had anything to lose by trying.

That was all right with Bear. He had enough confidence in himself for the both of them. Besides that, he knew Shenandoah was real. *Knew* it, with everything in him. And with the words on the wall to guide them, he was sure he and Dragon would find it.

They left in the cool gray twilight just before sunrise the next morning, slipping out a side door while the nomads still slept in the weed-ridden space beside the cistern. Bear breathed easier once they'd walked far enough to escape the stench of burnt human flesh. He wondered if the smell of sex, blood and fear was real or just his imagination playing tricks on him.

"Will they come after us?" Dragon asked after they'd walked in silence for nearly an hour. His fingers tightened on the handle of his knife.

Bear shook his head. "They'll probably sleep most of the day. We'll be long gone by the time they wake up."

Dragon didn't answer, but some of the tightness went out of his shoulders. A smile tugged at Bear's mouth. He knew how Dragon felt. He'd actually had nightmares the first time he'd encountered a gang like this, right after his initiation into the Pack. Time and experience lessened the impact, but not much.

"Maybe we could've helped them," Dragon said a long time later, when they'd left the thickest part of the old city behind and the ruins no longer blotted out the sky around them. "The nomads didn't know we were down there. We could've snuck up on them. At least rescued a couple of those captives, maybe."

Bear shot a sidelong glance at Dragon. The gray eyes were thoughtful and a bit sad. Bear sympathized. He felt bad for the men and women who'd suffered and died last night, but he knew for a fact that if he and Dragon had tried to help, their own dismembered remains would've been scattered among the brambles or heaped in piles of still-smoking bones beside the bonfire along with the rest of the dead. There was no point in regret or wishing things were different. At least there hadn't been any children among the victims this time.

"There were nearly enough of them to make a Pack, and only two of us. And I know they sounded like they weren't paying attention, but trust me, they were. There's no sneaking up on them." Bear clambered atop a pile of rubble blocking their path, reached down and grasped Dragon's hand to help him scramble up. "We couldn't have saved any of those people."

Balancing on a particularly large piece of stone, Dragon shielded his eyes from the bright midmorning sun with one hand and surveyed the landscape of low, crumbled buildings that surrounded them. "How much longer before we're out of Char?"

Bear shook his head. He wondered if he'd ever get used to the abrupt way Dragon dropped a subject once he was finished with it. "I'm not sure, exactly. I've never been through this part of the city. But I've been around the northern edge before, and I know we can't have that much farther to go."

"Good. I don't like this area. Too many places to hide."

Can't argue with that. Bear sniffed at the humid air as they made their way down the far side of the mounded debris. He caught the scent of wild dogs on the sluggish breeze, but nothing human, thank the Mother. This part of Char might provide a wealth of spots from which to ambush an enemy, but it offered nothing in the way of safe shelter. If he and Dragon came across another gang like the one from last night, they were as good as dead. Luckily, the odds of two such groups sharing the same territory were slim to none.

As the day wore on, Bear and Dragon made their way through the wilderness of vines, briars and crumbled ruins that made up the outskirts of Char. The light breeze died before the sun reached its zenith, leaving them to struggle along in a heat so thick it pressed like a physical weight on Bear's back. Each breath felt like trying to suck air through a damp cloth.

They stopped in the shade of a young tree to eat a midday meal of fruit and dried venison and rest for a while. By the time they started walking again, the temperature had risen to near-suffocating levels. Bear stripped off his shirt and stuffed it in his bag before they'd gone more than a hundred paces.

After a few minutes, Dragon pulled off his own shirt. Bear took it and shoved it into the bag without a word. He slowed his pace to let Dragon pull ahead and watched, smiling, as he wound his hair into a loose knot at the nape of his neck. Sweat cut through the dust and dirt coating Dragon's back to soak into the top of his buckskins.

In spite of the crushing heat, in spite of the danger neither of them could afford to ignore, Bear wanted to rip those pants from Dragon's body, throw him to the ground and plunge balls-deep inside him. Sink teeth into the meat of his shoulder. Taste the salt on his skin and smell the sharp musk of his seed when he came.

As if sensing Bear's stare, Dragon turned his head and aimed a smoldering look over his shoulder. Bear grinned at him. Laughing, Dragon faced forward again. "Can we swim this river of yours? Because getting in the water sure would feel good right now."

Bear considered. They could, if they detoured south-southwest, to where the water flowed over a wide, shallow shoal before narrowing again, twisting through a dangerous current and finally emptying into a large lake. It was a little too close to the lake for comfort—the small but vicious Norman Tribe haunted the forest on the western shore—but fording the river at the shoals might end up drawing less attention in the long run than trying to find a way to cross farther north.

"There's a spot where we can swim it." Closing the distance between them, Bear gave Dragon's ass a hard smack. "Then we'll make camp, and I can lick you open and fuck you raw."

A tremor ran down Dragon's spine. He didn't speak a word, but the ridge in the front of his pants said it all.

Bear's blood surged at the sight. Strange, how he didn't even miss sex with his Pack Brothers. Oh, he missed his Brothers. He missed talking to them, laughing with them, sharing his days with them. After all, he'd known nothing but the Pack since he was a young boy. But he didn't miss the sexual bond he'd shared with them, even though it had been a daily part of his life ever since his initiation graduated him from trainee to full-fledged Pack Brother nearly ten years ago. In Dragon, the Great Mother had gifted him with a lover who not only satisfied his every carnal urge, but understood him like no one else ever had. What more could a man ask?

Giving Dragon's rear a final squeeze, Bear moved ahead to pick a path through the wilderness of rubble which had once been a thriving city. The sooner they got out of here and across the river, the sooner they could make camp, and the sooner he could sink his cock into the welcoming warmth of Dragon's body.

"That's it? The river we need to cross?"

"Yes." Bear frowned at Dragon, who was breathing harder than he should be just from climbing the small hillock where they stood. His normally dusky skin had taken on a worrisome pallor. "Are you—?"

"We're not crossing there, are we?" Shielding his eyes with one hand, Dragon squinted against the glitter of the afternoon sun on the water a few hundred paces away from their spot beneath a stand of fig trees. "The current looks pretty strong."

Bear gave a mental shrug. Either Dragon was all right, or he didn't want Bear to ask. Either way, he was more than capable of looking after himself. "It is, here. We're going to go south-southwest a little farther." He sniffed the sluggish breeze. It smelled like grass, earth and figs, devoid of anything human or even any dangerous animal life. He adjusted his bag on his sweat-slick shoulder. "We're safe enough. Come on."

Bear trudged down the slope. Dragon trailed behind him, munching on one of the figs they'd picked. Several more lay cradled in Bear's shirt inside his bag. As they walked, Bear gazed toward the west, at the broad river that wound across the land north of the Norman Tribe lake. West of that, currently hidden behind a narrow strip of forest, lay meadows which stretched as far as the eye could see. Bear hadn't stood on the river's eastern bank in a long time, but he vividly remembered his first sight of the slow-rolling brown water, and beyond that the yellow-green grass rippling to the horizon.

That experience had been many years ago and much farther north, but he remembered every detail with perfect clarity. He was glad to see the river again, and looked forward to crossing the water and striking out across the grasslands. He'd only camped there once, within a stone's throw of the water, but he'd never forgotten it. There was something incredibly peaceful about lying in the cool grass with the stars glittering overhead in a bottomless black sky. The thought of sharing it with Dragon made him smile.

He glanced over his shoulder. Dragon had fallen surprisingly far behind. Bear stopped to wait for him. When he caught up, Bear took one look at his ashen face and sweat-soaked chest and silently handed over one of the water skins. Dragon drew several deep swallows.

"Better?" Bear took back the skin and drank, watching Dragon from beneath his lashes.

Dragon nodded. "Better."

He didn't look any better, but Bear didn't say so. He knew the observation wouldn't be welcome. Tucking the water skin back into his bag, he started walking again.

If Dragon noticed that Bear's pace was slower than before, he didn't let on.

The sun hadn't sunk much further toward the tree line when they reached the spot Bear was looking for. The place where the river ran wide, slow and shallow over a bed of sand and small, flat rocks. In spite of the storm night before last, rain lately had been more scarce than usual and the river was low. At its deepest, the water ought not to reach any higher than Bear's hips. Crossing shouldn't be too difficult.

"This is it." Bear set his leather satchel on the ground a few paces from the low bank, mopped the sweat from his face with both hands and wiped his palms on his pants. "Strip off. I'll put our clothes in the bag and carry it across so everything stays dry."

Dragon was naked before Bear finished talking. Rolling his pants around his moccasins, he dragged the bag over by the strap, opened it and settled the bundle of clothing inside. "Come on, Bear. Hurry up."

"Okay, I'm hurrying." Bear kicked off his shoes and skinned out of his pants as quickly as he could. He studied Dragon's abnormally pale cheeks and drooping shoulders. Dragon looked terrible, and the concern Bear had felt earlier came back stronger than ever. "You okay?"

"Fine. Just..." Dragon blew out a short, harsh breath. "It's *really* hot. I'm dying to get in the water. That's all."

"Oh. Yeah." Rolling his pants and shoes together like Dragon had done, Bear stuffed them in the bag—careful to avoid crushing the figs—then cupped Dragon's face in his hands. Dragon's skin felt cool and moist. Not good. Dragon had been born and raised in the mountains farther west. He wasn't used to the blood-boiling heat in Char and the surrounding area. "It can get pretty bad here, I know. Let's get across the river, then we'll fill our water skins at the stream on the other side and head into the grasslands to make camp."

Dragon stared up at him as if he'd lost his mind. "Is it safe? Camping in the open like that?"

"Very. There's a tribe on the western shore of the lake, but they don't leave the forest. Nightfeeders and nomad gangs like the ones from last night stick close to tribal lands, for obvious reasons." Bear caressed the corners of Dragon's mouth with his thumbs, remembering the way those soft lips had stretched around his cock the night before. "The grasslands are the emptiest place you ever saw. We'll be much safer there than we were inside Char."

Dragon turned a thoughtful gaze toward the river for several long moments before rising on tiptoe to kiss Bear's lips. "Should we tie ourselves together or anything to cross?"

"No need. The current's not that strong here." Bear narrowed his eyes as a thought struck him. "Maybe we should, though, if you're feeling weak."

Something hardened in Dragon's eyes. "I'll be fine."

Moved by an inexplicable uneasiness, Bear slipped both arms around Dragon's waist and hung on when he tried to pull away. "Are you sure? It won't take but a minute for me to make a rope harness if you—"

"I'm all right. Really." Dragon twisted out of Bear's grip, his face unreadable. "Let's go."

"Okay." Bear hefted the bag, wound the strap around it and perched it atop his head. He stared hard at Dragon, trying to figure out why he'd turned so cold, but his expression revealed nothing. Swallowing his frustration, Bear forced himself to speak calmly. "Stay close. Step where I step. And if you need help, say so."

Dragon gave a single, terse nod. With no reason to delay, Bear led the way to the water's edge, in spite of the trepidation he couldn't help feeling.

As they went, Bear studied Dragon with growing alarm. His skin was an unhealthy shade of gray beneath the sweat beaded on his brow and upper lip, and the pulse fluttered far too fast in his throat.

When he stumbled, Bear was ready. He caught Dragon's arm and pulled him close enough to feel his shallow, gasping breaths. "Get on my back. I'll carry you across."

Dragon shook his head, but his eyes wouldn't quite focus on Bear's face. "No, I'm f—"

"You're not fine. You're about to pass out, and we don't have time for you to lie about it anymore."

Dragon said nothing, just stared through him. They hadn't known each other long, but it was long enough for Bear to know that the lack of argument from Dragon was a bad sign. Dropping the bag on the ground, Bear squatted down and lifted Dragon onto his shoulders.

No struggle from Dragon. Not even the slightest protest as Bear stood, one arm balancing the leather satchel on top of his head while the other looped through Dragon's leg to clutch his wrist.

Bear had carried his injured Brothers often enough to know when a man had lost consciousness.

Chapter Three

Dragon opened his eyes. His head hurt and his stomach rolled. He wasn't sure whether the nausea came more from the crippling heat of this Mother-damned place or the lurch and sway of Bear's body beneath him.

He frowned at the swirling brown water, then shut his eyes when the motion made his head spin. "Bear? What happened?"

"You're back. Good." The relief in Bear's voice was unmistakable. "Let me get across."

Reaching the other shore sounded like a wonderful idea to Dragon. Especially with the violent cramps in his stomach. He clenched his jaw against the surge of bile in his throat.

He counted thirty-four paces before the riverbed rose under Bear's feet and he splashed onto dry ground. It felt like much longer. Dragon's weight shifted, the world tilted around him and he felt scrubby grass prickle the soles of his feet. He opened his eyes to find Bear staring at him with worry stamped all over his face.

Slipping one arm around Dragon's waist, Bear led him toward the shade of the nearby pines. "Come sit down. You passed out, probably because you got overheated. You need to cool off."

Dragon leaned against Bear's side and let himself be led, though his cheeks burned with the shame of it. Allowing Bear to help him was better than collapsing, which would surely happen if he tried to walk on his own right now. At least it was cooler on this side of the river. The temperature had dropped considerably compared to the opposite shore.

Bear eased Dragon onto the ground, then handed him the one water skin with anything still in it. "Here. Drink the rest."

Dragon took the skin, mortified at the way his hands shook. "But the other one's empty. Who knows how far we'll have to go to find water? We need to make this last."

"No, there's a stream over that way." Bear gestured to his left, in the direction of the lake that was still out of sight. "It's just past the next bend in the river."

"Oh. Oh, yes." Bear had mentioned the stream before. Dragon wrinkled his nose as he lifted the pouch and drank. How could he have forgotten?

While Dragon finished half the water in that skin then poured the rest over his head, Bear dug the other one—emptied hours ago—out of the bag. "Just sit here and rest while I'm gone. Don't try to get up or anything. I won't be gone long."

"All right." Dragon handed over the now-empty skin. Humiliation kept his gaze fixed on the pine needles carpeting the ground.

"Hey." Bear's big hand cupped Dragon's chin, forcing him to meet Bear's gaze. He leaned in and kissed Dragon's lips. "Don't worry. You'll feel better in a few minutes."

Dragon forced a smile he didn't feel. It was worth it to watch Bear's face light up.

Scrambling to his feet, Bear rooted through the bag until he found his moccasins, slipped them on and trotted off along the river's edge with the water skins slung over his shoulder. Dragon watched him go with a mix of admiration and envy. How in the Mother's name did Bear manage to endure hours on end of this blistering heat—heat that seared the skin from your back and sucked the air from your lungs—without so much as a stoop to his shoulders or the slightest stumble in his stride?

Bear would say it was because he'd been born and raised in Carwin, so he was used to it. But Dragon didn't buy that argument. It hadn't been nearly this hot on the journey from the outlying forest, where Bear and Lynx had captured him, to Carwin's walls. The unbearable heat only seemed to affect the Char ruins, which stretched almost as far as the river. Dragon and Bear had spent enough time talking about their Packs that Dragon knew Bear hadn't been on more than a couple dozen patrols into Char, and they mostly hadn't lasted but three or four days each.

In other words, Bear shouldn't be any more accustomed to the heat than Dragon.

I'm weak. A liability.

Resting the back of his head against the tree, Dragon stared at the muddy swirl of the water. Maybe Bear could still cut him loose and go back to his tribe. Lynx was going to tell the Carwin Tribal Council that Bear had been killed by nightfeeders. Bear could always say that Lynx was wrong, that he'd escaped. His council and his Pack might even buy it. Dragon, well... He had clothes and a weapon now. It was more than he'd had when Bear and Lynx found him. And Bear would leave him food and a water skin if he asked.

After all Bear had sacrificed for him, Dragon didn't want to be the cause of Bear's death. And he wasn't stupid enough to think it would never come to that. Alone in the wild, without the protection of a Pack or a tribe's city walls, he and Bear were vulnerable. Mother only knew what dangers would face them as they traveled farther north, outside the sphere of Bear's experience.

"Better to fight alone than with a weakling at your side," he whispered to the branches rustling overhead, echoing the growl of his first Sarge and the one lesson no Ashe Tribe Pack Brother ever forgot.

It all seemed like another lifetime ago now—the big, solid fists slamming into his jaw, into his gut, the hands gripping his hair and smashing his face into the dirt, the lesson growled into his bloodied and ringing ears every time he failed to take down the enemy during a training exercise. He'd always been proud of making it through the Pack training. Lots of whelps didn't. Many quit. A few didn't survive.

When Bear had told him the Carwin Tribe's seer picked out the boys who were destined to become Pack while they were still children, Dragon had felt just a little bit superior. Because he'd competed for a coveted spot in his own Pack, fought hard for it and won it rather than it being part of his fate, he'd thought that made him better somehow. Stronger.

He'd been wrong.

He didn't doubt his skills in battle. But another bout of faintness at the wrong time could get them both killed. It could get *Bear* killed, and he didn't deserve that. Better for them to part now while Bear still stood a chance of reaching Carwin safely.

Movement caught the edge of his vision. He turned toward it. Bear strode toward him along the riverbank. The water skins swung full and dripping from his shoulder. He lifted one hand and waved, a wide grin on his face. Dragon waved back, smiling in spite of himself. No one had ever warmed his heart with sheer, simple joy the way Bear did. The thought of leaving him hurt something vital deep in Dragon's core.

But I have to do it. It's for the best.

Dragon nodded. It *was* for the best. Of course it was.

Wasn't it?

Hours later, after the furious crimson of the sunset cooled to black and the stars came out, Dragon still didn't know. Unable to meet Bear's eyes, he stared into the campfire instead as if it held the solutions to all his troubles.

Logically, he knew leaving Bear was the right thing to do. He'd felt tired, sick and shaky right up until the sun went down and a fresh night breeze dissipated the lingering heat of the day. Bear hadn't said a word against him—had, in fact, been solicitous to the point of annoying—but Dragon wasn't fooled. He knew what Bear must be thinking—that he'd saddled himself with a burden, not a man capable of pulling his own weight. Certainly not the warrior he had a right to expect from a Pack Brother. Any normal, sensible man would be glad to be released from the promises Bear had made.

The problem was, Bear was hardly a normal, sensible man. A normal, sensible man wouldn't have left everyone and everything loved and familiar to him to chase after a dream with a man he barely knew. Even if he was wishing Dragon were stronger—as he *must* be, he was only human after all—it would never occur to him that they should part ways in order to keep himself safe. He'd probably find the very idea horrifying.

As horrifying as I find the thought of being the cause of his death?

Dragon stifled a sigh. He knew he couldn't delay his decision much longer, but what in the Mother's name was he supposed to do?

Bear plopped onto the blanket beside him and nudged his shoulder. "Here."

Shaking himself out of his thoughts, Dragon took the chunk of fire-roasted rabbit from the wooden skewer Bear held. He popped it into his mouth, chewed and swallowed. "Thanks."

"Sure." Bear tore open a fig and scraped out the meat with his teeth, watching Dragon the whole time. "How're you feeling?"

"Much better."

"Really?"

"Yes, really." Dragon fought down a spike of mingled irritation and shame at the unabated worry in Bear's eyes. Taking another chunk of rabbit, he tore off a strip with his fingers. "Bear, I'm all right now. I really am." He tucked the meat into his mouth.

"Okay. Good." Bear gave him a lopsided smile and hunched over to slurp up the rest of his fig.

Dragon finished his hunk of rabbit, then reached for a fig and made himself eat it, but he had no appetite. All he could think was, *This might be the last time I'll sit beside a campfire with Bear. The last time we'll eat figs and fresh rabbit together while the stars shine.*

A sharp ache twisted deep in his chest. Closing his eyes, he lifted his face to the cool wind. The night air brought the smells of grass and wood smoke, the pop and crackle of the fire, and the endless whisper of the meadow. Something about it made him want to walk out into that swaying green sea, lie down at its heart and sleep until the world forgot he'd ever existed.

The thought was as frightening as it was seductive. He opened his eyes. Bear was staring at him with a thoughtful gaze.

Dragon hunched his shoulders. "What?"

"You tell me." Bear tossed a rabbit bone into the fire. "Your mind's been somewhere else ever since the river, and it's not just because you've felt bad. What's wrong?"

Dragon stared deep into Bear's eyes. He saw the ever-present concern, but behind that, a belief as wide and solid as the earth beneath them. Nobody had ever looked at him with such unquestioning faith before, not even his Brothers, and as simple as that, his decision was made.

He would stay with Bear, whatever happened.

Sarge would tell him he was willfully endangering his Pack. That he'd brought unforgivable shame upon himself. But Bear wouldn't see it that way. To Bear, the only shame would be in giving up, and Bear *was* his pack now. He would prove to Bear that he was worthy of that honor, no matter what it took.

Throwing the empty fig skin he still held into the flames, Dragon turned to face Bear. "I was just thinking, that's all."

"About what?"

"About my old Pack, and how different they are from your old Pack, and from you." Dragon wound two long blades of grass around his fingers. "I'm sorry you had to leave your tribe for me."

Bear was shaking his head before Dragon finished the sentence. "You're still sun-addled. Leaving Carwin was my choice. You know that."

"Yeah, I know. I just..." Dragon shook his head and stared into the fire again. He wished words came easier to him. He didn't have the right vocabulary to express the confusing mix of things he felt and thought Bear ought to know. Like how he felt responsible for Bear's current situation even though he knew it had been Bear's decision. Or how he wished Bear had never had to leave his home and his Pack, yet at the same time thanked the Mother every morning and every night that he had.

"Hey. Listen to me." Bear laid a palm on Dragon's cheek, forcing him to turn his head and meet Bear's stern gaze. "It was my choice. *Mine*, and no one else's. You might have given me the final push I needed to make it, but you didn't make it for me. This was *my* decision, and no one can take that away from me. Not even you."

Dragon nodded. He wanted to protest that he wasn't trying to claim actual credit for Bear's choices, but he knew better than to say any such thing at that point. When Bear's voice took on that particular note of command, you didn't argue. You shut up and agreed with whatever Bear said.

He let out a surprised yelp when Bear's big hands closed

around his upper arms and pulled. His cheeks burned with humiliation as he was dragged across Bear's lap. He struggled, but he may as well have been a child in Bear's hands for all the good it did.

He met Bear's glare with one of his own. "What—?"

A bruising and thoroughly unexpected kiss cut him off and startled him into stillness. He obediently parted his lips for Bear's tongue.

"We're Pack now," Bear whispered when the kiss broke. One hand uncurled from around Dragon's arm to grasp his chin none too gently. "You and me."

Bear's eyes burned with something that made Dragon's pulse thunder in his ears. He swallowed. "I was thinking the same thing."

A wide grin lit up Bear's face. "See, that's why we were already Brothers before we even met. We think alike." Bear's hand slid off Dragon's chin and down his chest to the front of his pants. A swift tug undid the leather laces. "Take them off."

The thought of disobeying didn't even cross Dragon's mind. He kicked off his moccasins and worked his pants down over his hips with Bear's help. His cock was already half-hard, just from the raw lust in Bear's eyes.

Tossing the pants aside, Bear hauled Dragon up to straddle his lap. Dragon lifted up enough to let Bear loosen his laces. "I thought you were going to lick me." He fished Bear's cock out of the gap in his pants and closed his fingers around the shaft. It stiffened in his palm.

"Another time." Bear managed to wriggle his buckskins halfway down his thighs. He leaned sideways to shove his free hand into his bag. After rummaging around for a moment, he pulled out the small glass bottle of oil. He nudged Dragon's chest with it. "Pour."

Taking the bottle, Dragon uncorked it with his teeth,

drizzled the bare minimum needed into Bear's palm, then replaced the cork. "We're either going to have to fuck less or find a way to make more oil soon. That bottle's only three quarters full." He set it on the ground.

"I know." Bear's big fingers slicked Dragon's hole. "Shut up."

Dragon opened his mouth to wonder aloud where they might find the right kinds of plants, and how they were supposed to press the oil from them. Then Bear spread him open and breached him with one swift upward thrust, and he forgot all about talking. Digging his hands into Bear's shoulders for purchase, he slammed himself down onto Bear's cock with all his strength. Bear's oil-coated fingers slipped from Dragon's butt to his hipbones and dug in with painful force.

Dragon rocked his pelvis, but the angle wasn't right. Growling, he planted both palms on Bear's chest and shoved. Bear fell backward with a grunt. Dragon rode him down, hole clamped around his cock to keep him lodged deep inside.

Bear let out a low groan. Behind him, Dragon felt Bear's legs bend. Dragon barely had time to brace his thighs against Bear's sides before Bear's cock slid partway out of him, then drove back in so hard his teeth clacked together. A thin pain sliced the inside of his cheek, and he tasted blood.

On the next thrust, Dragon leaned back a little, and *oh Mother* that did it. Bear's solid length dragged over the spot inside him that always lit a hot spark low in his gut. He cried out, the flesh pebbling along his arms and up his spine.

For once, Bear didn't silence him with a kiss or a glare, or a hand over his mouth. Instead, he brushed an oddly reverent touch across Dragon's lips before curving a palm around the side of his thigh. The other hand remained on his hip, holding him in place astride Bear's groin.

Bear's harsh grunts, Dragon's sharp cries and the wet slurp of Bear's cock pistoning in and out of him mingled with the rustle of the grass in the wind. The amber glow of Bear's eyes in the moonlight burned all thoughts of guilt, weakness or shame right out of Dragon's brain. He clung to Bear with hands and legs and lost himself in the wild joy of fucking under the vast night sky.

It didn't last long. All too soon, Dragon felt the familiar tingling pressure spread from his groin along the insides of his thighs. His balls drew up tight to his body. Catching his bottom lip between his teeth, he took his cock in one hand and started stroking himself with the quick, firm touch he liked best. He spread his other hand flat on Bear's belly. The muscles flexed beneath his palm with each of Bear's increasingly brutal thrusts. *Mother, yes, almost...*

"Oh, yes," Bear whispered, the sound barely audible over the hiss of the breeze. He arched and trembled between Dragon's legs, his hand kneading Dragon's thigh hard enough to bruise.

Strangely enough, the thought of carrying Bear's marks on his skin played as large a part in triggering Dragon's release as the pulse of Bear's cock inside him. He came staring straight into Bear's wide-open eyes, his seed spilling over his hand and Bear's stomach and seeping into the place where their bodies joined together.

As the rush of orgasm ebbed, Dragon's head swam. Before he could embarrass himself by collapsing, Bear sat up, hooked an arm around his waist and pressed a soft, lingering kiss to his lips. "Mmm. I think I like you riding me like that."

"So do I." Dragon hissed as Bear's cock slipped out of him, followed by a trickle of semen. He rested his head in the curve of Bear's neck. "We should clean up." He yawned.

Bear's laugh rumbled against Dragon's ear. "I think the river is farther than either of us wants to walk right now."

"Mm. But we don't want to smell like sex when we're out in the open, do we? Even if there's no nightfeeders or nomads around, there might still be animals." Dragon yawned again. His eyelids felt heavy as stones. It would be so easy to just fall asleep right here, cradled in Bear's lap.

"The only animals out here at night are too small for us to worry about. The fire'll keep them away anyhow." Grasping Dragon's wrist, Bear lifted the hand coated in come and washed it with several long swipes of his tongue. "Better?"

Grinning, Dragon wiggled his still-sticky fingers. Bear obligingly sucked each one clean. "Much better," Dragon mumbled into Bear's throat.

"Not done yet." One arm under Dragon's rear and the other still snug around his waist, Bear lifted him and laid him on his back on the blanket. "Hold still."

It wasn't easy, especially when Bear lapped the drying seed from the sensitive tip of his cock, but Dragon managed. He bunched the rough fabric in his hands and held himself motionless except for the faint tremors he couldn't stop.

Human tongues weren't made for bathing, but Dragon didn't mind. It was good enough, as far as cleanliness went, and Bear's touch always soothed him in the aftermath of their coupling. He didn't mind returning the favor either, especially since it meant he got to curl up with his head against Bear's belly and lick the warm, salt-tainted skin to his heart's content.

Afterward, Bear eased out from beneath him so he could lie down. "Get some sleep. I'll take first watch."

Dragon didn't bother to argue. He knew he was in no shape to keep watch. Safe, fed and sexually sated, the stress of his earlier illness caught up with him, and his head buzzed with the need for sleep. He rolled himself in the blanket without bothering to put his clothes back on. The night was warm, and he could fight as well naked as clothed, if it came to that.

Just as he realized his knife lay out of reach in the grass, Bear lifted the corner of the blanket and pressed the sheathed weapon into his hand. "Here. Thought you'd want this."

"I do. Thanks." Dragon tilted his face up for Bear's kiss. "Promise you'll wake me later. Don't want you to stay up all night." His words came out slurred with exhaustion.

"Okay." Smiling, Bear touched Dragon's cheek. "Sleep."

Before Dragon's eyelids shut, a flare of the fire lit Bear's profile. The way the curve of his back shone in the orange light caused a peculiar catch in Dragon's chest.

I can't let him down again. I have to be strong for him.

Bear would be angry, since he didn't think Dragon *had* let him down. But Dragon's promise was for himself alone.

What Bear didn't know wouldn't hurt him.

Chapter Four

Dragon was hiding something.

Had been for more than half a moon cycle, ever since the river. Bear was sure of it.

Not that Dragon had been secretive, exactly, Bear reflected as the two of them hacked their way through yet another patch of brambles. Just quiet, and...driven. As if he had something to prove.

But we're Pack now. Brothers. Why would he hide anything? And what could he possibly have to prove to me?

Those were the questions Bear had been asking himself all the long trek from the grasslands to this wilderness of green, rounded slopes climbing higher and higher toward the sky. Dragon had done more than his share of hunting—especially in the forest, where he'd proven to be lethal with the bow and arrows Bear took from the abandoned farmhouse they'd found three days from the river—and had let Bear sleep through his watch so often that Bear had threatened to cane him if he did it again. Bear didn't quite know how to take the single arched eyebrow he'd gotten in response.

Up ahead, Dragon stopped and looked over his shoulder at Bear. "Stay there for a second. I'm going to check over there." He pointed sideways through the trees toward a tumble of huge boulders.

Bear nodded. "Okay."

He leaned against a white-barked tree and watched Dragon stride off through the undergrowth as if they hadn't spent the better part of two days struggling up steep slopes covered in a tangle of brambles, ferns and the spreading bushes Dragon called mountain laurel.

Bear shook his head, a smile tugging at his mouth. Dragon had been so mortified by his sickness at the river, as if he was the only one who had ever been overcome by the oppressive heat in Char and the lands to the north. What would he think if he knew how Bear's legs shook right now? Especially since Dragon hadn't so much as broken a sweat or breathed harder than normal.

From the corner of his eye, Bear saw Dragon emerge from the rocks and beckon to him. He pushed away from the tree and resumed his uphill trudge, grateful that Dragon was carrying the supply bag today.

"We lucked out," Dragon said when Bear drew near. "There's a cave here, and it's empty. It'll be perfect shelter for tonight. In fact, we can rest here for a couple of days, if you want."

"That sounds great to me." Bear mopped sweat from his forehead and wiped it on the back of his pants. "Were your mountains like this?"

Dragon's head tilted sideways. "Like what?"

"So *steep*." Bear used a particularly sturdy laurel to haul himself up the last few feet and stood beside Dragon, trying not to pant. "It feels like we've been climbing straight up for ages."

The look he got in answer told him Dragon was on to him. "It was pretty much the same where I came from, yes." Dragon's gray eyes held a sparkle of amusement.

At least he's not angry with me. It was a risk Bear ran every time he tried—in his admittedly clumsy way—to show Dragon that he wasn't the only one with weaknesses. Even the strongest Pack Brother was only human, after all. Dragon seemed to think he had to be better than that. Stronger than any man *could* be.

It made Bear wonder what exactly Dragon hadn't told him about life in the Ashe Tribe Pack. What he *had* told him had been brutal enough.

The corners of Dragon's mouth quirked into a wry smile, as if he knew what Bear was thinking. He turned and started off in the direction he'd gone before. "Let's gather some kindling on the way. There's a dead tree not far down the slope on the other side of the cave. We can get some larger logs from that after I show you where the cave is."

"Okay." Bear hitched the sturdy bow farther up his shoulder. It was shorter and thicker than the type he was used to, strung not with ox hair but some kind of treated plant fiber that itched even through his shirt. "How are we doing for meat? Do we need to hunt?"

Dragon shook his head. "Not yet. There's enough venison for a few more days." He grinned over his shoulder. "And there's a blackberry patch near the cave."

The thought made Bear's mouth water. They still had enough apples to add several pounds to their bag, courtesy of an orchard growing wild at the north-east border of the big meadow, so they weren't hurting for fresh fruit. But Bear loved blackberries. They were a rare treat in Carwin, where the crows attacked anyone bold enough to venture out to the few meager vines growing alongside the river that ran just east of the city walls.

Bear would have passed right by the cave if Dragon hadn't led him to it. Ferns and tree roots trailed over the tumble of boulders, hiding the triangular opening so that you had to look hard to realize it went anywhere. Dragon lifted the vegetation out of the way and ducked inside. "It opens up once you get past the entrance," he called when Bear hesitated. "Don't worry, you won't get stuck."

The amusement in Dragon's voice got Bear moving. Shoving the trailing plants aside, he crouched and managed to squirm sideways through the crack in the rocks.

Just as Dragon had said, the space was much larger inside than the cramped entry promised. Bear was able to stand up straight. Once his eyes adjusted to the low light, he saw that the ceiling rose toward the rear of the cave, about twenty paces back. Weak sunlight filtered in through a narrow crack in the rock at the apex of the ceiling. The floor was smooth and relatively flat, except for a short but steep downward slope near the wall to Bear's right.

Dropping the bow and quiver of arrows on the floor, Bear wrapped both arms around Dragon's waist and pulled him close. "This is perfect. We'll be safe here. Even the smoke from our fire'll get drawn up through that crack and get lost in the rocks up above, I'll bet."

"It should." Dragon slipped his arms around Bear's middle. He settled his hands on Bear's butt. Gave it a squeeze, something he never did unless he wanted to fuck, because he *knew* it turned Bear on. Bear raised his eyebrows, and Dragon bit his chin. "I've been hard for you all day, Bear."

Something caught in Bear's chest. "You *know* I'm hard for you. I'm always hard for you." Smiling, he nuzzled Dragon's hair. "I found a bottle of oil at that farmhouse where we got the bow and arrow." Bear undid the laces on Dragon's buckskins with one hand. "Did I tell you that?"

"I was there, remember?" Dragon sent his pants slithering to his ankles with a practiced wriggle of his hips. "We don't need oil right now."

"No, look, we tried it with spit that one time, and—"

Dragon laid a hand over Bear's mouth. "Hush."

Bear hushed. Moving his hand, Dragon opened Bear's

pants with a couple of swift tugs at the laces, then dropped to his knees and took Bear's cock into his mouth.

"Oh, Mother, yes." Bear dug his fingers into the thick hair at the root of Dragon's braid and hung on.

When it was over, Bear lay on the cold stone floor of the cave with Dragon naked in his arms and the residue of Dragon's seed coating his tongue and thought he might be the luckiest man ever born. He let out a happy sigh.

Dragon stirred, planted an elbow on his chest and peered at him with glazed eyes. "Mm? Okay?"

"Yeah. Happy." Bear tilted his head to press a kiss to Dragon's swollen lips. "I was just thinking how lucky I am."

To his dismay, Dragon's eyes clouded. He pushed to his feet, tangled hair falling over his face. "I should go gather some logs for the fire before it starts getting dark."

Bear had no clue what he'd said wrong, but he was bound and determined to find out. He stood and hooked an arm around Dragon's chest. Dragon didn't struggle. Bear supposed he'd learned by now that there was no point.

"We're Brothers," Bear whispered in Dragon's ear. "That means we don't keep secrets from each other. We tell each other everything." *Like the way you didn't keep any secrets from your Brothers in the Carwin Tribe Pack? Like the way you told them everything?* He ignored the accusing voice in his head and plowed on. "We help each other. Especially now, when there isn't anybody else." He rubbed his cheek against Dragon's, where the smell of sex nearly overwhelmed him. "What's wrong? What're you thinking?"

Dragon stood still and silent as a tree. Bear waited. He'd never been a particularly patient man. But for Dragon, he could wait forever.

It was a surprising thing to learn about himself.

"I was just thinking that... Well, shouldn't we be looking for some sort of sign to guide us to Shenandoah?" Dragon shifted in Bear's arms, just enough to keep Bear from seeing his face. "I mean, this mountain range is huge. It's easy to get lost here, and this tribe we're looking for could be anywhere, and I...I just think that we need something else to guide us."

A brief vision of the city in the green valley flashed behind Bear's eyes. He shook off the strange sense that the knowledge of how to get there lay deep inside himself—somewhere, somehow—if only he knew how to get to it. It was a ridiculous notion. Wishful thinking. Besides, there were more important things to think about here. Like why Dragon was lying. Because he *was* lying. Or at least not telling the whole truth. The stiffness of Dragon's body—and more than that, the fact that he refused to look Bear in the eye—told Bear all he needed to know.

He wanted to shake Dragon until he told the truth. Instead, he forced himself to nod and smile. "You're right. If all we have to go on is 'north' at this point, we could easily spend a year wandering around these mountains. We've already spent longer than the stories said. If we're on the right track at all, surely someone else who traveled to Shenandoah left some sort of sign to guide the way."

Dragon didn't answer, but Bear could almost feel the surprise rolling off him. As if he hadn't followed his own thought to its logical conclusion. That, more than anything else, told Bear that Dragon hadn't been truthful. That he didn't believe they needed to "find a sign" to Shenandoah, but only said that to cover up whatever he was *really* thinking at that moment.

It made Bear sad and furious at the same time. He'd never wanted the silent, submissive follower Dragon had halfway become since leaving Char. He wanted the strong, fierce warrior he'd found in the forest that fateful night. The one he'd left his tribe, his Pack and his home for.

He'd thought Dragon was his Pack now. His Brother. Where had they gone wrong?

Bear gave himself a mental shake. Whatever had happened, whatever had gone wrong, he couldn't go back and change it now. And he couldn't *make* Dragon talk to him, apparently.

Maybe a few days of hunting through the woods for the signs he didn't believe existed would loosen Dragon's tongue. For his own part, Bear thought Dragon had a point about needing something to point them toward Shenandoah. They had nothing right now. The strange, vivid dreams Bear had been having lately didn't count, and he wanted to be safe inside Shenandoah's walls by the time winter hit. The more time they spent wandering around the mountains with no clear path, the less likely Bear meeting his goal became.

Taking hold of Dragon's shoulders, Bear turned him around so that they faced each other. He cupped Dragon's face in his hands, leaned down and kissed him. The sweet little sound he made flooded Bear's chest with warmth. He kissed Dragon again, soft and quick, then let him go. "Okay. So, let's go get some wood, huh?"

"Yeah." Dragon picked up his pants and started pulling them on. "We can, um, start looking around for clues about Shenandoah tomorrow."

"Tomorrow. Sure thing."

Bear flashed his widest, most innocent smile. Dragon flushed. He pulled his shirt over his head and stepped into his moccasins in one motion, then stooped to grab the water skins. "I'm going to fill the water skins and gather some berries. The dead tree is about ten paces down the slope to the northwest. You can't miss it. I'll be there in a few minutes."

He ducked out of the cave before Bear could say a word in answer. Bear smiled without humor. The next few days were going to be hard.

Two days later they still hadn't found any signs to guide them to Shenandoah.

Not that Dragon had expected anything different. He hadn't *really* wanted to spend any time here searching for *signs*, for the Mother's sake. And of course Bear knew that. It was obvious in the way he looked at Dragon—sidelong glances brimming with worry—whenever he thought Dragon wasn't watching.

As if there was ever such a time. Dragon *always* watched. *Always know what's going on around you, but never let 'em see you looking.* Another of Sarge's lessons. A particularly good one too.

Dragon scowled as he hacked through a patch of some vine which was clearly once cultivated but now ran wild. At this point, he wondered if he shouldn't just come clean with Bear. Tell him about his fears and insecurities. It would be better than chasing after some mythical sign to a tribe that may not even exist. He certainly hadn't expected Bear to cling this stubbornly to his ridiculous statement about "finding a sign" when they both knew it to be false. Never mind that they were both still pretending it was true.

He let out a quiet laugh. *Great Mother, but we're both being stupid.*

The wind which had been blowing steadily from the east all day stilled for a moment, then shifted. The smell it brought from the hollow to the southwest nearly made Dragon gag. If it was an animal, it was too far gone to be of any use to them. But it didn't smell quite like an animal...

Bear came slipping silently through the brush to the north. "I smell a body nearby."

Dragon had to laugh. "Even *I* can smell it, Bear."

That got him a grin and a smack on the ass before Bear turned serious again. "We should probably see how they died. I know we haven't seen anyone nearby, but still. Whoever it is, they died not long before we arrived. We need to know what it was that killed them."

So it *was* a person. Dragon shook his head. It never ceased to amaze him how Bear could gather so much information just from a scent. "You take point. I've got your back."

With a brief nod, Bear set off down the slope in a half-crouch, his knife gripped loosely in his right hand. His head turned side to side, nostrils flared. Dragon followed a few paces behind, peering between the trees and into the ferns, briars and mountain laurel huddled among the trunks. He hadn't seen a single soul in this forest other than the two of them, but it wouldn't do to turn lazy now.

At the bottom of the hollow, Bear eased aside a dense clump of some shrub whose name Dragon didn't know. "Hey, Dragon?"

"Yeah?" He wrinkled his nose at the stench. Maybe they should bury the body. It was a fair distance from their cave, but still. They didn't want it attracting predators, animal or otherwise.

Bear motioned to him without looking up from the ground. "Come look."

That couldn't possibly mean anything good. Darting one last glance at the surrounding woods, Dragon hurried down into the hollow. He didn't bother with being quiet. If there was anyone around, they would've already heard Bear calling to him anyway.

He stopped at Bear's side. "What?"

Bear stepped out of the way. Dragon leaned around through the gap in the undergrowth to look, and groaned. "You're sure he's only been dead a couple of days?"

"Yes. Maybe even less." Bear dug a toe into the leaf mulch at their feet. "It's pretty damp around here. That can speed up the decaying process. It's possible he might've been killed as recently as yesterday morning."

Dragon studied the dead man with a critical eye. He wore buckskin pants, a shirt similar to Bear's and a pair of leather moccasins. Decay mottled the skin of his face, neck and hands. Flies buzzed around his open, sunken eyes. A single arrow penetrated his rib cage, straight through his heart. There was hardly any blood.

He was killed so quickly he didn't even have time to bleed. And whoever killed him is still out there somewhere.

"Wonderful." Dragon turned to stare out into the forest. "We can't stay here any longer. We need to move on."

"Agreed." Bear crouched beside the body, a strange expression on his face. "At least we know we're on the right track to Shenandoah."

Dragon frowned. "I don't understand."

Rising to his feet, Bear gave Dragon a sad smile. "I recognize that man. He's from the Carwin Tribe. He must be the one who wrote that message on the wall in Char."

Chapter Five

Even though they'd followed the unknown author of the words on the wall, Dragon had never expected to actually find him. Especially dead in the vast, uncharted wilderness many days' travel from his home.

Dragon had never even considered the possibility that Bear might *know* the man.

Not knowing what to do or say, Dragon laid a hand on Bear's chest. "We can bury him. If you want."

"I think we should." Bear rested his hand on top of Dragon's. "I wish he hadn't died. But at least we found him. The Mother led us to him, to let us know we're going the right way to Shenandoah."

Dragon didn't answer. He'd learned enough about the Carwin Tribe on their journey to know how unheard of it was for anyone to leave voluntarily. Nomads and nightfeeders took the occasional unwary citizen, and the rare crime might be punished with banishment. Few survived that particular brand of justice. Knowing those things, he was willing to believe the dead man might be the one who'd written the words on the wall. How many Carwin Tribe citizens could there be out here? But taking the presence of the corpse in this place as a sign from the Great Mother was more than Dragon could do.

He pressed close to Bear, because he couldn't look Bear in the eye but neither could he bring himself to pull away when

Bear looked so sad. "I passed a hollow tree on the ground a little ways back. I think we could break it up enough to use the pieces for digging." Bear's heart thudded slow and steady beneath Dragon's cheek. The sound soothed some of the tension from his mind.

"Good idea." Cupping Dragon's chin in one big hand, Bear lifted Dragon's face. He stared into Dragon's eyes with the penetrating gaze that seemed to see right through him. "Dragon?"

Instinct told Dragon to get away before Bear started asking uncomfortable questions. He pulled out of Bear's arms. "The tree's not far to the south. Come on."

He turned his back to Bear and began the trek back the way he'd come. Behind him, Bear's feet rustled through the mulch of brambles, rotting branches and fallen leaves. Bear didn't say a word, but the weight of his stare was practically a physical pressure on the back of Dragon's head.

He clenched his hand around the handle of his knife. Why the idea of arguing with Bear bothered him so much, Dragon had no idea, but there it was. He'd allowed Bear to lead without challenging any of his decisions so far, telling himself that there was no need. That one direction was as good as another, and there was no point in dissent for its own sake. It wasn't like Bear never listened to Dragon. He did. In fact, he'd let Dragon lead them through the thick forests of the foothills, recognizing that he was more familiar with that type of terrain.

Bear was a good leader. The two of them worked well together. Dragon figured there was no point in telling Bear what he thought about the body being a sign from the Mother, because it didn't make any difference.

No point in giving him a reason to leave you.

Dragon ignored the silent voice which had haunted him ever since the river. It was ridiculous, and he knew it. Bear wouldn't leave him, especially not for something as stupid as a

53

disagreement. They were Pack now, and Pack Brothers didn't desert each other. Not ever. Not even in death.

The knowledge did nothing to explain the icy hook that buried itself in Dragon's gut at the mere thought of having Bear look at him with disgust.

Bear grabbed him by the arm before he'd gotten more than thirty paces from the dead man. Dragon knew by the gentle but firm way Bear gripped him that he wasn't going to get away without talking this time. He swallowed.

When Dragon stopped walking, Bear turned him around by the shoulders. "Dragon. You're avoiding me. Stop it."

Dragon's stomach clenched. "I'm not." *Liar.*

"Yes, you are." Bear's fingers dug hard into Dragon's upper arms. "You won't *talk* to me. You won't tell me what you're thinking, and it's driving me crazy."

Tell him. Dragon opened his mouth. Part of him wanted to tell the truth, tell Bear the dead man was nothing but a corpse in the woods and not a sign, that even if Shenandoah really existed he wasn't sure they'd ever find it, but he needed Bear more than he needed to be heard and he just. Couldn't. Say it.

"You're wrong," he whispered instead, hating himself for the lie but unable to do anything else.

Bear's eyes narrowed. "You're afraid. You're *afraid* to talk to me."

The words cut deep, mostly because they were true. Dragon shook loose of Bear's grip. "Believe what you want. I'm not hiding anything from you."

"Yes you are."

"I'm not." Dragon turned away and started moving again. "Stop wasting time. We need to get busy burying your Carwin friend there if we want to get out of this area before nightfall."

He should've known Bear wouldn't let it go. Footsteps thudded behind him, then Bear's hand closed over his arm and yanked him around until they stood face to face. Bear's eyes burned with fury.

"You're lying," Bear accused, his voice low and rough with barely controlled anger. "I thought you were stronger than that. I didn't think you were so weak that you can't even be honest with your Brother."

Rage stained Dragon's vision red. Before he realized what he was doing, he unsheathed his knife and dug the tip into the pulse point in Bear's throat.

Everything stopped. Dragon's heart pounded against his breastbone, the only thing moving too fast in a world gone still.

You're Pack. You kill. You even kill members of other Packs if you have to. But you never. Ever. Draw a weapon on your Brother.

His second Sarge had hammered that particular lesson home at the public hanging of Sarge number one, who'd been witnessed stabbing a Brother in the back.

Dragon sheathed his knife on the first try in spite of his shaking hands, turned and walked away without a word. This time, Bear didn't follow him.

By the time Dragon returned to the corpse a few minutes later with two large, sturdy chunks of tree in his hand, the tremors had stopped. He tossed a piece of wood toward Bear, who was already digging with his bare hands, and started on the other end of the trench Bear had begun.

He didn't look at Bear. Couldn't. *I drew a knife on him.*

If Bear ever had a *real* reason to leave, this was it. Dragon swallowed the bile rising in his throat and dug into the loam of the forest floor as hard as he could.

They worked in silence. The sun passed the midday position and sank a couple of hours toward afternoon before Bear tamped the last of the loose dirt over the makeshift grave.

After they finished, the two of them stood on opposite ends of the mound of earth. To Dragon, it felt like he stood on a whole other world, separated from Bear by a wall of things unsaid.

He had to change it.

Drawing himself up straight, Dragon forced himself to look Bear in the eye. "I'm sorry, Bear. I shouldn't have drawn my weapon on you. It was wrong."

Bear stared back, his face expressionless. "Yeah, it was."

A cold, sick feeling settled in the pit of Dragon's stomach. He rubbed a hand over his face. *Mother, how do I fix this?*

"But I shouldn't have called you weak. You're not weak. I..." Bear ran one hand through his hair. "I was angry. I didn't mean it."

Dragon let out a harsh laugh. What a pair they were.

Bear made an impatient noise. Dropping his piece of wood, he stalked up to Dragon and cradled his face in both hands. "We said we were Pack. *Brothers*, Dragon. We chose each other. What does that mean, if we can't tell each other the truth?"

He's right. Bear was right, and Dragon knew it was time he acknowledged it.

He wound both arms around Bear's neck and tilted his face up. He knew everything he felt was there for Bear to see. It made him feel as if he'd wandered into a battle without a weapon, but he reminded himself that Bear was his Brother now. If a man couldn't trust his Brother with his deepest secrets, he couldn't trust anyone.

"Bear, I—" He stopped.

"What?" Bear ran a thumb over Dragon's chin. "Tell me."

The expression on Bear's face hid nothing. Dragon felt he could look straight down to Bear's soul, if he chose. It terrified him, but he wanted that kind of closeness more than he'd ever wanted anything in his life. All he had to do was open himself

56

up to Bear, and he could have it.

He licked his lips. "I..."

Say it. Tell him you think he's wrong about that body being a sign. He won't leave you. Tell him.

He couldn't. Couldn't. He wanted to, Mother, he did, but it felt like a huge risk, and he didn't even know why.

Confused, angry with himself and needing to make the world simple again, Dragon tightened his arms around Bear's neck and pulled him down into a hard kiss.

Bear stiffened for a second, then relaxed and opened his mouth wide for Dragon's tongue. He didn't try to resurrect the conversation, which was fine with Dragon. As far as he was concerned, fucking in the cool, moist earth was better than fighting any day.

After they pulled their clothes on again and went on their way, Bear didn't ask Dragon any more questions about Shenandoah and the signs, and Dragon didn't offer to share his thoughts.

A day and a half later, they came through a narrow pass in the mountains and stood on a high stone shelf overlooking a valley set like a green jewel in the surrounding slopes. In a clearing in the midst of the valley, a tall wooden fence surrounded a collection of rough buildings.

They didn't need to say anything. Side by side, they made their way down the pathless slope toward the town.

Chapter Six

The valley was bigger than it had looked from the pass. Wider, more rugged, the forest older and thicker than any Bear had ever seen before. A river with a vicious current crossed the path they threaded through the trees and waist-high ferns along the valley floor. Luckily, it was narrow and shallow enough to cross on foot.

"Great Mother, that water's freezing," Bear said as he and Dragon redressed on the opposite bank.

"The rivers and streams in the mountains are always cold like that." Dragon stood and slung the bag over his shoulder. He shook his water skin. "Speaking of water, I'm still good. What about you?"

"Nearly full." Bear took a good look around. The afternoon sun shone through the canopy overhead, surrounding him and Dragon with green-gold light. "The town was northwest from the pass, right?"

Dragon nodded. "There's a path there, about ten paces away." He gestured toward the west, where the trees grew thinner. "We need to be very, very careful. We're lucky we haven't run into their Pack yet."

"I know." Bear sniffed the air. It smelled like earth and running water, with a sharp whiff of urine where a wildcat had marked its territory. "I don't smell any people. No one's been out here for a long time."

A very, very *long time.* He wondered about that, but there was no point in puzzling over it right now. They'd most likely find out more than they wanted to know about this tribe and its Pack soon enough.

"The wind's in our favor, for now. If we're careful, we can get close enough to get a good look at the village without being noticed." Dragon flashed the rare grin that always made Bear's blood sing. "Ready?"

"Ready." Bear stalked up Dragon, swept him close with an arm around his waist and kissed him. "Let's do it."

At it turned out, their caution was unnecessary, since the village was utterly deserted.

Not that they realized that right away. The wall around the town was tall, sturdy and well-maintained, without a single gap. From their hiding place beneath a spreading mountain laurel where the forest crowded relatively close to the eastern edge, even Dragon's sharp eyes couldn't spot a chink through which to see what was happening on the other side. It wasn't until they noticed a lack of chimney smoke, workers in the fields around the town or in fact any other signs of life that they decided a closer look was in order. Dragon shimmied to the top of a tall chestnut tree and announced that there was no one inside the walls.

"There's a gate in the western wall," he said as he dropped to the ground. "It's open. Let's go take a look inside."

Bear rubbed his chin, thinking. It was several hours past midday. They should probably move on, sooner rather than later. A deserted village never meant anything good. If the people here had simply moved on because their fields had gone barren, that was one thing. But if it was something else, if there were nomad gangs or nightfeeders who'd gotten bold and found ways inside the wall...well. Better to be somewhere far away when the sun went down.

On the other hand, they were running low on dried meat and fruit. Maybe they'd find some in the town. And Mother, if this tribe had left behind a single wheel of cheese, he'd praise them forever.

Bear squinted into the sky. Surely they had time for a quick foray into the abandoned town for supplies. They could always leave if either of them sensed danger.

"No signs of danger?" Bear hadn't smelled anyone—or any predatory animals for that matter—ever since they'd entered this valley, but he had to ask. Dragon could see much farther than Bear could smell.

"Nothing." Dragon brushed his palms against his pants. "And there's lots of game in the forest. Deer, rabbits, boar. You probably smelled them already. There's another river on the far side of the town too, so we can probably catch some fish."

Bear watched the back-and-forth sway of Dragon's braid as they crept single file around the edge of the forest to the west side of the village, still careful even though they both knew there was really no need. Something in the way Dragon talked about this place tolled an alarm in Bear's mind. He figured he knew why—Dragon probably thought the same thing Bear had thought at first, and had dismissed it the second he saw how small and primitive this place was.

Dread curled in Bear's gut. *This is not going to end well.*

He pushed the unpleasant thought away. Maybe he was wrong. Maybe he was reading too much into Dragon's words. After all, it was likely they'd find it safe to spend the night here. Or at least as safe as camping in the open. If they stayed here, even for a night, why *not* fish? Or hunt? They'd done it plenty of times while traveling through the trackless wilderness. Why shouldn't they do it here? It was perfectly reasonable.

He'd nearly talked himself out of his unease by the time they'd skirted the fields, the empty livestock pens and the barn with its door banging in the breeze and stood in the eaves of the forest about a hundred and fifty paces from the western wall. The gate stood wide open. Through it, Bear saw a dusty, pocked path cutting through thin grass. The corner of a house showed on one edge of the space.

The sight burned like a beacon. Mother, to have a real roof over his head again. To sleep in a *bed.* After most of a moon cycle spent journeying, it seemed like an unimaginable luxury. Great Mother, he hoped this place was safe to spend the night. He'd almost forgotten what it felt like to rest on a feather mattress, or even a grass-filled pallet. It had been even longer for Dragon.

What would it be like to make love to Dragon in a real bed, instead of a blanket on the ground?

With a jolt, Bear realized that except for the one time inside Char, he and Dragon had never fucked anywhere but outside, under the open sky.

He darted a sidelong glance at Dragon and was startled to find Dragon staring back at him with a familiar heat. His cock rose in response to the need in those gray eyes and the scent of lust rolling off Dragon in waves.

Dragon's face broke into a grin. Pressing his body to Bear's, he fisted a hand in Bear's hair and kissed him hard. "Soon as we know it's safe. We can get supplies after."

"Except oil. We might need that now."

Dragon raised his eyebrows. After finding that bottle of oil in the abandoned farmhouse, they had a pretty decent supply left. The only way they could possibly need more *right now* was if Bear planned to fuck Dragon for days on end, and they both knew it. Bear grinned, shoved a hand down the back of Dragon's buckskins and rubbed a finger over his hole.

The way Dragon's eyes fluttered shut and his mouth fell open made Bear's cock pulse against his laces. For some reason, the threat of a dry finger up his ass aroused Dragon strongly and instantly. Bear didn't understand it, but Mother, he *liked* it.

He pulled his hand out of Dragon's pants before either of them could get carried away. "Ready?"

Dragon's eyes opened. The lust vanished, replaced by his usual cool alertness. He drew his knife. "Ready. I'll take point."

Bear agreed with a single curt nod. Knife in hand and all senses on alert, he followed Dragon down the weed-ridden path between the forest and the village gate. They passed three empty livestock pens. He sniffed at them as they walked by. He caught the distinct whiff of goats from one, but he wasn't sure about the other two. The smell wasn't familiar, and neither was the dung left behind—large, round, dry pellets with a sweet, grassy scent.

"They had goats," he told Dragon as they walked. "I don't know what the other animals were, though, I don't recognize the smell."

Dragon stopped long enough to peer into the nearest pen. "Sheep, I think. Looks like their droppings, anyway. There's a tribe north of Ashe that keeps them." He moved on, kicking a round dungball out of the way. "It'd be great if there were still some around, actually. We could use the wool when winter hits." He plucked a long, coarse, dark hair from the rough wooden rail of the third pen as he passed. "Looks like they kept horses too."

Bear trailed behind, frowning. He'd seen photographs of horses before, from the old world, but didn't realize anyone still kept them. Sheep, though, that was a new one. "What's wool?" he asked.

"It's the sheep's fur, only it isn't really like normal fur. It's thick and rough and really curly. You can shave it off and weave a nice warm fabric out of it." Dragon paused at the gate, one hand on the wood of the wall, and cast a narrow-eyed stare through the gap. "I don't see anything moving in there."

62

A deep sniff confirmed what Bear already knew. "And I don't smell any people. I think this place really is deserted."

Dragon didn't answer, and Bear couldn't read anything in the set of his shoulders or the watchful line of his profile. They stood there in silence for another few seconds before Dragon moved forward. Bear followed with his nostrils flared and his knife at the ready, just in case.

Inside, tiny log houses crowded close together on either side of the path. Weeds and grass had begun to creep into what had obviously once been a well-maintained road. To their left, a tall, narrow gatehouse stood with the door hanging open. A hefty spear with a wicked stone head leaned against the wall.

Dragon glanced over his shoulder. "Bear?"

He shook his head. "Nothing." The only scents were dirt, grass, a riot of herbs and flowers—kitchen gardens, most likely—and a faint, musty smell he couldn't quite place. All the smells people normally carried with them and left behind were gone.

"Good." Dragon turned to face Bear. He rubbed his thumb over the handle of his knife, something he did a lot when he was thinking. "We'll do a walk-through first, get the layout of the place. You can do the sniff test on each house we pass to see if there's any people or dangerous animals, and we can make note of which places we think are most likely to have the supplies we need. After that, we can go through each place for supplies and decide where we want to stay."

To stay? Bear frowned at the odd wording but decided not to mention it. They'd already come to the unspoken understanding that they'd be staying overnight, at least. That was probably what Dragon meant.

It took them less than an hour to skirt the inner perimeter of the village wall and walk the main street and the short lanes sprouting from it. The whole town contained only twenty-four buildings, including the gatehouse and a large public hall set against the north wall. A row of four chicken coops sat apart from the houses, in a cleared area on the east side of the enclosure.

Not one chicken remained, to Bear's disappointment. After so many long days of dried meat supplemented by hunting wary deer and swift rabbits, it would've been nice to eat something as easy to catch and kill as a chicken. They tasted good too.

Dragon bumped his arm as he stood gazing mournfully at the empty coops. "At least they left the gardens."

Bear laughed, and Dragon grinned. Most houses had small but fruitful kitchen gardens packed with marigold, feverfew, sage, thyme, violets, chamomile, valerian, hemp and other plants Bear didn't recognize but assumed had some value as food or medicine, or both. A few houses even had small fruit trees growing nearby. One house, larger than the rest and set apart in a sunny clearing, boasted several wooden trellises heavy with ripe greenish-brown scuppernongs. Bear and Dragon both figured that house must've belonged to the tribe's Mother.

Privately, Bear hoped they'd find a stash of scuppernong wine. If they did, he planned to take a couple of bottles with them—one for themselves, and one to help ease their way into Shenandoah if need be. Hopefully they'd be welcome without it, but it never hurt to be prepared.

"So, I guess this solves one mystery."

Bear glanced at Dragon in surprise. "Huh?"

"The grapes. All of these gardens, in fact." Dragon swept one hand in a wide circle. "They're thriving. That vine's full of scuppernongs, all the plants in the gardens are healthy. Obviously nothing's wrong with the soil here, so..."

"So that can't be why they picked up and left," Bear finished, catching on. He scratched the back of his neck. "And we haven't seen any signs of violence in the town, so it doesn't look like they were having trouble with nomad gangs or anything."

"No." Dragon swiveled in a slow circle, his brows drawn together in a thoughtful frown. "What happened here, I wonder?"

Bear shrugged. "Maybe they just outgrew it. There's really no room to expand in this valley, not without cutting down more of the forest than is healthy, and the houses are really close together here. Wouldn't surprise me if they just picked up and moved somewhere with more space to grow."

"Maybe." Dragon strode forward, plucked a plump grape from the vine and popped it into his mouth. He chewed for a moment, watching Bear the whole time with an appraising gaze, then spit the seeds onto the ground. "You know, I'm kind of surprised you're taking this so well."

"Don't know what you mean." Ignoring the voice in his head that said he knew exactly what Dragon meant, Bear bypassed the vine and headed for the garden at the side of the house. It was larger than any of the others. He told himself he just wanted to see what grew there and wasn't trying to avoid what Dragon was going to say next.

Not that it mattered, since Dragon followed him. "What? You mean after we've come all this way, after we've traveled nearly a moon cycle to get here, you're not the least bit upset or disappointed to find Shenandoah deserted?"

Bear scowled. He'd hoped Dragon wouldn't say it. That way, he could pretend Dragon hadn't been thinking it, and that he hadn't known Dragon had thought it, or that he himself had ever thought it. But now it was out there, voiced out loud, and he couldn't avoid the inevitable fight. Because he knew they would fight over this. Knew it, as surely as he knew the cycles of sun and moon and the seasons.

Maybe you're wrong. Maybe Dragon only wants to stay here for a day or two. Rest, restock our supplies, then move on. He never believed in Shenandoah anyway, not really.

Bear knew he was kidding himself, though. He'd heard Dragon's desire to stay here in the way he spoke of it, in the words he chose. He wouldn't want to leave. But they couldn't stay. Not with Shenandoah still out there somewhere.

"Bear. *Look* at me, will you?"

Reluctantly, Bear turned to face Dragon. The gray eyes were troubled, Dragon's body radiating tension. He had to sense Bear's anxiety.

Bear drew a deep breath and blew it out. "This isn't Shenandoah."

Dragon blinked. "Yes, it is."

"It isn't."

"Yes, it *is*. For the Mother's sake, it fits the description on the wall perfectly." Dragon looked around, arms out at his side. "A hidden valley, in the mountains far away? Bear, come on."

"I know, it's just..." Sighing, Bear raked both hands through his tangled hair. "Look, I know it looks right on the surface, but this isn't it, okay? It just isn't."

Dragon raised his eyebrows. "Oh? All right then." Sheathing his knife, he crossed his arms over his stomach and pinned Bear with a cold stare. "Explain why not."

Bear debated telling Dragon about his dreams and the strange waking visions he had now and then, but decided it wouldn't go over well. "All the stories say Shenandoah is a big tribe. This place is—was—tiny. And it's supposed to be hard to find. And well-defended. We just walked right up to it, right over the pass and into the valley. Anybody could've done that. And, well..." *And this place is empty and small and depressing.* Frustrated, Bear glared down the dirt lane toward the village gate.

Dragon made an irritated noise. "I know you wanted Shenandoah to be better than this. And I know you wanted a tribe to belong to again. So did I. But it is what it is, Bear. It could be a lot worse. At least the buildings are intact, the soil's good and the gardens are still growing. We can take this house here. We can hunt, just like always. We can build a smokehouse if they don't already have one, and then we can have venison all winter without hunting."

In the time they'd been traveling together, Bear had grown used to Dragon backing down on the rare occasions when they disagreed about anything important. So it came as a shock to hear Dragon standing by his opinion for a change. Part of Bear ached with pride, because he'd wanted Dragon to do that for so long.

Another part cringed inside, because he couldn't back down and let Dragon have his way. Not on this. They'd set out in search of Shenandoah, and Bear refused to give up until they'd found it.

He licked his lips, trying to find the best way to say it. Mother, but he wasn't good with words. "Dragon—"

"Look, no, don't." Stalking forward, Dragon laid a warm hand on Bear's chest. He peered up at Bear with a set jaw and a stubborn crease between his eyes. "We could have a good life here. It doesn't really matter what it was or wasn't. It's *here*, now, with everything we need. There's no real reason to go on."

Bear searched for the best words. The kindest words. They eluded him, so he decided to go with the truth. "Except that we still haven't found what we set out to find. This isn't Shenandoah, and I don't want to stop until we find it."

Dragon's expression turned stormy. "So you'd throw away something good—something *real*, something here right now, something we can have *right now*—to keep chasing after something that might not even exist? Or worse, something we might have already found, only you won't believe it because the reality of it isn't as nice as the dream? Is that right?"

Anger seeped like poison through Bear's blood. "I won't be

tempted away from what we both *agreed* to do just because we found one fairly nice place. I'm not that weak."

The twitch that meant Dragon was angry, scared and hurt all at the same time started up in his cheek, but his gaze held Bear's. "I know you like to be in control. And that's fine, most of the time. But not when it might mean both of our lives. Just this once, I think you ought to listen to me."

Just this once? In his mind, Bear pictured all the times he'd thought he and Dragon had worked so well together. All the times Dragon had led them through the pathless mountains and Bear had followed, meek as a mouse. All the times Bear had tried, in his clumsy way, to encourage Dragon to open up to him. And now Dragon wanted Bear to completely disregard his own wishes in favor of Dragon's, *just this once*, in the one single thing that really mattered to Bear?

The anger simmering in Bear's gut surged up and took over.

Hands clenched so he wouldn't grab Dragon and throw him into the nearest solid object, Bear took a big step backward to put some space between them. "There's a time for listening and a time for taking charge. And right now, I'm taking charge. This isn't Shenandoah, and we're not staying here. We'll spend a night or two, stock up on supplies, but that's it. I'm not giving up on Shenandoah."

Dragon's cheeks flushed red. "And I'm telling you, this *is* Shenandoah. This, right here, where we're standing." He stared at Bear, his expression hard. "It's stupid to go back out there when we've already found it. You're blinded by your fantasy of what you wanted Shenandoah to be."

"Shut *up!*" Bear growled low in his throat. "Great Mother, when I said you should speak up I didn't mean you should nag me like a fucking old woman."

The instant the words were out, Bear wished he could take them back. But he couldn't. The damage was done. All the fire and fight drained out of Dragon's face, leaving a cold mask behind, but not before Bear caught a glimpse of the raw pain in his eyes.

Bear stepped forward, instantly remorseful. How often had his Pack leaders—and even his parents, in the long-ago days of his early childhood—told him to keep a check on his temper? "Dragon, I'm sorry, I—"

"We need food." Dragon clenched a hand around the strap of the satchel still slung over his shoulder. "We should probably take care of that first, since we'll have to spend the night here. We can check the town for clothes and other supplies after that."

He didn't mention sex. Not that Bear expected it at this point.

At least he's not suggesting you split up. Bear breathed a little easier knowing that. He'd been half afraid Dragon would insist on staying here even if Bear moved on.

Not knowing what else to do, Bear forced himself to speak as if nothing was wrong. "I'll go hunt. You can start gathering some fruit and whatever other food you can find." He bit his lip. "Is that okay?"

Dragon gave him an unreadable look, then turned and started toward the small shed behind the empty house. He didn't say a word.

Bear waited until Dragon was out of sight before heading for the village gate. He had no idea how he was going to fix this new rift between them, but he had to find a way. He couldn't let Dragon drift away from him. Not when he'd just started to crack the hard shell Dragon kept around himself.

Confused, angry and dejected, Bear left the village and headed into the forest. Maybe he'd find some answers out there along with the game.

Game was as plentiful in the forest as Dragon had said. Deer, rabbit, boar, even ducks swimming in a small pond not far from the village. The problem was, Bear couldn't seem to summon the concentration he needed to kill anything. He kept seeing the swift flash of hurt in Dragon's eyes, over and over again, until it drowned out everything else.

Guilt twisted Bear's insides. He wouldn't have felt so bad about what he'd said if it had been true, but it wasn't. And because of that, because he'd let his anger and his fixation on his goal get the better of him, everything he'd done to get Dragon talking was for nothing.

You're such an idiot. When you get back, you need to tell him how wrong you were to say that to him, and start all over again.

Bear breathed a near-silent curse as the deer he'd been sighting bounded off through the underbrush. Keeping the arrow nocked, he lowered the bow to the side and slipped through the forest in the buck's wake. The wind had picked up in the hour or so since he'd left the village, and kept shifting directions so that he'd given up trying to stay downwind of his prey. If he could just get a second's clear shot, that's all it would take. He didn't care if the buck knew he was there or not.

He followed the deer for another half hour before losing all sight and scent of it. Berating himself for letting the argument with Dragon distract him so much, he sniffed the air for traces of other nearby game, but the crazy swirl of the wind defeated him. It carried such a mix of smells from so many different directions, he couldn't pick out which was which and where it led.

He bent to inspect the forest floor. Boar tracks punched through the leaf mold to pockmark the soft black earth beneath. They were only a few minutes old. Bow at the ready, he trotted off in the direction they led.

It wasn't long before he heard the sounds of the wild pig snuffling up ahead. He slowed his pace until his feet made no sound. At least the wind was in his favor at the moment, wafting the overwhelming smell of boar right in his face. He rounded a thick oak tree, and there was the pig, rooting in the earth just ahead.

He raised the bow. *Steady, steady.*

He drew the string back. The wood creaked. The boar lifted its head, but by that time Bear's arrow was already flying through the air. It hit the pig's side with a solid *thunk.*

The boar immediately took off through the forest, squealing. Bear dropped the bow and his quiver and ran after it. His shot was a good one. The animal wouldn't get far before its wound overcame it. He could return for the bow and arrows after he had his kill.

He was so focused on catching the pig, the smell of human didn't register until it was too late. The boar tore through a thicket of mountain laurel. Bear followed, and nearly fell over two naked women lying on the ground.

Time slowed to a crawl while Bear's prey escaped and he stood there staring in shock at the first live people he'd seen— other than Dragon—in more than a moon cycle.

One woman lay sprawled on her back, long black braids spread out beneath her dark body like a blanket. The second, blonde and pale, knelt between the first woman's spread thighs. It was obvious what Bear and his lost pig had interrupted.

The first woman's gaze met his. Her cold eyes narrowed, her hand reached for the sheath by her side and Bear's world lurched into motion again.

He sprang backward out of the thicket, turned and ran, drawing his knife at the same time and wishing he had his bow. The two women were Pack. He couldn't have said how he recognized that in them, but he did, somehow. Pack nearly always recognized other Pack, and these women were clearly warriors.

Good ones too. He could smell them coming after him but couldn't hear them. He bit his lip, thinking hard as he ran. He needed to retrieve his bow and arrows, then get back to the village. He wasn't worried about leading these two to Dragon. Between the two of them, they could take on the two women and it would be an even fight. He hoped.

They would have to think about the implications of this *after* they'd dealt with the immediate danger.

A sudden, searing pain in his left thigh made Bear stumble. He reached back and grimaced when he felt a hefty knife buried hilt-deep in the muscle. Since he didn't dare risk the blood loss he'd get if he pulled it out now, he left it there, gritted his teeth and ran on.

He could ignore the pain. The torn muscle in his leg, though, slowed him down. No amount of willpower would make the injured muscle move any faster. And the exertion of running sent blood spilling from the wound in spite of the knife still in it. It was inevitable that they would catch up to him.

They cornered him against a boulder. He dealt the blonde one a wicked slice across the abdomen before they brought him down. Maybe he shouldn't have, since it seemed to bring out the protective instincts in the dark one. She came at him with pure fury in her eyes and punched him so hard he saw colored lights for a moment. By the time he shook off his daze, he was lying on his side with his wrists and ankles bound.

The blonde woman smiled sweetly at him. "Sorry about this." She took hold of the knife handle sticking out of the back of his thigh and dragged the blade upward through the meat of the muscle.

Great Mother, but nothing had hurt like that in a long, long time. He bit his tongue and held the blonde's gaze in silence. If they were waiting for him to scream, they could forget it.

The dark woman let out an impatient noise. "Wasp, quit playing. We need to get back to camp before his Brothers find him."

"Maybe he's alone." Wasp—and a perfect name it was, Bear realized—dug the blade a little deeper, pale eyes gleaming, before pulling it out finally. "C'mon, Hawk. Can't we have a little fun with him?"

Hawk pinched the bridge of her nose. When she looked at Wasp again, her expression brimmed with a mix of revulsion and adoration that made Bear's gut clench with fear. Clearly, Wasp's idea of "play" didn't sit well with Hawk at all. But it was just as clear that pretty little Wasp usually got her way, just because Hawk loved her to distraction.

Bear could deal with torture, if he had to. He'd been captured by the Norman Tribe once, and no one did torture more creatively than them. But he had a feeling Wasp's playtime involved knives and blood, and he was already bleeding too fast. If he died out here, Dragon would never know what happened to him. He might think Bear had left him, and that was the one thing Bear couldn't stand.

After what seemed like forever, Hawk shook her head. "No. He's Pack, obviously, and Pack never travel alone. Clean my knife and give it here, then dress that wound in his leg. I'm going to make a litter to carry him."

Wasp looked disappointed, but set about doing as she was told. "So we're taking him back?"

"You *know* we are." Hawk stared at him with hard eyes. "I wouldn't do this if I didn't have to. But I do, for the good of my tribe. I'm sorry, Brother."

He sneered at her. "You don't have the right to call me Brother."

Her feet were bare, but he still lost consciousness when she kicked him in the head.

Chapter Seven

By the time Dragon returned from the shed with two large baskets woven of the same sturdy grass they'd used in the Ashe Tribe, Bear had gone. Dragon was glad. He'd never felt so utterly gutted, yet at the same time so furious. He'd barely found the strength to hide both extremes from Bear long enough to make his escape. If Bear were here right now, Dragon had no idea whether he would hit him or crumble at his feet. Neither option held any appeal, so finding himself blessedly alone was a relief.

He spent a couple of peaceful hours harvesting scuppernongs and other fruits and vegetables from the town's gardens. One garden, larger than any but the Mother's, overflowed with sage, feverfew, chamomile and other medicinal herbs. Dragon figured that house must've belonged to the tribe's healer. After a moment's thought, he plucked a healthy clump of chamomile and put it in his basket. They could always come back for more herbs later, but in the meantime he thought it a good idea to have at least one plant he knew how to use for wound healing. If nothing else, it made a tasty tea.

Back at the Mother's house, he set the second full basket beside the first one and went to draw a bucket of clean water from the well at the north end of the enclosure. He used the water to clean the soil from the fruits, vegetables and chamomile, then used a length of rope he'd found in the shed to hang the chamomile out in the sun to dry.

Those chores finished, he squinted into the sky. The gentle breeze from earlier in the day had become a stiff wind that changed direction every few seconds. High, thin clouds hazed the sky and blurred the sun's disc where it hung just above the humps of the mountaintops.

It's only been about three hours, he reminded himself. *Just because there's a lot of game out there doesn't mean it's easy to catch.*

Ignoring the tiny, fearful part of him that whispered *he's leaving, he's leaving you,* even though he knew that wasn't so, Dragon decided to explore inside the Mother's house. Just to kill time until Bear returned. Because surely he'd be back soon. Bear was a good hunter. He'd be back any minute now, a big buck slung over his wide shoulders, and everything could go back to normal.

But it can't. Nothing can ever be like it was again. Bear's going to get both of you killed chasing Shenandoah, or his ideal of it. You can't just let it go. No matter how angry it makes him, or what he thinks of you for it.

Dragon hadn't the slightest idea how to heal the breach the subject had already created between them. And Mother help him, but he yearned body and soul to be with Bear forever. He didn't know if he was strong enough to risk losing that.

There was no point in thinking about it right now. With one last worried glance down the dusty dirt road toward the gate, Dragon opened the door and went into the house.

Inside, it smelled musty and stale. Dragon rolled up the thick fabric covering the windows to let in the fresh air and waning daylight, then started searching through the cabinets and cupboards. They'd mostly been cleaned out, but he found a couple of thick wool blankets, a roll of cheesecloth and three down pillows, and the bed still had sheets on it.

When the western sky turned orange with the sunset and Bear still hadn't returned, Dragon knew something had gone terribly wrong. He loaded the bag with both full water skins, some scuppernongs, a couple of apples and several pieces of fire-roasted venison wrapped in sage leaves. After a moment's consideration he cut off a long strip of cheesecloth, rolled it up and stuffed it in the bag as well, along with both of the blankets he and Bear had brought with them.

The bag held everything, barely. He hoped he wouldn't need it all, but he didn't know what he might find. He and Bear might have to spend a night or two in the forest. They might even have to leave and abandon the town altogether. Best to be as well prepared as possible.

At the village gate, Dragon paused long enough to fashion an arrow in the dirt out of white stones, pointing the direction he planned to go to begin his search. He had no idea which way Bear had gone. If he returned while Dragon was away, he wanted Bear to at least know which direction he'd taken, and understand why. He hoped the single symbol in the earth was enough.

Even using what he knew of his Brother's usual hunting habits, it was nearly midnight before Dragon found any sign of Bear. The bright silver light of the full moon pierced the thin clouds to outline the shape of Bear's bow and the quiver of arrows lying abandoned on the ground. Not far off, black drops darkened the leaves.

Blood.

Dragon's pulse sped up. He swallowed down the rush of fear that wanted to come. He didn't think this was Bear's blood. It looked like Bear had shot an animal, a deer or boar most likely, then dropped his gear to run after it and finish it off. What worried Dragon was that the bow and arrows were still here, long after the blood had dried. Bear hadn't come back for them. Which meant something had happened. Something bad enough to prevent Bear from retrieving his gear or making it back to the village.

Picking up the bow, Dragon slung it over his shoulder along with the satchel, then shoved the quiver into the bag. He peered at the ground. It didn't take long to find the trail of blood left behind by whatever animal Bear had shot. Moving as quickly as he dared while still keeping it in sight, Dragon followed the trail of blood and boar tracks into the moonlit woods.

The spoor led him on a wild, looping path through trees, ferns, briars and mountain laurel. It doubled back and crossed itself more than once. Dragon held back his frustration and kept going. He might be able to find Bear if he left the blood trail and struck out blindly into the forest, but his chances weren't good. Better to stick with a more or less sure thing.

He could have called out for Bear, but instinct told him not to. They hadn't seen any signs of people anywhere near the village or the surrounding woods. But if they were wrong, if nomads or unfriendly tribe members had somehow captured Bear, Dragon didn't want them to know about him. Retaining the element of surprise could mean the difference between rescuing Bear and losing him.

If that was what had happened. Dragon hoped with everything in him that it wasn't.

He got his first real inkling of the truth when the trail led him into a laurel thicket exactly like a thousand other laurel thickets he'd already gone through. The pig tracks swerved sideways around a flattened place in the dirt. Broken branches on the opposite side showed where the animal had continued on its way.

Dragon stopped, frowning. Something was off. Something about the tamped-down spot in the soft earth, and the way the tracks veered around it. Why would the boar take the time and energy for a detour, even a small one, when it was running for its life? It wouldn't, unless...

Overhead, the sheer cloud layer parted enough to let the moonlight shine through unchecked. It picked out something thin and silver-white half buried in the leaf mold. Mouth dry, Dragon strode forward and bent to look.

It was a hair. A single long, blonde, human hair.

And now that he'd seen it, he saw others. Not just blonde ones, but thicker, courser black ones as well.

Two of them. Maybe more.

Dragon's stomach dropped into his feet, but he didn't have time to waste with worry. Whoever these people were, they had Bear. If they didn't, Bear would've come back to the village right away. Dragon had to find him, the sooner the better.

He refused to think about the possibility that the strangers might not take prisoners.

It didn't take long to figure out which way Bear had gone from the thicket. His path wasn't much more difficult to follow than the boar's blood trail. He'd been running hard, with no thought to hiding his tracks.

Dragon's gut clenched when the tracks stumbled and blood splattered the trail. His pulse pounding in his ears, Dragon upped his pace to a silent trot. The amount of blood on the path increased with every step. It wasn't a life-threatening amount yet, thank the Mother, but it was more than anyone—even a warrior as strong as Bear—could afford to lose. Especially while trying to escape enemies.

The trail of blood ended in front of a large boulder, with a puddle so large it hadn't yet congealed completely. Dragon dropped to his knees, searching the ground for any signs at all that Bear was still alive. All he saw was the blood. Blood everywhere. None of Bear's tracks led away from this place.

"Mother, please," he whispered, desperate. His chest hurt

and his eyes stung. *Mother, please. Please don't let him be dead. Not like this.*

Shaking off the despair that wanted to swallow him, Dragon pushed to his feet. There was still a chance Bear was alive. If he was, Dragon couldn't waste time on useless grief. He had to find Bear and save him. If Bear was dead...

Dragon gripped the handle of his knife as hot fury rose to replace the desolation inside him. *If he's dead, I'll avenge him or die trying.*

Dragon bent to inspect the ground with renewed purpose. Even if Bear was dead, his body had been moved. Therefore, there must be more tracks of some sort, leading to Bear.

He found them after a moment's study. Parallel grooves in the dirt, with the marks of bare human feet on either side. He cursed. The marks told him nothing, except that two people— probably the same ones Bear had been running from—made a litter and used it to drag Bear away. It didn't tell Dragon whether Bear had been dead or too injured to walk, or if his captors simply hadn't wanted him on his feet.

Dragon slipped through the night at a dead run, one arm clutching the satchel and bow close to his body and the other holding his knife at the ready. His feet picked out the most silent path by instinct. *I'm coming, Bear. I'm coming.*

He slowed down when he spotted the flicker of flames through the trees. A campfire couldn't be anyone but the Mother-damned bastards who'd taken Bear. All his attention focused on the orange glow, Dragon flitted from one bit of cover to the next, closer and closer. Eventually, he heard murmured voices and saw two figures huddled close together between him and the fire.

He hunched down and crawled as close as he dared. He couldn't see anything with any clarity but the tops of their heads. One blonde, one black. Bear had to be near. Had to.

"I just don't see any point, that's all," one of the voices said. "I mean, aren't we coming back here soon anyway? Why can't we just take him back to Lexin now? It's three whole days back to Bath City."

A deep sigh from a different voice. "Wasp. Look. We're under orders to bring back all prisoners to Mother Stella. You *know* that."

"Then let's kill him. Mother Stella doesn't need to know we ever captured anyone alive."

Dragon's heartbeat faltered. Bear was alive. *Mother, thank you, thank you.*

On the other hand, unless the other Pack Sister—because who else could these two be but Pack?—was less practical and more compassionate than Wasp, he wouldn't be alive for much longer.

Setting his satchel on the ground, Dragon sheathed his knife, swung the bow into position and nocked an arrow. He aimed between the dark head and the blonde one. He couldn't see Bear from where he knelt, but by the Mother, the first of the women to threaten him would get an arrow through the head.

"He can tell us about the Lexin Tribe," the dark woman said.

"They're gone. The town's empty. It's ours now, and about time." Wasp shrugged. "What more do we need to know?"

It didn't take much for Dragon to put two and two together and realize Bear had been right all along. His chest constricted. *I'm sorry, Bear.*

There was no time for regrets, though. He ignored the ache inside him and concentrated on listening.

"Idiot." The dark woman sighed again, a long-suffering sound as if she had to put up with this sort of thing from her partner a lot. "After all these years of fighting over this valley, the people of Lexin have gotten very clever. They could have moved all but their Pack into the hills and left the Pack to ambush us when we come here to move in. Or they could've poisoned the water, or the soil. If they've done any of those things, or something else we haven't thought of, this Brother may know. And if he does, Mother Stella and the council will get it out of him."

The unpleasant way Wasp laughed then told Dragon all he needed to know about what was in store for Bear if they took him to Bath City. Dragon didn't need any more information than that. Sighting on the shine of blonde hair in the firelight, he drew back the bowstring and let the arrow fly.

Dropping the bow, he jumped up and ran forward with his knife drawn as the blonde woman fell sideways with the arrow in her throat. He burst into the small clearing where the women had made camp and jumped on the dark woman's back, tackling her to the ground. She was bigger than him, and strong. She writhed like a cat, nearly throwing him off.

He stabbed his knife into her wrist, pinning it to the earth. She grunted. He planted his knee on the elbow of her free arm when she tried to push herself up. Snatching up Wasp's abandoned knife, he yanked his captive's head back by the hair and dug the point of the knife into her throat. "Where's Bear?"

She managed to turn her head enough to glare at him with one eye. "I don't—"

He opened up a long, shallow cut alongside her windpipe. "You captured him tonight. You were just talking about him. Where is he?"

"Fuck you," she wheezed.

A thump sounded from the other side of the fire, followed by a muffled voice. Dragon stared, but couldn't see anything through the flames other than a couple of blankets. "Bear?"

The voice sounded again. There were no obvious words, but it was Bear. No doubt about it. The knot in Dragon's gut

Ally Blue

unwound just a little. "Hang on, I'm coming."

The woman beneath him bucked. He dug his knee harder into her elbow, forcing a sharp cry from her. "Are you alone? Is there anyone besides you two out here?"

She let out a wheezing laugh. "Lexin's ours now. Can't stop it."

"We're not from Lexin. I don't *care* about Lexin." He shook her head hard. "I'll ask again. Are. You. Alone?"

She bared her teeth at him. "I say again. Fuck. You."

Looking into her defiant face, he knew she wouldn't tell him anything. With no reason to postpone the inevitable, he cut her throat. Blood poured out in a hot flood. She jerked and gurgled beneath him. He dropped her head and wiped the knife clean on the back of her pants. It took a moment to wrench his own knife free of the dead woman's wrist. Once he did, he cleaned and sheathed it, then rose to his feet.

He ran back to fetch his and Bear's bag and the bow. Dropping the extra knife he'd just acquired into the bag, he trotted over to where Bear's voice had come from.

Bear lay curled on his side, a stained white blanket covering him from the neck down. A wadded-up cloth was stuffed in his mouth and tied in place with a strip of rope. His eyes were shut. Even in the warm firelight, he looked frighteningly pale. Dragon thought of the huge puddle of blood in the woods, and tasted fear on the back of his tongue.

Setting the bag and longbow down, Dragon knelt beside Bear and cut the gag off. He threw the rag and rope aside. "Bear? It's Dragon. I'm here."

Bear's eyes opened slowly, as if it was an effort. He smiled. "Figured you'd find me."

"Of course." Dragon laid a hand on Bear's forehead. His skin felt much cooler than it should have, and sweat beaded his upper lip. Dragon frowned. "You lost a lot of blood out there.

Where are you cut?"

"My leg. Hawk—that's the dark one—threw her knife at me, then Wasp...well, sort of played around with the wound after they caught me. She's the one who actually made it bleed so much."

Rage thumped through Dragon's blood. Tribal councils might sometimes engage in torture, when they thought it was necessary for the safety of the tribe. But Pack didn't do such things. Especially to other Pack, even enemies.

He resisted looking over his shoulder at Wasp. *Just be glad you're already dead, Sister.*

Bear let out a hoarse chuckle. "I can see what you're thinking. Let it go. Just untie me and let's just get out of here."

"Right." Dragon pulled the blanket off and started cutting through the ropes wound around Bear's wrists and ankles. The left leg of his pants had been cut away, and his bare skin was covered with drying blood. *Mother, so much of it.* "Do you have any idea if there are more of them? Or where this Bath City Tribe of theirs is? I brought food and blankets, so we can leave straight from here if we need to, but I'd rather go back to the town—Lexin?—first if it's safe. We're, what, southwest of it, so we'd have to pass by it anyway, most likely."

"I think they were alone. From what I could figure out, the Bath City Tribe's been after the Lexin Tribe's valley for a long time. Been trying to drive 'em out. I think maybe Bath City sends out scouting parties now and then to see if Lexin's abandoned the town yet, and that's what those two were doing here. Sounded like they were on their way back to Bath City. I'm not sure where Bath City is, but I'm guessing it's west of here, from the way they were talking." Bear grasped Dragon's arm. His eyes gleamed in the wavering light. "I'm sorry, Dragon. About earlier. About what I said."

Dragon blinked, surprised. "But...but you were right. This isn't Shenandoah at all. I should be apologizing to *you.*" *No time like the present, in fact.* He drew a deep breath. "I'm sorry, Bear. About everything."

Bear shook his head. "No. We're Brothers. I didn't have any right to talk to you like that. You don't nag, you never have, and, and I acted like...like I was your *Mother* or something, and that was wrong."

The quiet passion in Bear's voice made Dragon's chest feel warm and tight. Dropping his knife, he clasped Bear's hand in both of his. "We both said things we shouldn't have. But we know better now." He leaned down and pressed a soft kiss to Bear's lips. They tasted dry and salty. "You need some water. Here, sit up. I'll help you."

With Dragon's help, Bear pushed to a sitting position. He didn't make a sound or say a word, but the way his jaw tightened told Dragon how much pain he was in. He took the water skin Dragon handed him and drank several long, deep draughts. When he finished, he was breathing hard enough to worry Dragon.

Taking the skin, Dragon set it aside, dug a handful of scuppernongs out of the bag and handed them to Bear. "Here. Eat these. Then I need to take a look at your leg." He cast a worried glance at the bloody cloth wrapped around Bear's thigh. "One of the houses in Lexin looks like it might've belonged to a healer. When we get back, I'll check and see if they left any dried herbs to help with the pain. And I picked some chamomile and hung it up to dry earlier. It won't be dried out enough yet, but that's okay. I'll make you some tea anyway. It'll help you sleep."

"Yeah. That sounds good." Bear shifted his leg, grimacing. "Don't bother with the wound right now, though. It's dressed. The bandage is good and tight, and it's stopped bleeding, for now." He popped two grapes into his mouth and chewed. "Better to wait until we get back to Lexin before we start messing with it."

Dragon ran a hand over the bandage. It seemed sturdy enough. "Will it hold up for the trip back, or do you think I need to reinforce it?"

"I think it'll hold up." Bear spit out a mouthful of seeds. "I'll keep my weight off that leg as much as possible." He smiled, amber eyes shining. "I have you to lean on, don't I?"

Something warm and sweet lodged in Dragon's chest. He returned Bear's smile. "Yes. You do."

The sun had begun to rise behind the clouds thickening above the eastern mountains by the time Dragon half-dragged Bear over the threshold of the house back in Lexin. He got Bear to the bed through sheer willpower and lowered him to the mattress. Brushing Bear's sweaty, tangled hair from his brow, Dragon kissed his forehead. "Roll onto your stomach. Let me look."

Bear groaned, his face gray with exhaustion and blood loss, but he did as Dragon said. His wound had started bleeding again a couple of hours ago. Not too heavily, but it hadn't stopped, even when Dragon had called a halt long enough to reinforce Bear's bandage using some of the cheesecloth he'd brought.

Dragon's body blocked the pale dawn light coming in from the window. He moved to the side and bit back a curse when he got a look at the bandage. Fresh blood saturated the cloth and cut glistening swaths through the dirt and dried red coating the back of Bear's leg.

"You're bleeding worse than I thought." Setting the bag on the bed, Dragon dug out the rest of the cheesecloth. He stripped off his shirt, fashioned it into a long roll and placed it over the bloody bandage, then slipped one end of the cheesecloth beneath Bear's thigh. "This is going to hurt."

"Not as much as it hurt getting cut, I bet." Bear hissed, but held still when Dragon used the cloth to tie his shirt tightly to Bear's leg in a makeshift pressure dressing. "Ha. That's all you got?"

Dragon laughed, but it sounded as strained as Bear's joke. "I'm only getting started. That's just to slow down the bleeding while I collect some herbs, start a fire and boil some water. After that, the *real* fun starts."

The way Bear scowled then said he'd had bad wounds cleaned and dressed before, and knew exactly how painful it could be. In the back of his mind, Dragon knew Bear had experienced such injuries. He'd seen the scars on Bear's body, he just hadn't given any real thought to how Bear had gotten them. All Pack had battle scars, after all. Now, though, the fact that Bear had evidently survived severe wounds before gave Dragon hope. And Mother, but he needed hope right now, to counter the cold terror coiled in his stomach.

Kneeling beside the bed, Dragon kissed Bear's too-pale lips. "I'll be back soon. Don't you move, or I swear I'll fetch the whip from the guard house and give you ten lashes."

Bear's mouth curved into the wicked grin that always scrambled Dragon's thoughts. "Don't worry. I'll be good. For you."

Closing his eyes against the sting behind his lids, Dragon rested his forehead on Bear's temple. Just for a second, he told himself, caressing Bear's face with his fingertips. Just until the sharp, sweet ache inside him eased and let him breathe again.

Bear curled a hand around the back of Dragon's head. "It's okay," he whispered. "I'll be okay. Don't worry."

Dragon drew away and opened his eyes. Bear gazed back at him with the directness and honesty which had drawn Dragon to him from the start, and guilt squeezed Dragon's heart like a fist. *If I'd been truthful with him when he asked, maybe none of this would have happened. Maybe we wouldn't have fought when I told him what I thought about this place.* Maybe that wasn't so, but Dragon couldn't shake the feeling that it was.

He couldn't change the past. But he could fix things between them from here on out. All he had to do was talk to Bear, finally. Trust Bear with his fears, ridiculous as they seemed after everything that had happened in the past half a day.

Too bad Bear was too busy slowly bleeding to death to listen to Dragon spill his guts right now.

Forcing a smile for Bear's sake, Dragon kissed him again, then stood. "Believe me, I'm going to do everything in my power to make sure you're okay." He picked up the satchel and put it well within Bear's reach. "Here. Both water skins are in here, and the scuppernongs and apples are right on top. I'll be back soon."

Bear nodded, but said nothing. His eyes had already drifted closed by the time Dragon reached the door, and he didn't even move when Dragon lifted the latch and went outside.

Having mentally mapped out the healer's garden on his previous expedition through the town, it didn't take Dragon long to gather what he needed. He returned not even half an hour after he left with a basket full of yarrow, sage, violets and more chamomile. Not a scrap of dried herbs had been left inside the healer's home, so he was forced to start with all fresh plants, but that was okay. He could work with it. Leaving the basket in front of the house where Bear lay, Dragon hurried to the well for fresh water, then carried everything inside.

Bear hadn't budged. His chest rose and fell in slow, deep breaths. To Dragon's relief, the bleeding seemed to have stopped since he'd tied on the pressure dressing. He hated to disturb Bear *or* his injury, but there was no help for it. Leaving the wound alone wasn't an option. Some degree of infection was likely no matter what, but massive, probably fatal infection was inevitable if it wasn't thoroughly cleaned, sooner rather than later.

Dragon just hoped there was enough yarrow and chamomile in the town's gardens to last until Bear was healed. Dragon had made plenty of travel plans during the arduous trip back to Lexin, and those plans included bringing enough of the herbs with them for daily wound poultices and teas to help ward off infection. They might find some growing in the wild, but Dragon wasn't about to bet Bear's life on it.

The woodbox next to the fireplace still had several logs of various sizes in it, plus an abundance of kindling. To his relief, he also found a flint and a hunk of metal on the hearth. He was definitely taking those with him when they left here. It would make starting the campfires *much* quicker and easier.

A matter of minutes later, he had a fire burning and water on to boil in a metal pot hanging from a large hook over the fire, obviously set there for that purpose. He wondered, briefly, where the tribe members got the metal and how they fashioned it into pots and the other utensils he'd spotted around the house. The Ashe Tribe certainly didn't have any such ability, and he knew from Bear's stories that the Carwin Tribe didn't either.

Maybe they're artifacts. Left from the old world.

Normally, the idea would've excited Dragon. He would've showed the pot to Bear, and they would've speculated about where the tribe might've found such a thing. Whether there might be an ancient city nearby, and if so, the possibility of exploring it themselves.

Now he couldn't bring himself to care. Not with Bear lying face down on the bed, still and bloodied and too silent, his breathing the only sign that he was still alive.

Moving closer to the bed, Dragon stared at Bear for a long moment. His face was grayish-white, its pallor stark in the hazy morning light. He hadn't even twitched, in spite of the noise Dragon had made getting the fire started and the water on to boil. More to the point, his sleep had none of its usual alert, listening edge. If Wasp and Hawk's Pack came charging through the door right then, Dragon half-feared Bear still wouldn't wake.

He fetched the satchel from the bed and dug out the clump of chamomile. It hadn't really dried enough yet, but it would have to do. A quick search of the drawers and cupboards turned up a small wooden mallet and a paring knife made of polished bone. While the water bubbled in the pot over the fire, Dragon found a large earthenware bowl and poured clean water into it, then set about washing and preparing the herbs he'd harvested for use.

Some time later, Dragon carried a yarrow poultice, a bowl of cooled boiled water infused with chamomile flowers, several fresh strips of cloth from the cupboard and a cup of tea to the bed. He set the poultice and cloths on the bed and the water bowl on the bedside table. Rain had begun to fall outside. It pattered on the roof in a soothing rhythm. Dragon found a few candle stubs in the back of the cupboard, set them on the table beside the water bowl and lit them using a bit of wood from the fire.

With everything ready to go, he sat on the mattress beside Bear. "Wake up, Bear."

Bear's eyes blinked open. He smiled when he saw Dragon. "Hi."

"Hi." Dragon ran his fingers through Bear's tangled hair. "I'm sorry to wake you, but I need to take that bandage off and clean your wound."

Bear grimaced. "Let's get it over with."

"I made you some tea from chamomile and feverfew. It'll help with the pain, and help you sleep some more after." Dragon reached over and picked up the steaming cup. "Here, sit up and drink it while I cut the bandage off."

The grimace didn't fade, but Bear obediently propped himself up on his elbows and took the large brown mug Dragon handed him. He took a sip. "This isn't nearly as bad as I thought it would be."

"There's some honey over there in the cupboard. I put some in the tea to make it taste better." Dragon lifted the top layer of cheesecloth and started cutting, careful to keep his knife well to the side of where Bear's wound lay. "Bear?"

"Yeah?"

Dragon pushed the words out before he could change his mind. "You were right, before. I *was* afraid. I was afraid of being weak. And...and afraid of what you'd think of me if you knew that. How weak I was, and how afraid I was." It didn't even come close to expressing the insane jumble of fears and insecurities that Dragon only half understood himself, but it was the best he could do.

Too bad Bear didn't seem to have anything to say in answer. The silence stretched on, broken only by the drum of the rain on the roof. Dragon wanted to look at Bear's face, but he didn't have the courage. He kept his attention firmly fixed on his blade slicing through the layers of bandage and tried to ignore the sickening gallop of his pulse.

Bear shifted, forcing Dragon to lift his knife so he wouldn't slice Bear's skin. "Be still, Bear, I almost cut you." He scowled at the faint quaver in his voice.

"Hey. Look at me."

Dragon could never resist that tone of gentle command. He looked up. Bear was gazing over his shoulder at Dragon with a smile that made him think of his grandmother. Sweet and tender, strong and proud. He swallowed against the tangle of emotions crowding his throat.

"We're all scared about things like that sometimes," Bear said, his voice soft. "But nothing you do, or say, or think, would ever make me think less of you."

For the first time in over a moon cycle, the tight knot in Dragon's chest eased. Maybe Bear could live up to his statement, and maybe he couldn't. But he *believed* it, and his sincerity made Dragon believe it too.

Holding his knife carefully to the side, Dragon leaned forward to give Bear a kiss that said all the things words couldn't. When the kiss broke, he felt the tension which had kept them apart ever since the river melt away.

"Drink your tea," Dragon ordered, smiling. "You're going to need it."

Bear groaned. "I know." Settling back onto his belly, he sipped at his tea.

Dragon tossed his bloodied shirt onto the floor and cut the last of the bandage away. He managed not to curse out loud, but he couldn't hold back a tiny, dismayed sound.

"It must be pretty bad." Bear turned his head just enough to catch a look at Dragon's face. "Dragon? Tell me."

"It's bad. Deep, almost to the bone. And the edges are ragged, like she worked the knife to pull the wound open as much as she could. Unless the knife was dull?" Dragon aimed a questioning look at Bear, who shook his head. *So she widened the wound on purpose, either to disable him or just to hurt him.* It made Dragon wish he could kill Wasp all over again, more slowly this time. "Okay, here's what we're going to do. I'm going to help you get out of these pants first, or what's left of them, then I'm going to pour water into the wound. Then you can roll onto your side to drain out as much of the water and old blood as possible. We'll do that a couple of times, then I'll clean the outside and bandage it with the yarrow poultice in place. That should stop the bleeding, and the chamomile in the water should hopefully stop any infection from taking hold."

Bear regarded him with solemn eyes. "We both know it'll

get infected, Dragon. It's just a matter of when, and how badly. And how far from here we can get before it happens."

The matter-of-fact tone in Bear's voice hurt Dragon's heart. He wished he could switch places with Bear. It would be far easier to face his own possible death than his Brother's.

He stared straight into Bear's eyes. "I know. But I will fight it with every breath in me, and by the Mother, I will *win*, because I will *not* lose you." He reached for the water and strips of clean cloth, embarrassed by way Bear beamed at him. "You're not drinking your tea."

Lifting his mug in a mock salute, Bear downed half of the remaining contents in a few gulps while Dragon wadded one of the bedsheets beneath Bear's leg to catch the water he was about to pour on it. Bear set the empty mug on the bedside table. "All right. Let's get this done."

Dragon didn't know how long it took to clean and dress Bear's injury, since an unrelenting curtain of rain hid the sun, but it felt like forever. Bear's stoicism couldn't possibly mask the agony of having such a horrendous wound washed out and re-bandaged, the edges held together by strips of cheesecloth tied around his thigh. The way his back tensed with each touch to the raw, bleeding flesh told Dragon exactly how much it hurt.

He worked as quickly and carefully as he could, but Bear's body shook from head to foot by the time Dragon tied the last knot of the new dressing. Blood still oozed out, but it had slowed from a red river to a trickle after he tied strips of cheesecloth around Bear's thigh to hold the edges of the gash together and secured the poultice directly on the wound. The yarrow should stop the bleeding completely before long.

"Okay. Done." Pulling the wet sheet from beneath Bear's leg, Dragon tossed it on floor. He grabbed the last of the cloths he'd brought, wet it in the bit of clean water remaining in the bowl and set to work swabbing the blood and dirt from Bear's body. "Take your shirt off. I'll get you cleaned up, then you can sleep."

Bear obeyed without argument. He rolled onto his back with Dragon's help and lay there shivering while Dragon washed him. "They cut the leg off my buckskins. They won't be any good for keeping the dirt out of this wound. Are there any clothes around here?"

"Nothing in this house. I'll check the other houses in a little while. If I can't find anything..." Dragon shrugged. "I can rig a new pant leg out of a blanket. Tie it on with rope, if no one around here left a needle and thread for sewing. It's not great, but it's better than nothing. And I'll wash our clothes, too, in chamomile water if I can't find any soap."

Bear waited until Dragon had tossed his cloth aside along with the rest, then grabbed his wrist. "Rest first."

Dragon shook his head. "No, I should get started. We can only stay here for a couple of days, and—"

"Dragon. Stop." Bear ran his thumb over the bones in Dragon's wrist. "There's no one around here now but us. No one from Bath City can get here any quicker than three days, and it's seriously doubtful they'd be here any sooner than six days, since they aren't expecting Wasp and Hawk back yet."

Bear was right. Dragon's resolve wavered. Maybe he could afford to rest just for a little while. Now that they were safe and Bear was taken care of, he was *so* tired...

"You were up all night rescuing me," Bear murmured, as if he himself hadn't spent the night limping through the woods dribbling his life's blood all over the forest floor. "You're exhausted." He tugged on Dragon's arm. "Lie down here with me. Sleep for a while."

Sleep. The very thought made Dragon's eyelids feel heavy as stones. He yawned. Bear raised his eyebrows, and Dragon let out a weak laugh. "Okay, yes. You win. Move over."

"You're making me *move*, after all that?"

"This side's all wet now." Dragon kicked off his moccasins and skinned out of his pants. "I thought you'd be more comfortable on the dry side of the bed."

Bear smiled, his eyes shining. He dug the heel of his good leg into the mattress and scooted himself to the other side of the bed. "Come here."

Picking up the thick, soft blanket he'd set on the end of the bed earlier that day, Dragon unfolded it and spread it out over Bear. He crawled beneath the blanket and cuddled against Bear's side, his head pillowed on Bear's chest and one arm tucked around Bear's middle. "You okay? I'm not hurting you?" He yawned again. His eyelids closed. He dragged them open again.

"I'm fine. Think I can actually sleep." Bear's arm tightened around Dragon's shoulders. He kissed Dragon's forehead. "Rest now."

Dragon relaxed in Bear's embrace with a deep sigh. He drifted off to the thrum of the rain outside and the steady rhythm of Bear's heartbeat against his cheek.

Chapter Eight

In the end, they stayed in Lexin four days before setting out again.

If Bear were to be completely honest, he'd have to admit he didn't want to leave so soon. Limping around town on the makeshift crutch Dragon made him set his leg to throbbing after no time at all. Spending hours on end trudging through trackless lands and sleeping on the ground would probably mean constant, unrelenting pain. And he didn't look forward to the inevitable infection.

They couldn't stay in Lexin, though. Every hour they lingered increased the chances of a confrontation with the Bath City Tribe. The need to get out nagged at Bear's brain more each day. The only reason they'd stayed as long as they did was because Dragon was worried Bear's wound would start bleeding again if he tried to walk on it too much too soon. Bear hadn't argued. Dragon was right, and he knew it. Getting out of town earlier wouldn't help them any if they had to stop dangerously close to the valley because of Bear's injury.

At least it wasn't raining anymore.

They reached the northern head of the valley just after midday on the first day. Dragon halted beneath a spreading beech tree and set down the new, larger bag he'd fashioned out of deer hide. "Let's stop here. We can rest for a while."

"I don't need to rest," Bear protested. "I can go a while

longer."

Dragon arched an eyebrow in obvious disbelief. Bear clenched his teeth and managed to keep the stomach-churning pain in his leg from showing on his face.

Sighing, Dragon shook his head. "We're stopping here. We're going to rest and eat something." He linked his arm through Bear's. "Sit. I've got you."

Bear knew that stubborn glint in Dragon's eye. He dropped his crutch and let Dragon ease him down to the patch of scraggly grass.

They sat in silence for a while, munching on grapes, apples and the venison Dragon had dried while Bear recovered. Dragon handed Bear the skin full of willow bark tea liberally sweetened with honey. It still didn't taste very good, but Bear gladly drank several long swallows. It usually helped, even if it didn't kill the pain completely.

"Why are you doing this, Bear?" Dragon asked, interrupting Bear's contemplation of the valley below.

Bear turned to look at Dragon. His face held the same mix of worry, irritation and sadness as his voice. Bear's stomach flip-flopped. "What're you talking about? What am I doing?" He thought he knew what Dragon was going to say, but he asked anyway.

"I know how much pain you're in. I can see it. And you *know* you shouldn't keep going when you start hurting really bad, because you're not healed enough yet." Dragon squinted out over the sun-drenched valley. "You want me to tell you everything. I thought you were willing to do the same. So why are you trying so hard to hide this from me?"

Bear stared at the side of Dragon's head, stunned. "I... Well, you'd make us stop if I said anything, and we need to keep moving. That's all. I didn't think of it that way. I'm sorry."

"Yeah. I know. Just..." Dragon rubbed a hand over his face.

He looked tired, black smudges shadowing the skin beneath his eyes. "Look. We need to be honest with each other, okay? *You* made me realize how important that is. And it's especially important now." He turned a pleading, almost angry look to Bear. "The wound's starting to close. What do you think'll happen if it opens up again, out here?"

Bear looked at the ground. If the gash in his thigh broke open again, he might bleed to death. What good would his hurry do them if that happened?

He lifted his head and met Dragon's eyes. "You're right. I'll do better. It's just hard, you know?"

The corners of Dragon's mouth turned up. "Yeah, I know."

Relieved, Bear smiled back. "I've just had a feeling all day, like we needed to hurry. I don't know why."

"Hm." Shading his eyes with his hand, Dragon gazed out over the valley. He stilled, his body going tense. "Well, apparently your instincts are good. And it seems we got out not a minute too soon. Look." He pointed toward the thin part of the forest to the west of Lexin.

Bear followed the direction of Dragon's gaze. He could just make out a line of figures moving through the trees. They were heading toward the town. Several hours' travel away yet, but definitely going that way.

Picking up his water skin, Bear took a long draught of herb tea, then pushed to his feet. "I've rested long enough, for now. We need to move on."

To his relief, Dragon didn't argue. He gathered their things, handed Bear his crutch and followed him through the trees.

For the rest of the day, they kept up a slow but constant pace, pushing relentlessly north. Bear led the way. Dragon trailed a few steps behind, sharp gaze on both the surrounding forest and, Bear knew, on him. They took two short rests, only a few minutes each. It wasn't enough, really, but it eased the ache in Bear's thigh from a scream to a whimper. It would have to be good enough, for now.

They made camp that night in the ruins of an ancient house built of what looked like river rocks. All that remained were the four walls, the roof having collapsed generations ago. Daisies and purple coneflowers sprouted where the floor had once been.

Bear sat on one of the blankets Dragon had taken from Lexin while Dragon started the fire. He studied the ragged opening of the door and windows while he dug food from the bag. "Who do you think lived here?"

Dragon sat back on his heels, a thoughtful expression on his face. "Good question. It's so far away from everything. No tribe anywhere near. I wonder if there were any other houses out here, back when someone lived in this one? I wonder if it was safe then?"

Bear had no answer for that. He mulled it over while Dragon bent and blew the flames higher. They were probably safe enough now, tonight, but they couldn't live here. Staying in one spot in the wild was never a good idea for long. Maybe it was different before the Change. Before the oceans rose and the old world vanished beyond recall. Maybe then, a person could live alone in a tiny stone house in the forest and never fear sudden death in the night.

He didn't care what anybody said. He didn't care what Mother Rose or the Carwin Tribal Council would've thought, or how much trouble he'd have gotten in back home for saying so. He would've given almost anything to live just one day back then.

"I've love to go back to the old world. Just for a day, you know?"

Dragon's voice jolted Bear out of his thoughts and reminded him why he'd taken this on to start with. Reaching over, he snagged Dragon's wrist and tugged. Dragon fell backward with a grunt, landing on Bear's uninjured thigh. He glared up at Bear, but his lips twitched with the threat of laughter. "What'd you do that for?"

"Because you just said the same thing I was thinking. You do that all the time. I like that about you." Bear cupped Dragon's jaw in one hand, tilted his head back and kissed his lips. "We should've left Lexin sooner, I guess."

"I don't see how we could have. You're not really healed well enough to travel as it is." Dragon scooted off Bear's leg and sat cross-legged on the blanket beside him. "But obviously it's a good thing you talked me into leaving when we did. The Bath City Tribe'll be in the town by now. If they'd found us there..."

He didn't have to finish the thought. They both knew what happened to outsiders when a tribe caught them. Especially members of strange Packs. And if the Bath City Mother and her council discovered the bodies of the two Sisters in the woods, any chance of survival Bear and Dragon might've had would be gone.

After a long, silent moment, Dragon pushed to his feet. "All right, I need to fill the water skins and the cooking pot before it gets dark and start getting everything ready to redress your leg." He leaned down to kiss the top of Bear's head. "You drink the rest of that tea and eat a little something, then lie down and rest. I'll make more tea when I get back, plus some with valerian in it for tonight so you can rest. We have plenty of dried venison for now so I'm not going to hunt yet."

"Okay." Bear grabbed the skin with the tea in it, drained the little bit that remained then set it next to the one they'd brought with them from Carwin and the new one Dragon had made during their stay in Lexin. He frowned when Dragon poured an entire skin and a half of water from the two other skins into the earthenware pot they'd found in the guardhouse and taken with them. "Great Mother, Dragon, you hardly drank anything today. You're going to get dehydrated. It was hot today."

Dragon shot him a defensive look that suggested the memory of the river outside Char still rankled. "It wasn't *that* hot. I drank all I needed. Believe me, I'm not about to weaken myself with unnecessary water rationing. Not when there are streams all over the place."

"Oh. Yeah, I guess so." Bear tucked his hands beneath his head and stared at the leaf-framed patch of blue sky above him. "You know, I'd always heard that Shenandoah was only a week's foot travel north of Char."

"Yes, I remember you saying that." Dragon set the pot on a ring of flat rocks near enough to the fire to boil the water. "But I suppose that would be for someone who knows where they're going. We don't. Which is why we've been traveling in a search grid, remember? So we wouldn't walk right past Shenandoah's valley and never see it. Plus we spent several days in Lexin. You have to keep all that in mind." Dragon pulled the satchel toward himself. "Of course, there's always the possibility that whoever said that was just wrong."

Bear craned his neck to smile at Dragon, who was rummaging through the satchel for the various herbs he'd packed away in the cheesecloth bags he'd made. "Thank you for that."

Dragon looked up, a puzzled frown on his face. "For what?"

"For encouraging me." Bear reached out to brush his fingers across Dragon's ankle. "I know you never really believed in Shenandoah. Not like I do. But you've stuck with me anyway, and...and even back in Lexin, before we found out about Bath City, you only did what you thought was right, and, well, it just seems like beyond the call of duty for *you* to keep *me* believing in Shenandoah. You know?"

For a moment, Dragon stared at him with a blank expression, and Bear cringed inwardly. He'd never been good at expressing himself. He should've kept his mouth shut, rather than spouting off something that only vaguely resembled what he felt.

He was on the verge of a stumbling apology when Dragon sank to his knees, cradled Bear's face in his hands and bent until his forehead rested against Bear's. "You're mine. My Brother. What keeps you going, keeps me going. Keeps *us* going." He ran his thumbs over Bear's cheekbones, kissed the tip of his nose. "We're in this together. Always together, Bear. Let's not ever forget that again."

Bear's throat closed up. Unable to answer any other way, he grasped Dragon's head in both hands and kissed him with all the pent-up desire from days on end of forced celibacy.

A needy little whimper bled from Dragon's lips. His mouth opened, his tongue stroking against Bear's. His breath came harsh and fast through his nose. Bear slid one hand downward and planted it over the center of Dragon's chest. His heart thudded against Bear's palm.

When Bear went for the laces of Dragon's buckskins, Dragon broke the kiss and pulled away. "Not now. It'll be dark in less than an hour. I have to go find water."

Dragon's voice shook with the lust Bear knew he was holding back. Bear wanted to wrap both arms around him, drag him to the ground and take him. But Dragon was right. Now wasn't the time, even if Bear's lame leg would've cooperated. The sun hung low over the treetops in the west. Even with Dragon's nearly supernatural night vision, Bear didn't want him wandering around unfamiliar country alone in the dark.

"Yeah, okay." Bear shifted his leg. The torn muscle twinged, and he grimaced. "I'll be here."

Worry cooled the heat in Dragon's eyes, but he didn't say anything. He rose to his feet, picked up the water skins and slung all three over his shoulder. "I'll be back as soon as I can. I don't think I'll have to go far. I'm pretty sure I heard running water nearby. But give a whippoorwill call if you need me."

Bear watched Dragon walk through the still-intact doorway arch of the ancient house and vanish into the lengthening shadows between the trees. Drawing his knife from its sheath, Bear rested it on his belly, his hand curled loosely around the handle. He hadn't smelled the faintest whiff of another human since they'd left the Sisters dead in the woods outside Lexin, but he wasn't taking any chances. He made himself as comfortable as he could and settled down to wait.

Bear woke from another dream of the bright city in the valley to slick, wet heat on his cock. He opened his eyes. Overhead, stars glittered in a bottomless sky. He peered down the length of his body. Dragon knelt at his side, naked, mouth stretched wide around Bear's half-erect cock. His pale eyes gleamed in the firelight as he looked up at Bear.

The sight brought Bear fully hard in a heartbeat. Groaning, he buried his hands in Dragon's hair. He'd unwound his braid, and the dark strands fell like a curtain around his shoulders. Bear loved to dig his fingers into the thick black mass, hold Dragon's head still and fuck his mouth.

It didn't take but a couple of upward thrusts to realize it wasn't going to happen. The movement sent sharp bolts of agony down Bear's leg. His pulse raced like he'd been running all day. He pressed the heels of his hands to his eyes, frustrated. Great Mother, if he didn't even have the energy for *sex*, he was in trouble.

The warm suction went away from his cock, leaving him bare to the night air. A cool breeze brushed the damp skin, and he whimpered. Fingers curled around his wrists and pulled his hands away from his face. Dragon leaned in to kiss him before he could say a word.

"Don't worry, Bear," Dragon murmured against Bear's mouth. His breath smelled like Bear's cock, ripe and musky with a tang of sweat. "I'm going to take care of you tonight. You don't even need to move." Dragon planted a hand in the center of Bear's chest. "You *shouldn't* move. You need to rest. So I'm doing all the work this time." Tilting his head, he pressed a tender kiss to the angle of Bear's jaw. "How do you want me? My mouth, my ass, my hand? Anything you want. Anything."

Bear licked his lips, catching a bit of his own taste along with Dragon's. Mother, but it made him hard just to hear Dragon whisper those things to him. "I want your mouth. But I want you in my mouth at the same time."

A tremor ran through Dragon's body. His breath caught, a sweet little sound Bear would've missed if Dragon's head hadn't been so close to his ear. Bear grinned. They'd only done it once before, but there was no missing how much Dragon had enjoyed it. And what excited Dragon tended to excite Bear too, since he loved to watch Dragon drown in lust.

After a deep, hungry kiss that would've had Bear humping the air if he could've done it without hurting himself, Dragon drew back. "I don't think we can manage that without you lying on your side like you did last time." He kissed away Bear's disappointment before he could voice it. "Don't worry. I'll take care of you. I'll make it good. Just relax."

Bear nodded, since he couldn't manage to get any words to come out of his mouth. His chest felt tight with a feeling he couldn't quite put a name to. He watched, his whole body thrumming with anticipation, as Dragon crouched at his feet to pull off his moccasins.

"I have to take your pants off to redress your wound anyway. Might as well do it now." Dragon crawled on hands and knees to Bear's side, sat back on his heels and eased the buckskins over Bear's hips. Dragon flashed the rare, childlike grin that always made Bear's heart thump. "Besides, it's so much easier to play with you with these things out of the way."

Bear's laughter turned into a hiss of pain when Dragon drew the pants carefully down over his thigh. "I think I'll go naked from here on out."

"Mm, no. As fun as that would be for *me*, your wound's much more likely to get dirty that way, which is no good for *you*." Dragon tugged the pants with their one makeshift blanket leg off Bear's feet, tossed them aside and clamped his hand around Bear's cock. Bear's erection, which had flagged a bit with the pain, came back with a vengeance. He moaned, and Dragon gazed at him with fire in his eyes. "I'm sorry for hurting you. Now let's see if I can make you feel better."

He swung a leg over Bear's middle and scooted backward until his cock and balls swung a few tantalizing inches from Bear's face. His hole clenched and relaxed, and Bear's mouth watered. Mother, but he wanted a taste. Just a little taste.

Bear started to push up on his elbow to try and get some of that dark, wild flavor. Then hot suction engulfed his cock, and Bear forgot all about everything else. His mouth opened in a soundless cry. He dug his hands into Dragon's bare buttocks and did his best to hold still. It helped to have Dragon's arms pinning his hips to the blanket.

It felt so good to have Dragon's mouth on him after five endless days. He'd had to go longer without sex, of course, but he never liked to. And sex with Dragon was always incredible.

Dragon pulled almost completely off, sucked hard on the head of Bear's cock, then swallowed him to the root. Dragon's throat constricted once, twice, three times in rapid succession before he drew back and started the cycle all over again. Bear bit back the yelp that wanted to come out. His body shook all over. None of his former Brothers had *ever* had Dragon's talent for sucking cock.

Wanting to make Dragon feel as good as he did but unable to suck him in this position, Bear wet two fingers in his mouth and shoved them into Dragon's ass. He was rewarded with a shudder and a muffled moan. Dragon's hole gripped his fingers tight. He pushed them deeper, searching for the spot that could sometimes make Dragon come without touching his cock at all. He found it and rubbed it in firm little circles. Dragon moaned again, his hips rocking. The vibrations around Bear's cock tore a soft cry from his throat.

He wanted it to last. With his leg in the shape it was in, who knew how often he'd be up to this sort of thing in the days to come? But it had been too many days, and Dragon's mouth felt so good. Bear came with his fingers buried in Dragon's ass and Dragon's throat milking his cock.

Dragon swallowed as fast as Bear's seed spurted out. When Bear started to squirm, Dragon let his softening cock slip from his mouth. Before he could move, Bear grabbed hold of Dragon's stiff prick with his free hand and gave it a tug. "Come here."

Thankfully, Dragon didn't need to ask what Bear meant, because he didn't think he was capable of more than those two words right now. Dragon scrambled backwards, planting his knees beside Bear's head and spreading his legs. His cock slid through Bear's parted lips and down his throat.

Bear would've let out a satisfied sigh if he hadn't had his mouth full. He delved his fingers deeper into Dragon's ass, curled his free hand around Dragon's thigh and swallowed his cock as deep as he could.

"Oh. Mother." Dragon's hips swayed, the movement slow and gentle as if he wasn't sure if Bear could handle anything more. "So good, Bear."

All Bear could do was hum his agreement. He lifted his head to take Dragon deeper.

Agony stabbed through his leg. He pulled off Dragon's prick, his head dropping back to the blanket. He couldn't hold back the sharp hiss of pain.

In an instant, Dragon yanked Bear's fingers out of his hole and turned around, his face inches from Bear's. "What? What's wrong?"

Bear stared up into Dragon's shadowed face. It was too dark to see the expression in Dragon's eyes, but Bear could smell the worry overlaying the strong musk of sex. He laid both hands on Dragon's cheeks. "Nothing. Just a little twinge in my leg, that's all." He grinned. "Who said you could take your cock out of my mouth?"

Dragon shook his head. "No."

"But—"

"No." Dragon stopped Bear's next protest with a kiss. "I know you want it. But I also know you were hurting just now."

Embarrassment heated Bear's cheeks. "It honestly wasn't that bad."

"I'm sure. But there's no need for you to hurt at all. This is good too, right? I think it is." Dragon kissed Bear again, tongue curling around Bear's, his cock digging hard and hot into Bear's belly. "I could come just like this. I want to. Let me?"

Part of Bear wanted to insist on bringing Dragon off with his mouth like they'd both wanted him to. It bothered him that he couldn't because of a damned injury. But he could never resist it when Dragon asked for something in that rough whisper, his breath scented with Bear's seed and the smell of desire rolling off him in waves.

Dragon no doubt knew it too. Knew it, and used it, to make sure Bear did what he wanted him to. Bear decided to forgive him, for now.

He buried one hand in Dragon's hair and slid the other down his back to his ass. "Anything you want."

Dragon drew a shaking breath. His groin moved, rubbing his cock against Bear's abdomen. "Kiss me."

Something in Dragon's voice hooked Bear's heart and

tugged hard. He pulled Dragon's head down and kissed him, rough and deep, sliding a finger into his already loose hole at the same time and drinking down the resulting whimper. Dragon braced one hand on the ground beside Bear's ribs and dug the other into the tangles at the back of his neck. His teeth knocked against Bear's, catching Bear's bottom lip and drawing blood. Dragon didn't seem to notice. Bear couldn't be bothered to care. Not as long as Dragon kept devouring his mouth and rutting against his belly, the grip of Dragon's body tight around his finger.

A sudden tightening of Dragon's grip on Bear's hair was the only warning he got before Dragon came in slick bursts between their bodies. Bear pulled his finger out of Dragon's ass, stroked his back and kissed his slack lips while he jerked and trembled his way through his release. The soft little keening sounds he made gave Bear a warm, full feeling in the center of his chest.

He brushed the hair from Dragon's face, kissed his brow, held him close when he sighed and tucked his head under Bear's chin. He didn't want to talk, didn't want to move. Most especially, he didn't want Dragon to get up, get his herbs out of the satchel and redress the wound in his leg. Bear was no coward, and no stranger to pain, but that didn't mean he had to like it. Holding Dragon's naked body to his was much preferable in his opinion, especially when they were both sticky with Dragon's seed and reeking of sex, and of their desire for each other.

Far too soon for Bear's liking, Dragon stirred and lifted his head. He smiled. "You okay?"

"I'm fine." Bear framed Dragon's face in his hands. "I'm sorry I couldn't suck you."

Even with Dragon's face half in shadow, Bear saw the reproachful look. "I wish you wouldn't worry about it. It's not like I didn't come. As I'm sure you noticed." Dragon wriggled enough for the fluid drying between them to catch at the hairs on Bear's stomach. He squirmed, and Dragon laughed. "Bear, when are you going to get it through your head? There's no bad sex between us. No way for you to touch me that isn't good." He touched Bear's cheek, traced the line of his jaw with gentle fingertips. "I love what you do to me. *Everything* you do to me."

The warmth in Bear's chest expanded, filled his throat until he couldn't speak. He pulled Dragon to him and put all the things for which he had no words into one more slow, searching kiss.

Dragon broke it an indeterminate time later, before the vague ache in Bear's groin could turn into anything more. He planted a kiss on Bear's forehead, then peeled himself off Bear. A few of Bear's body hairs went with him. Bear winced, and Dragon grinned. "Sorry."

"It's okay." Bear scraped at the fluid gelling on his skin. "I don't guess you'd lick it off?"

Dragon snickered as he stepped over Bear and headed for the fire. "I'll wash it off after I clean and redress your leg."

"Oh." Dread curled in the pit of Bear's stomach at the reminder. He stared at the stars overhead while Dragon bustled around the fire, digging herbs and food out of the satchel. "I don't think it's bled any today."

"That's good. I hope you're right." Dragon reappeared and knelt on the blanket by Bear's side, holding the earthenware mug he'd brought from Lexin. "I have tea. Do you think you can sit up, or would you rather lie on your stomach?"

"I can sit up." In actual fact, Bear wasn't sure he could. Now that the rush of sex had passed, his head pounded, his leg throbbed and he felt weak and dizzy. But he'd be damned if he'd lie here like an invalid when they still had Mother knew how far to go before they reached Shenandoah. If he couldn't even sit up to drink a cup of tea and eat something, he'd never make it. And he was determined to make it.

Dragon nodded, his expression solemn as if he knew exactly what Bear was thinking. Setting the mug on the ground, he moved closer and slid an arm beneath Bear's shoulders. He clasped the other hand to Bear's forearm. "Here. Pull."

Planting his free hand on the ground and bending his good leg, Bear used Dragon's arm as leverage to pull himself to a sitting position. The world spun around him. He hung on to Dragon and breathed through the rush of nausea.

When his stomach settled and everything stopped moving, he let go of Dragon's arm. Dragon handed him the mug of tea without a word, for which he was grateful. Either his weakness and sickness would go away with food and rest, or it wouldn't. There was nothing else to be done about it, and no point in talking about it.

Chapter Nine

They pushed north for three more days before infection began to set in. By the time they stopped to camp on the fourth night, after a day of slow and difficult travel, Bear ached all over with fever.

He clutched one of the wool blankets around his shoulders and tried to lie still while Dragon cleaned his wound. Even the gentlest touch hurt with a deep, sickening pain.

"It's bad, isn't it?" He knew the answer already, by Dragon's muttered curse when he'd first unwound the dressing, but he had to ask.

Dragon was silent for a moment, patting the skin dry and laying a fresh poultice over the wound. "It's swollen and red," he answered finally. "And it's obviously infected all around the outside. The good news is, the infection doesn't seem to run too deep." He ran his hand down the underside of Bear's knee in a brief caress. "It's bad. But it's not as bad as it could be."

"Well, that's good. I guess." Bear gritted his teeth and lifted his leg so Dragon could pull the old wrapping out from under him and slide the new ones beneath him. Dragon hadn't said so, but Bear knew they were about to run out of clean cloth. Soon, Dragon would have to start reusing the old ones. He'd been washing and saving them since day one. "I wonder how much farther Shenandoah is?"

Dragon's movements faltered, and Bear hid a grim smile in

his folded arms. He wouldn't be able to walk much farther. If they didn't find Shenandoah soon, he'd die out here. He knew it, and he knew Dragon did as well.

After he finished with Bear's dressing, Dragon rose, gathered the used dressings into the rabbit-skin bag he'd made for the purpose, then went to the fire. "I'll make you another cup of tea."

"It's okay. One's enough." Bear wasn't sure about that, not tonight. His leg hurt so badly he didn't think anything would help. But to be fair, the tea he'd had before Dragon started on the dressing hadn't had time to work properly yet. And who knew how long the herbs they'd brought with them would need to last? There weren't that many willows of the type they needed growing in these woods, so they hadn't been able to find much more bark since they left Lexin.

Dragon just shook his head and prepared another mug. He stirred in a generous portion from their precious stash of honey, then handed the mug to Bear. "Drink it. I still have chamomile and sage, and there's plenty growing wild around here. I can use that."

Bear obediently gulped the tea, trying not to grimace at the bitterness cutting through the sweetness of the honey. It might taste awful, but it eased his pain enough to let him sleep, which was more than any of the sweeter herbs could manage.

A few minutes later Dragon returned to the blanket with an earthenware pot full of the rabbit stew that had been simmering while he changed Bear's dressing. "Can you sit up? You need to eat."

"Yeah. Give me a second."

Setting the empty mug down, Bear rolled onto his side. He pushed into a sitting position, his good leg curled close to his body and his injured one stretched out in front of him. His head swam, but he dug his fingers into the ground at his side and forced himself to remain upright.

When he thought he could move without falling over, he handed Dragon the empty mug. Dragon dipped it in the pot to fill it and handed it back without comment, but the sharp gray eyes missed nothing. He leaned over the pot and scooped stew into his mouth with a clean, flat piece of wood, watching Bear the whole time.

He reached for Bear's mug after he'd drained the last of the broth from the bottom. "Here, I'll get you some more."

Bear shook his head. "No."

Dragon's eyes narrowed. "I've had my fill, and there's still some left. And you need to keep up your strength. So if you're just saying that because—"

"I'm not. I promise." Bear hunched his shoulders beneath the blanket still draped over him. Mother, he was cold. "My stomach's kind of unsettled. I'm afraid if I eat too much I'll be sick, and we can't afford for me to lose anything I've eaten. I'm already weak, and we don't know how far we still have to go."

The suspicion melted from Dragon's eyes. Setting Bear's mug beside the pot, he rose onto his knees and moved close enough to press his body against Bear's side. He wound both arms around Bear's shoulders and laid his cool cheek against Bear's hot one. Bear turned his head to nuzzle behind Dragon's ear, breathing in the scents of sweat, wood smoke and herbs. It smelled like comfort and safety. Like home.

Bear hoped he survived long enough to make a *real* home with Dragon.

Don't think that way. You'll make it. You have to.

Turning toward Dragon, Bear curled his body enough to rest his head on Dragon's shoulder. He yawned as a familiar languor crept into his limbs. "How much valerian did you put in that tea?"

"Only a little more than usual. You've had a rough hike today. Between that and the fever, you're worn out." Dragon stroked Bear's sweat-damp hair away from his face. "Lie down. Sleep. We'll start whenever you're ready tomorrow, but we're going to go easy, okay?"

"Agreed." Bear yawned again. His eyelids slid closed. When he forced them open, he was surprised to find himself stretched out on the blanket, with Dragon's shirt beneath his head and the thick wool blanket he'd been using earlier tucked around him from toes to chin. Dragon crouched beside the fire, rinsing the cooking pot with what clean water remained in the other pot. Bear frowned. "Dragon?"

Dragon's head whipped up. When he saw Bear watching him, he set both pots down and hurried back to Bear's side. "What is it? What do you need?"

"Nothing. I just..." Bear shook his head. It bothered him that he could fall asleep in the middle of a conversation and not even realize it was about to happen. "You should sleep too. I know you must be tired."

Dragon smiled, though the worry line between his eyes remained. "I will. Just let me finish cleaning up."

"All right." Freeing one arm from the blanket, Bear reached up to touch Dragon's cheek.

Dragon grabbed Bear's hand in both of his and pressed a kiss to the palm before letting go. Bear shut his eyes and let himself drift.

He half-surfaced when the blanket lifted and Dragon's warm body pressed close to his. Rolling onto his good side, he curled into Dragon's welcome embrace with a contented sigh. He sank back into sleep to the sound of Dragon's heartbeat in his ear.

When he woke the next day, Bear thought he was back in Carwin. It was only for a few seconds, but it scared Dragon badly enough that when he spotted the ruins on the horizon

that morning as he and Bear picked their painstaking way
down a wooded hillside, he decided to make for them. By that
night, the overgrown rubble of outlying buildings lay only a
stone's throw from their camp and tall buildings of the type
built just before the end of the old world loomed across a
treeless expanse of low hills.

Shenandoah *must* be near, but Bear no longer had the
strength to keep up the search. Not without guidance. Dragon
hoped to find some sort of clue in the remains of the ancient
city ahead. If nothing else, he and Bear could find a secure spot
to stay for a few days, where Bear could rest and recover.

Dragon refused to consider the possibility that Bear might
get worse instead of better. Or that he might not survive.

The suspicion that Shenandoah might be nothing but a
myth was something Dragon buried deep in the farthest
recesses of his mind. He couldn't let himself believe that. Not
when more and more it looked like Bear's only hope.

"We're heading for the ruins tomorrow," Dragon told Bear
that night, after wound care and a new dressing and a broth of
wild onions and leftover rabbit that Dragon had to feed Bear
because his hands shook too hard to hold the mug. The two of
them lay together between the blankets, Bear curled into a ball
and Dragon molded to his back, one arm around Bear's waist
and the other pillowing his head. "It isn't far. We should reach
the city center by midday tomorrow, no matter how slowly we
go."

Bear shook his head. "No." He clamped a hand around
Dragon's wrist. His palm burned against Dragon's skin.
"Shouldn't go to Char. It's not safe. Remember the nomads?"

Dragon's heart broke a little, hearing that, but he didn't let
what he felt come through in his voice. If ever he needed to be
strong, it was now.

Tightening his arm around Bear's middle, Dragon planted a
kiss on Bear's neck. The skin there felt damp and hot against

114

his lips. Bear's matted curls smelled sour with dried sweat and sickness. "It's not Char, Bear. I don't know *what* city this is, but it isn't Char. Don't you remember? We've been traveling north, more or less, for more than a moon cycle."

Bear twisted enough to look into Dragon's face. "Is it Shenandoah? Have we found it?"

It killed something inside Dragon to have to squash the hope in Bear's eyes, but there was no help for it. Letting him think they'd reached their goal was just cruel. Dragon owed him the truth. Even if his fever made him forget again by morning.

"No, Bear. It's not Shenandoah." Dragon clutched Bear closer, resting his face in the crook of Bear's neck when disappointment clouded his eyes and he laid his head on Dragon's arm again. "I'm sorry. I wish it was. I want to find it too." *Especially now, when you get worse every day and I can't stop it, and they might be able to help you.*

"Don't be sorry. You have no reason to be sorry." Bear's fingers tightened around Dragon's wrist. His voice sounded weak and slurred. Dragon hoped it was just the valerian in the tea, but he suspected it wasn't. "I'm the one who should be sorry. If I'd been paying more attention back in Lexin, I wouldn't have surprised those Sisters, I wouldn't have gotten injured, and I wouldn't... You wouldn't have to..."

He didn't finish the thought, but he didn't need to. Dragon knew exactly what came after those last trailed-off words, and Mother, he didn't know if his throat burned and his eyes stung because of that unspoken knowledge or because this was the most lucid Bear had been all day.

"It's all right," Dragon whispered into the tangles behind Bear's ear. "Everything's going to be all right. I'm going to take care of you, you're going to get better, and we're going to find Shenandoah." He tucked the blanket tighter around Bear's trembling body. "Go to sleep now, okay?"

Bear said nothing, about Dragon's impossible promises or

anything else. Within a few minutes he lay limp in Dragon's embrace, twitching now and then, his breathing rapid and shallow with his fever.

Dragon splayed his hand over Bear's galloping heart. He lay awake for a long time.

Bear woke before dawn, insisting the Great Mother had taken him on a spirit journey to Shenandoah during the night and they had to go immediately. Since they needed to travel on anyway, Dragon didn't bother to argue. He refilled the water bottles from the nearby stream and force fed Bear the rest of their scuppernongs, a mug of willow-bark tea with honey and two strips of dried venison. By the time he'd packed up the blankets and slung the satchel across his back, gold light rimmed the eastern sky and Bear had forgotten all about his fever dream.

They reached what Dragon judged to be the city proper by midmorning. Most of the buildings were nothing but burnt-out husks. Others had been reduced to piles of rubble so long ago that grass had grown over them, turning them into rounded green hillocks that seemed out of place in the otherwise stark, flat landscape of stone, ragged weeds and ancient metal.

Bear leaned against Dragon's shoulder, panting. "Lynx? Are we going to Char again? Do we have patrol?"

Dragon knew it was just the fever, but it still hurt a little to be forgotten so completely. "This isn't Char, Bear. And I'm not Lynx."

"Oh. Oh, yes." Bear pressed a fiery kiss to Dragon's cheek. "I'm sorry, Dragon. This fever's making my head fuzzy."

"I know. It's all right." Dragon tightened his arm around Bear's waist. He'd been helping Bear along most of the morning, once it became clear that the crutch no longer provided enough support. "We're going to find a secure place in this city and let you rest while I look for some sort of sign to show us how to get to Shenandoah. Maybe if you rest for a while instead of hiking through the woods for hours on end, you'll get better."

Bear laughed, the sound weak and raspy. "Better. Yeah."

His teeth chattered in spite of the heat of the sunny day, and Dragon had to swallow hard against the sudden tightness in his throat. "It looks like the more intact buildings are on the other side of the city center. We'll head for that area."

Bear sagged against Dragon's side, his burning forehead pressed to Dragon's temple. His body shook and his breath came harsh and far too fast. Dragon held him up without a word. What was there to say? Once Bear lay down this time, they both knew he might not be getting up again until the fever abated and the worst of the infection had passed.

If it ever does.

Shoving the morbid thought away, Dragon nuzzled Bear's cheek. "Hey. Are you ready? The sooner we get moving the sooner you can lie down and rest."

"Yeah. Ready." Bear lifted his head enough to look at Dragon. "'M sorry."

He could've been apologizing for needing so much help to walk today, or for having been injured in the first place. He'd done it before. But something in his eyes said different, that this particular "sorry" was for the thing that hadn't happened yet, but they both knew probably would.

Dragon's chest went tight. He fought to draw a full breath.

Get hold of yourself. Your Brother needs you now. Be strong.

He tilted his head, brushed a kiss across Bear's chapped lips. "Don't. I will not accept your death, so save your apologies." Dragon started forward, one arm snug around Bear's waist and the other holding on to the arm Bear had slung around his shoulders. "Come on now. We'll go as slow as you need to. Tell me if you need to stop."

They moved down the weed-ridden canyon in silence. The midday sun shone directly into the narrow space and through the metal latticework looming around them.

"I won't be able to walk out of here," Bear said after they'd gone deep enough into the city to lose sight of the open spaces beyond. "You have to go on without me. Find Shenandoah. Bring 'em back here to get me."

This idea might actually work, depending. At least he hadn't suggested that Dragon abandon him to a lonely death in the ruins. Dragon would never be able to do such a thing.

"I know you won't be able to walk. If it's safe here and Shenandoah is close enough, I'll think about leaving you long enough to get help. If not, I'll make a litter and take you with me." Something moved in the shadows at the edge of Dragon's vision. He whipped his head around, but saw nothing. "Bear? Do you smell anything? Humans, or any predators we need to worry about?"

Bear shook his head. "All I can smell anymore is myself."

Fear curled in the pit of Dragon's stomach, the shadow forgotten. Bear's leg had looked awful the previous night, dark red and badly swollen, draining thick yellow-green fluid onto the bandages. It didn't have the putrid smell that Dragon had encountered a few times in the past—and which had always meant swift, unpleasant death—but his nose wasn't as sensitive as Bear's. If Bear detected the first signs of something worse...

"It's not that." Bear gave him a weary smile. "It's not rotting. Not yet, anyway. I just smell sick, that's all. I can't even pick up anything else." He narrowed his eyes. "Why did you ask?"

"Oh." Dragon glanced toward the tottering pile of odd reddish stone where he thought he'd seen the shadow before. "It's nothing. I thought I saw something move, but there's nothing there now."

Bear followed Dragon's gaze, but didn't say anything. He was breathing hard. Talking seemed to have used more strength than he could spare.

At least he hadn't lapsed back into delirium. He hadn't remained this clearheaded for this long at a stretch in a day and a half. It gave Dragon hope, and he needed hope right now.

As the two of them made their painstaking way along what had clearly once been a road, the buildings on either side grew taller and better preserved. Dragon became more curious about the place with each passing minute. He didn't have a lot of experience with old-world cities, but there'd been a much smaller ruin only a half day's walk from the Ashe Tribe's walls, and the vision of Char was permanently burned into his brain. Both those places had enough of a mix of styles for him to know that these enormous structures reaching for the sky and blotting out the sun were the newer ones, built only a short time before the Great Mother rose against the people of the old civilization to take back Her Earth.

Neither Ashe nor Char, however, showed this weird divide between older and newer. It was almost as if hundreds of tribes had all moved here at once and built these monstrosities of black and silver to house themselves. Though why they should make them so terrifyingly *tall*, Dragon had no idea.

"Mother Rose said they were trying to reach the sky. She said it wasn't natural, and it made the Great Mother angry."

The sound of Bear's voice, weak and shaky but perfectly lucid, brought Dragon out of his thoughts. He glanced at Bear. His face wore the animated expression he always got when he talked about the old world, and Dragon couldn't help but smile. "Mother Holly said pretty much the same thing. Sarge Cougar said she was full of shit."

Bear let out a shocked laugh. "Bet he never said that where she could hear him."

Dragon's grin widened, remembering. "Never. He was sadistic and arrogant, not stupid. I always thought he had a good point about that, though. It's not like people can live in the sky, after all."

"They could *fly*, though." Bear turned wide, glazed eyes to Dragon. "I've seen it. There's the photograph things in Char, and in the council chambers in Carwin. They had these big metal things that looked like birds, but they weren't. People *rode inside* them, in the air. I saw it in the photographs. If they could fly, maybe they could live in the sky too." He stopped his slow, halting progress, his crutch angled in front of him and his arm slack around Dragon's shoulders. His brow creased. "Lynx? What's this place? It doesn't look like Char."

Mother, not again. Dragon smothered a rush of irritation. Bear's body temperature was so high the heat of his skin burned Dragon even through both of their clothes. It was a wonder he was conscious and on his feet. Expecting him to make sense all the time would be too much.

"I don't know." Dragon took a step forward, urging Bear along with him. "Come on. We need to find a safe place for you to rest."

"Rest." Bear planted his crutch on the ground and moved to match Dragon's pace. His injured leg dragged behind him. "I'd like to rest. I don't feel very good. And my leg hurts really bad."

"I know. As soon as we find a place to settle, I'll build a fire and make more tea."

Dragon surveyed the surrounding area. Just ahead, a building wider than it was tall stood between a pile of rubble and a silver tower that seemed to vanish into the heavens. The low, wide building was completely intact, with only a single door. It was a place a single man might defend against any attack in the night.

He kissed Bear's burning cheek. "Okay, Bear. We're heading for that black building over there. The short one. It's no more than a hundred paces. Hang on to me."

Dragon was relieved to find that the building's door wasn't stuck, or locked, or otherwise blocked to entry. His left arm shook from holding up a man heavier than himself for half the day, and an indefinable tension made him anxious to get inside. The back of his head itched with the feeling of being watched, though he hadn't seen anyone or any sign of human habitation.

Inside, he found a completely intact room with a single heavy metal door and a small, square window set high in the corner of the thick wall. It was possible that someone might be able to scale the sheer wall outside and spot them through the window, but it wasn't likely, and it was a risk he felt he had to take. He didn't want to leave Bear alone in the pitch dark. No one would be able to get in through the tiny opening anyway.

He spread a blanket on the strangely dust-free floor and helped Bear lie down. "I'm going to look around this building a little bit, just to make sure there's no one else around. I'll be back soon." Kneeling beside Bear, Dragon handed him the water skin containing the willow bark and chamomile tea he made fresh every night for each day's travel. "Drink some of this. Drink as much as you need. I'll make some more once I find a place where I can build a fire."

And something to burn. He kept that thought to himself. He didn't know if Bear had noticed the scarcity of trees in this part of the city, but if he hadn't, Dragon didn't see any point in worrying him when he couldn't do anything about it.

Bear grasped at Dragon's hand. "Be careful. Feels wrong here. Like someone's watching."

The hairs stood up along Dragon's arms. He stared into

Bear's fever-bright eyes. "You felt that too?"

Bear nodded. His hand dropped from Dragon's. "Char's never empty, even when you think it is. Watch your back."

Dragon couldn't tell if the warning was a general one using Char as an example, or if Bear actually thought they were back in Char like he'd done on and off since the previous day. Not that it mattered. Just because the nameless city outside Ashe had been utterly deserted didn't mean any of the other ancient cities were. Dragon had never been one to ignore his own instincts in any case. That sort of thing got you nothing but killed, inside the tribal walls as well as out.

"Don't worry. I'll watch myself." Leaning down, Dragon kissed Bear's damp brow. He made sure the other two water skins—one full and one nearly so—were within Bear's reach. "I'll go outside and look around, but I won't go out of sight of this building. If anyone else comes in here, I'll know, and I'll come back."

Bear's lips quirked, but he didn't say anything. Dragon was ridiculously grateful for that. They both knew the dangers of separating in unfamiliar territory, especially with one of them injured and gravely ill. He didn't think he could stand to have those risks pointed out to him right now, when he had no choice but to leave Bear alone and vulnerable.

He dug Bear's knife out of the bag, drew it from the sheath and laid it on the blanket by Bear's side, then rose to his feet. He waited until Bear curled his fingers around the handle before turning and walking out the door.

Dragon took the time to explore the first level of the building before doing anything else. All the rooms were empty. The building had only one other entrance—a narrow door in the rear, opening into a squalid lane between that structure and the one behind it. Animal bones and bits of rotting fruit dotted the ground, as if someone had dumped the remains of many meals there. Dragon glanced at the building across the way. The windows gaped like empty eye sockets. Nothing moved inside, and he heard no sound in the still air.

So, people come here, at least sometimes, and they throw their scraps out those windows. We'll have to be careful. It was not much more than he'd already suspected. He shut the door carefully to avoid making any sound. After a moment's study, he figured out the metal tongue-and-groove locking mechanism and slid it into place, marveling that the material had remained undecayed and unblemished after hundreds of years.

He detoured back to check on Bear before going outside. Bear lay in a restless sleep, his injured leg bent at his side and his fist still closed around his knife handle. His face, neck and chest were blotched red with fever, and his lips moved as if in a silent conversation. The sight made Dragon's chest ache with helplessness, fear and the fierce need to protect.

Moving as silently as he could, he shut the door and made his way down the long hallway to the open space just inside the door to the old street. Daylight filtered in through the outside walls. Walls that looked like solid black metal from the outside, but from the inside were as transparent as glass.

Whatever they were made of, they *felt* solid enough. Dragon rapped on one nearly invisible expanse with his fist, still half-expecting it not to be there next time he checked. His knuckles made a dull *thud* on the strange stuff. Shaking his head, he drew his knife and headed for the door.

Outside, narrow bars of sunlight striped the tall grass in between the shadows of the buildings. The shade felt cool and damp. Now that he was able to turn his full attention to his surroundings, Dragon noticed the silence. No birds, no insects, not even the rustle of squirrels and other small animals through the weeds.

It made the back of Dragon's neck prickle. He curled his fingers tighter around the handle of his knife.

A survey of the immediate area revealed nothing more exciting than the skeleton of a rat tangled in the weeds between the building they'd chosen for their camp and the silver tower next door. But the deep, ringing quiet didn't abate. If anything, it grew more intense. By the time Dragon came to the solid black tower with the broken top a couple hundred paces across the road, he felt anxious and jumpy, every nerve on edge.

He stopped at the entrance to the old structure. It gaped into dusty, fetid gloom. Not far past the shattered door, the weak sunlight fell on a flight of stairs leading upward out of sight. Something about the place felt unhealthy.

Dragon turned to look over his shoulder at the place where Bear lay sleeping, alone and unable to defend himself. The door was still shut tight. Dragon could see no signs of anyone having entered.

Biting his lip, he considered what to do. He didn't like the silence here, and he *really* didn't like the atmosphere of this particular building. His gut told him to run back to Bear's side. But he couldn't. Not yet. He and Bear were all alone in this place. If any threat lurked here, he needed to know about it, and he would learn nothing without a little risk. Besides, he still hadn't found water, and he needed to. If he couldn't find water, they'd have to move on, and his every instinct screamed at him that when they left this city, they'd better get far, far away before dark.

There were no windows between the door and the far corner of the building. No way for anyone to attack him from behind if he kept his back to the building. Hugging the wall, Dragon edged toward the place where the tower nearly butted up against the one beside it. He estimated no more than four long strides between the two structures. It didn't seem like much space to separate buildings of such mind-numbing size.

When he reached the corner, he peered around the edge with his knife held in front of him. The ground here looked much the same as the little lane behind the other building, the grass thin and scrubby, covered with a layer of bones, fur and fruit pits. It smelled musty and rank.

The skin along Dragon's scalp prickled. His shoulders tensed. He peered into the shadows. Nothing moved. But he heard a sound that made him curse under his breath.

Water. The unmistakable trickle of water.

Great Mother, why here?

There was no help for it. Their two skins of water wouldn't last much longer. He had to find more, today if possible, and this was the first sign he'd found of fresh water in the city.

He eased forward a few tentative steps on the balls of his feet, ready to run at the slightest provocation. Nothing happened. Putting his back to the solid metal wall, he moved sideways, deeper into the alley. The sound of water running got louder. It seemed to be coming from behind the building next door. Encouraged, he eased farther into the darkness, trying to see into the narrow space behind the next building.

A movement overhead caught the tail of his eye. He gazed upward and froze. High up, the height of at least four tall men above Dragon's head, hemp ropes hung at intervals between the two buildings. The skins of small animals and other things dangled from the ropes. Some of the hides swaying in the air looked disturbingly human.

Now that he looked, *really* looked, some of the bones on the ground appeared human as well.

A great icy fist reached into Dragon's chest, closed around his lungs and squeezed.

Water would have to wait. Dragon ran.

He'd almost reached the open air when something caught him around the throat and cinched tight, lifting him off his feet.

Chapter Ten

Shoving the burst of panic ruthlessly aside, Dragon grabbed at the rope above his head and started sawing at it with his knife. It was no use, though. He'd barely made a start on cutting through before he was dragged through a window and into the building. He managed to sheath his knife beneath his too-long shirt before being yanked over the windowsill. Whoever his captors were, they'd certainly take away his weapon if they knew he had it, and he couldn't let that happen. With any luck, he'd managed to hide it before they'd spotted it.

Inside, he was pulled across a room smelling overpoweringly of urine and unwashed human and dumped in a dark corner. As soon as the pressure on the rope let up, he gulped air as discreetly as he could. The spots in his vision and the burning in his chest both cleared soon enough. His throat ached, but he could breathe now and he was able to swallow just fine, even though it hurt like fire. There didn't seem to be any permanent damage.

Although, judging from the skins and bones outside, staying that way didn't seem very likely. He lay sprawled on his back where they'd left him and watched through slitted eyelids as a filthy man with a long white beard and a fur cap crouched beside him. The man wore a vest that appeared to be fashioned of human skin. Shriveled fingers ringed the neckline, a grisly decoration. His lower body was naked except for a skunk's hide tied around one thigh. His feet were bare and black with grime.

Dragon lay still, breathed shallowly and waited. This man might be old, but he was big, nearly as big as Bear, and looked strong. If he knew how to fight, he wouldn't be easy to take down. And he wasn't alone. The sheer number of ropes and skins hanging outside told Dragon there were more people here than just this one man. He would have to wait for the right time to make his escape.

The man poked at Dragon's legs, arms and torso. "Good meat on this one. No sickness neither. Not like that other one it come in with."

"I still say we can cut the leg off a that one an' use the rest," said a female voice from Dragon's left. He didn't dare turn toward it. Someone tugged on his hair, and he caught a whiff of a body reeking of blood and feces. "I want this un's hair."

"Have it, then." The man bent so close Dragon could smell the rank odor of rotten teeth. Dark eyes glinted at him in the dimness. "It's awake."

The woman shrieked, making Dragon's ears ring. "Kill it! G'on, kill it now! Don't want it awake while we's asleep."

Leaning over Dragon's body, the man dealt the woman a blow that sent her tumbling backward across the floor. "Shut up. Don't like 'em 'less they's fresh. Kill it later, when it's time to eat. We got rope enough off a the last ones we caught to tie it up 'til then."

The woman rushed at the man, growling, and bowled him over. The two fought like wild animals, with teeth and nails, drawing blood. Dragon took the opportunity to open his eyes and search out the lay of the room. A door stood open only about ten paces away, in the direction from which the woman had come. The problem was, he had no idea how to get out of the building, or how many other people were inside. He'd have to take his chances going back out the window.

He waited until the woman bit the man's earlobe off, ensuring his attention was on her and her alone. While the old man howled, one hand clamped to his bleeding ear, Dragon jumped to his feet and ran.

He heard their cries, knew they'd seen him, heard scurrying footsteps and knew they'd abandoned their disagreement in favor of recapturing their evening meal, but he couldn't let that stop him. Drawing his knife from its sheath, he leapt for the window.

Hands caught his wrists. Too many hands. His knife was knocked from his grip, hit the windowsill and tumbled to the ground below. His forearms were yanked into a painful angle behind his neck and bound together. Half in and half out of the window, he twisted in his captors' grip, steeling himself to fight his way free with no weapon and no hands.

The old man in the fur cap grinned at him with black front teeth. A younger man, dressed only in smears of blood, shoved him out the window.

Dragon realized then what they intended. He drew a lungful of air before the rope brought him up short and cut off his breath, but it didn't matter in the end. Whatever else you might or might not be able to say about these people, they knew how long to hang a person before he passed out from lack of air.

Dragon turned his gaze toward the sunlight he'd never see again. He hoped Bear would somehow find his way out of here. Find Shenandoah, and the life he wanted.

Mother, take care of him.

Darkness rose and dragged Dragon under.

Bear's spirit roamed.

On his otherworldly journey, he walked northwest, where the mountains rose tall against the sky. He climbed slope after steep, wooded slope, leaving behind the strange, silent city in the foothills to follow the irresistible call in his head. The call leading him to his ultimate goal.

To Shenandoah.

He traveled for a day, a night, and well into the next day, though he knew the passage of time might be no more than a few minutes in the waking world. His path curved due north during the final morning's walk. As the sun's disc met the top of the highest western peak, he emerged from a narrow pass and looked down into a wide green valley. In its midst sprawled a large town ringed by a high fence. People passed in and out of the gate, bustled through the town's wide lanes and rode ox-driven carts between the many outlying fields and the city wall.

He'd dreamed of it before. Even seen flashes of it in his waking life. But it had never seemed so real before, so vivid and full of life. Bear longed to be a part of it.

He ran down the slope. His leg, healed and whole in his incorporeal form, carried him with a speed he'd never experienced while awake. As he came out of the woods and neared the town, the crowds parted for him. The people smiled at him, called greetings to him, welcomed him as if he were family, and his heart felt like it might burst. *This* was what he'd been searching for, the reason he'd been willing to brave the long journey north from Carwin.

A home. A real home, for himself and for Dragon.

A figure waited for him at the open gate to the city. Bear slowed as he approached and saw that the figure was a reed-thin woman nearly as tall as himself. She wore buckskin pants and a long purple shirt that billowed in the breeze. Her dark hair curled all the way to her hips, and her golden brown skin gleamed in the sun. A thick silver chain hung from her neck and a matching ring circled the middle finger of her right hand. Her feet were bare.

She smiled as Bear walked up to her. "Hello, Brother Bear.

Welcome to Shenandoah."

"Hi." Bear returned her smile. "Are you Shenandoah's Mother?"

She laughed. "We have no Mother here, other than the Great Mother we all share. I'm the tribal Seer. My name is Willow."

"Willow." It was a fitting name, Bear thought. "I'm Bear. But you already knew that, it sounds like." She nodded, and Bear went on. "This is my second spirit journey here. The Great Mother brought me last night too. That was different, though, like flying. And I didn't meet you, did I? I would've remembered."

Willow shook her head. "The Great Mother didn't bring you here, Bear. Not then, and not now."

He frowned. "Of course She did. There's no other way this could happen. My body's asleep, and the Mother's showing me the way to Shenandoah. She knows that my Brother Dragon and me have to get here soon, or I'll die."

"You're not on a spirit journey. You're dreaming."

"I am?" Bear looked around. Everything seemed sharp and clear. Not like his usual dreams, where the world was hazy and strange and he didn't even realize it wasn't real. "This doesn't seem like a dream. It seems more like a spirit journey."

"That's because I'm guiding this dream, much like the Great Mother would guide you in a spirit journey. I don't have Her powers, obviously, but I can sense the mind of a seeker like yourself, and I can speak to you in your dreams."

"A seeker?"

"A person who is seeking our tribe. You aren't the first. I've guided many seekers to Shenandoah through their dreams." Her gaze dropped to Bear's leg. "I can feel the sickness in your body. You don't have long."

A hollow feeling lodged in Bear's chest. "I know. I can

barely even walk now, and I keep forgetting where I am. I keep thinking I'm back with my old Pack. I told Dragon to go on without me and find your tribe. I was hoping you'd send someone back with him to help me. Will you?"

"Yes. In fact, a scouting team from our Pack is already on the way to you. They should arrive in Harrisonburg by midday tomorrow."

"Harrisonburg?"

"That's the name of the city where you and your Brother are right now. You're safe enough where you are. There are nests of cannibals in many parts of the city, but they usually only come out at night. Don't go inside any of the other buildings, and bar the doors to your own building after dark. If something happens and you must leave before our team arrives, follow the path I've shown you in this dream. You'll meet the team on the way." Stepping forward, she took Bear's hands in hers. "We can help you, Bear. We can heal you. Everything will be all right."

She smiled, her face radiant, and the longing to be there in reality rose like a wave of fire in Bear's gut. His throat closed up and tears blurred his vision. He squeezed his eyes shut.

When he opened them again, the green, sunny valley was gone, along with Willow's welcoming smile. He lay on the sweat-soaked blanket in the dark, musty room in an ancient building in an equally ancient city—Harrisonburg, Willow had called it— with watery afternoon light slanting through the single tiny window high up in the corner. The only sounds were the rush of his pulse in his skull and his own too-rapid breathing.

Dragon was nowhere to be seen.

Bear wasn't sure exactly how long ago he'd drifted off to sleep. But he knew it had been several hours, judging by the angle of the sunbeam cutting across the floor. Dragon should've been back long ago.

Something's wrong. Something's happened to him. Bear knew it as surely as he knew Willow was real.

He sat up. Too fast. He splayed his hands on the floor and shut his eyes until the world stopped moving and he no longer felt like throwing up, then opened them again. Finding his sheath in the tangle of blankets, he strapped it to his good leg and slid his knife into it, carefully because his hands still trembled with fever.

Mother, he hoped he wouldn't need to fight. He'd be all but useless in this condition.

Now for the hard part. Scooting the few feet over to the corner where Dragon had leaned his crutch, Bear gritted his teeth against the pain he knew was coming and used the wall to push himself to his feet.

The burst of agony nearly sent him back into unconsciousness. He fought it with every ounce of willpower he possessed. His rising sense of urgency told him if he didn't find Dragon soon, he may never see him again. Or worse, he might find a few scraps of clothes and a pile of bones picked clean.

There are nests of cannibals in many parts of the city.

The thought made Bear tuck his crutch under his arm and limp as fast as he could to the building's front door.

The hall was a long one. Bear frowned when he emerged into a wide, shallow room fronted by a tremendous window. He crossed to the window. It looked out on a city full of black and silver metal buildings so tall the tops of them vanished into pinpoints in the sky. Bear stared. He couldn't remember this place. Not that that was so strange, really. Even now, there were still parts of Char no one had ever explored. But he was sure Char had never had buildings like that. So where was he? Why was he here alone? How had he gotten here?

He gingerly bent and straightened his leg, which hurt with a bone-deep pain. *And what happened to my leg? It's infected.*

I'm sick. Feverish.

Sickness. Fever.

The memories came back in a dizzying rush. His stomach churned. Clenching his teeth, he rested his aching forehead against the cool glass—only it wasn't glass, was it? He remembered that, now—until the nausea passed. He couldn't afford to throw up. He was too weak already. If he lost any more fluids, he wouldn't have the strength to even walk, never mind rescue Dragon.

Assuming he could find Dragon in the first place. He had no idea where to look. He thought he remembered Dragon saying he would stay within sight of this building, but that was the only clue he had. And if Dragon had been taken, whoever took him wouldn't be bound by that promise.

Head still pressed to the not-glass, Bear gazed out into the waning afternoon light. He wished he had some idea where to start. He could waste precious hours—hours Dragon might not have to spare—searching through all the empty places in this vast, sinister old city.

Well, the one place he isn't, is here. And the sooner you get started, the sooner you can find him.

He nodded to himself, as if to firm his resolve. He could search through the nearby buildings first. The ones on either side of this one, then the ones immediately across the way. After that, he'd try the ones to the north. That's probably what Dragon would've done, looking for water and firewood.

His plans in place, Bear pushed away from the wall. He gazed up the ancient street, measuring the distance with his eyes. He could probably manage to search the few buildings within two or three hundred paces north before he had to rest. If he hadn't found Dragon by then, he'd—

The glint of sunlight off a polished surface stopped his thoughts cold. He leaned closer.

"Oh, Mother." Heart pounding, Bear hopped to the door as fast as he could on his good leg and his rough crutch, flung it open and went outside. He shaded his eyes against the sun's rays and looked again.

It was still there. Not a dream.

About two hundred paces away, at the entrance to a shadowed passage between two enormous towers, lay a shape blurred by distance, but familiar enough for Bear's memory to fill in the details he couldn't make out—the finely honed edge to the long stone blade, the colored stitching on the leather-wrapped handle.

Dragon's knife. It was Dragon's knife, abandoned on the ground.

Bear could think of a lot of reasons it would be there. None of them meant anything good for Dragon.

Bear's own knife was a comforting weight against his uninjured thigh. He rubbed his thumb over the worn leather of the handle. It was a good weapon. It had killed its share of enemies over the years. He hoped it would be up to the challenge this time.

With no need to wait and every reason to hurry, Bear started toward the spot where his Brother had been taken.

Dragon woke to a tender, swollen throat and a pounding headache. He lay still, trying to remember where he was and what had happened to him. His shoulders ached and his hands throbbed. His arms, twisted behind his head, refused to budge when he tried to move them, but he felt the bite of coarse ropes binding each wrist to the opposite arm just above the elbow. More rope dug into his ankles and the raw skin of his neck.

Apprehension fluttered in his belly. *What in the Mother's name is going on here?*

Something scuffed the ground—*the floor,* Dragon realized as the sound echoed in the way sound only did indoors—a few paces to the right of where Dragon lay. A male voice mumbled. A female one hissed at it to shut up. The sound of flesh connecting with flesh followed, then a cry and a thud.

There was a brief scuffle and some muttering before silence fell. By that time, Dragon remembered it all. The horror of human skins swaying overhead and human bones underfoot. The shocking suddenness of his capture. Freedom so close he could taste it, only to be snatched away again.

He'd been so certain he was going to die. But he hadn't died. He was alive. *Alive.* His life was a gift, and he swore a silent vow to make the most of every precious second.

Dragon thought he knew why this particular time felt so different from every other time he'd slipped away from death at the last minute.

Bear. It all came down to Bear. To the man who needed him almost as much as he needed Bear.

Someone coughed to Dragon's left. He bit back a startled cry, mentally cursing himself for letting his attention slip. He already knew there were at least three people in here—the old man, the younger man and the woman. How many more were there? In this room, and in this building? He didn't dare open his eyes to assess the situation. Not yet. As long as his captors believed he was still unconscious, he had a chance. If they knew he was awake, there was no telling what they would do. If they decided that caution was more important than fresher meat, they'd kill him. He couldn't take that chance.

The strain on Dragon's shoulders sent shooting pains down his back and up his neck into his already-aching skull. He longed to move, to ease some of the tension from his body, but he didn't dare. So he lay motionless and tried to come up with an escape plan. The woman had said something about him being awake while she and her companions were sleeping, which meant they must be planning to sleep at some point before killing him.

He had no idea *why* they would do that, but it didn't matter. If they were about to settle down to sleep for a while— and it sounded as if they were—that worked in his favor. All he had to do was wait until all of them were asleep, then free himself and get back to Bear.

Free yourself...how?

That was the real question. It all hinged on whether or not the rope around his neck was secured to anything. Dragon hoped not. The three who'd captured him were clever hunters, but they didn't seem particularly intelligent. With any luck, they would count on the ropes around his arms and legs to keep him from escaping. Getting out of here while tied up wouldn't be easy, but he could do it. Bear could cut him loose once he got back to their camp.

Bear. Mother, just the thought of Bear alone and vulnerable in his sickness made Dragon's heart hurt. Bear was defenseless without him right now. He needed him.

All the more reason to be careful, and bide your time.

With a mental sigh, Dragon forced himself to remain still and wait.

By the time Dragon's captors finally settled down, his arms had long since gone completely numb and his skull felt like it was coming apart at the seams. The woman and the older man kept getting into minor squabbles, and once the younger man crossed the room to piss in the corner, from the sound of it. At last, though, after what felt like hours, all three lay unmoving long enough for their breathing to grow slow and deep.

Dragon waited a while longer before opening his eyes. He still had no idea how many people inhabited the rest of this building, but there was nothing to be done about it. He had to get out of here, and his only chance lay in freeing himself while the three in this room slept.

He looked around, careful not to move in case one of the three was awake after all. His head was tilted to his right, where the two older ones slept. The woman lay curled in the corner to the right of the window, one arm over her head. Blood trickled from her split lip. The old man sprawled on his back near the woman's head, snoring.

Good. That took care of the two of them. Now he just had to make sure the younger man was asleep. Which meant he had to turn his head and look.

Dragon shut his eyes again first. He believed the other man was asleep, judging by the slow, regular rhythm of his breathing, but there was no sense in taking chances.

He let his head flop to the other side, as if he were turning in his sleep. The movement sent a sharp, sickening pain shooting through his head like an arrow. Ignoring it as best he could, he cracked his eyelids open just enough to peer through his lashes. The younger man lay on his side atop a large animal skin. His eyes were closed, his mouth slack with sleep.

Dragon let out the breath he'd been holding. So his captors were all asleep. Perfect.

Moving as slowly and carefully as possible, he rolled onto his right side. Mother, it hurt. Not a surprise, really. It was a miracle his neck hadn't been broken. A few pulled muscles or a bone in his spine out of place would hardly be unexpected. Grimacing in pain and concentration, he used his bound feet to move his body while keeping his head still. If the rope around his neck was loose at the other end, fine. If it was tied to something that might fall over and wake everyone, though, he didn't want to find out the hard way.

He'd almost gotten himself maneuvered into position when the rope pulled taut around his neck. He swallowed a curse. This didn't bode well. Arching his back to create some slack on the restraint around his throat, he rolled his eyes upward until he could follow the line of the rope. It was knotted to a thick metal bolt in the wall.

He shut his eyes. For several minutes he just lay there, fighting despair. How was he supposed to get out of this? His knife was on the ground outside. It might as well be back in Ashe for all the good it would do him. Maybe he could get the rope untied, if he could reach one of the knots.

And if I could feel my fingers. He clenched his fists a few times, but it didn't help. His hands were dead as wood. Useless.

Desperate, he hunched his shoulders up as high as he could and tried to force his bound arms over his head. Maybe, if he could just get them in front of his body instead of contorted behind his neck, the feeling would come back and he could untie himself.

It didn't work, and not just because his arms were tied too tightly together. When he tried to move them forward, the rope pulled against his windpipe.

Those Mother-damned cannibals must've tied his arms to the noose.

Fuck.

The old man rolled onto his side. His hand flopped only a couple of paces from Dragon's foot. Dragon froze. The man mumbled in his sleep for a moment before settling again.

Dragon lay still until his pulse slowed and he was positive the old man was still sound asleep, then started pushing himself toward the wall where his rope was tied.

Once he got close enough, he wrestled himself into a sitting position as quietly as he could. The change in position made his head pound. He ignored the discomfort and studied the thick bolt embedded in the ancient metal wall. It was too far above his head to reach while sitting, but would be too low if he were to stand. Which made his escape plan difficult, but he had to try. He'd figure out how to untie the knot without being able to feel it once he got to that point.

Turning around, he sat with his back to the wall. He was about to push himself up toward the bolt when he heard noises from somewhere outside.

No. Not outside. The noises—soft, shuffling footsteps—came from inside the building.

They were close. And coming closer.

Not knowing where this new person was going or what they might do, Dragon slid back down to the floor and stretched out where he was. He didn't have time to move the few paces back to the spot where he'd been before. He'd just have to hope that if the three sleeping around him woke up, they wouldn't notice he'd moved.

He'd no sooner gotten himself in position than the footsteps sounded not far from the door to the room where he lay. Silence fell for a moment. Outside, someone breathed fast and harsh. The tread resumed. Faint *clunks* sounded in between the uneven, halting footsteps.

Something about the stealthy sound made Dragon's pulse quicken, though he couldn't say why. He cracked his eyelids open just enough to watch the doorway as the footsteps reached the threshold.

What he saw almost gave him away with the exclamation he barely held back.

Bear. Bear had come to rescue him.

Chapter Eleven

The sight of Dragon with his arms bound behind his head and raw rope burns around his neck made Bear want to leave bloody pieces of Dragon's captors splattered all over the walls of the filthy little room. He stomped down the killing urge. Much as he'd love to slice the bastards to quivering ribbons, he knew he wasn't up to the task right now. He needed to free Dragon, then the two of them had to get out of here as fast as they could.

Why the three had taken Dragon in the first place, Bear couldn't say for sure. But the fact that Dragon was strung up like a goat for slaughter—not to mention the human skin the older of the two men wore and the scattered human bones—gave him a pretty good idea. He'd dealt with enough nomads and nightfeeders to know the signs. And Willow had told him there were nests of cannibals here.

He pressed a finger to his lips when Dragon's eyes went wide with surprise and relief, though he knew Dragon wouldn't make a sound. Dragon nodded when Bear held up his knife. Biting his lip in concentration, Bear hitched himself the few paces across the dirty floor to where Dragon lay. His crutch slipped in a small puddle of blood. He stumbled against the wall not far from the bolt to which Dragon was tied.

For a few seconds he stood perfectly still, barely breathing, his knife at the ready. The man curled on the pile of skins to the left of the door didn't move a muscle. Neither did the older man, sprawled on the bare floor only a few paces away and snoring loudly. The woman grumbled something unintelligible, rolled over and settled with her back to the door.

Mother, that was close. Heart racing fast enough to make him dizzy, Bear put his back to the wall to steady himself, then gestured at Dragon to sit up. Dragon rolled sideways and squirmed himself silently into a sitting position, knees bent. Leaning over, Bear hooked his hand through Dragon's elbow and helped haul him to his feet.

He paled, swayed and fell back against the wall, eyes closed. For a horrible moment, Bear thought he'd passed out. Then the gray eyes opened again, sharp and clear, and Bear grinned in pure relief.

Okay? he mouthed.

Dragon nodded. He jerked his head toward the bolt in the wall. *Hurry.*

Bear cut the rope tethering Dragon to the wall first. Next came the one around his ankles. That one was trickier. Bear had to lean his crutch against the wall and lower himself onto his good knee to do it. He felt something give deep inside his wound just before his knee hit the floor. Fluid oozed from the gash in his thigh and ran down his leg when he stood after cutting the rope binding Dragon's legs. Blood, pus or both, he didn't know. Not that it mattered right now. They could deal with it later, when they weren't both in immediate danger of becoming someone else's meal.

Dragon was already nodding toward the door by the time Bear regained his feet. He didn't bother to argue. They needed to leave, right now. He could finish cutting Dragon loose outside.

Tucking his crutch under his arm, Bear followed Dragon out of the squalid room and into the dark, musty hallway. The whole place stank of blood, shit and death. The smell pierced

141

right through the illness that had been fogging up his senses these last few days. His gorge rose with a mix of the building's stench, lightheadedness from his fever and the gut-punched feeling of blood loss. It must be blood, or mostly blood, running faster and faster down the back of his leg. He hoped he'd make it outside without throwing up. They couldn't risk the noise.

Navigating the stairs seemed to take hours. Bear cut Dragon's arms free before they started down, despite the danger in lingering there, partly because he didn't think it was safe for Dragon—still unsteady from having his legs bound for hours—to try the stairs with his arms tied, but also because Bear didn't think he could make it himself without help. Not that Dragon could provide *much* help. As he wordlessly indicated, he couldn't feel his arms at all, and he was unable to manage even the weakest grip on Bear's hand. But he slipped an arm around Bear's waist anyway, tucking his useless hand into the top of Bear's buckskins, and provided him with a pair of strong shoulders to lean on.

It made Bear nervous to be without his weapon in his hand in this place, even for a few minutes, but he was forced to sheath his knife because he couldn't hold on to it and Dragon at the same time. As soon as they reached the bottom of the steps, he pulled away from Dragon and drew his knife again. A bar of watery sunlight from the open door to the outside cut through the gloom. Only about fifteen paces away. So close.

As they approached the door, Bear took Dragon's knife from beneath the leather belt from which his sheath hung—he'd had nowhere else to put the weapon and hadn't wanted to leave it behind—and tucked it into the sheath still strapped to Dragon's thigh. Shooting Bear a grateful smile, Dragon flexed his fingers around the handle in a still weak but improving grip.

Upstairs, back the way they'd come, an indignant roar sounded, followed by pounding footsteps. Adrenaline shot through Bear's blood. "Fuck."

"Yeah." Before Bear could object, Dragon slipped beneath his arm again, supporting him on the side opposite his crutch. "Come on. Lean on me."

Bear didn't dare look back as Dragon practically dragged him the last few paces to the door and out into the leveling rays of the late-afternoon sun. His ears told him well enough that their pursuers were practically at their heels.

Dragon didn't even slow down when they reached the relative openness of the ancient street. Bear didn't argue, in spite of the dizziness and fatigue threatening to overtake him. Willow had said these people mostly came out at night, but Bear didn't doubt for a second that they'd charge straight out into blazing sunshine to salvage their food source.

Sure enough, feet thudded through the weeds behind him, a man's voice growled close enough that Bear caught the rotten-meat foulness of his breath and quick as thought, Dragon was snatched backward. Instinctive balance and his grip on his crutch saved Bear from a fall.

Knife in hand, Bear pivoted toward the sound of struggle. The younger of the two men had one hand wound in Dragon's hair and the other clamped onto Dragon's right wrist, wiry muscles standing out ropelike under his grimy skin as he fought to make Dragon drop his knife. So far, it wasn't working. Dragon held on, though his whole arm shook with the effort.

Relief blossomed through Bear's fear and anger. The strength in Dragon's arms and hands must be coming back, which was good. But it wasn't enough. He was losing the battle. In the brief second Bear watched, Dragon's attacker dragged him backward several paces toward the building they'd just left.

Bear didn't stop to think. Dropping his crutch, he lunged forward and plunged his knife into the cannibal's neck.

The man let go of Dragon and dropped to the ground, clawing at his throat. He yanked the knife out and tossed it aside. Blood fountained from the wound. A wheezing gurgle

143

accompanied each labored breath he drew. Bear realized he'd punctured the man's windpipe as well as severing the big blood vessel that ran alongside it.

Good. It shouldn't take long for him to die.

Dragon kicked the man onto his back, where his body convulsed in the dirt, then grabbed Bear's knife from the ground where it had fallen. "I don't think the other one's going to follow us out here."

Bear squinted toward the doorway. The older man huddled in the shadows just inside. The smell of his fear drifted to Bear on the cooling breeze. "He's scared because I killed that other one. Don't know about the woman, though." Bear stopped, his breath coming short. He shook his head to clear it. Mother, he couldn't afford to pass out. "Let's move. We need to get back to camp."

"Yeah." Dragon wiped Bear's knife clean on a nearby patch of grass and replaced it in Bear's sheath. With a quick glance at the younger cannibal—who now lay still and silent in the weeds—Dragon resumed his spot at Bear's side. The hand around Bear's waist now dug into his side with reassuring strength. Dragon kept his knife gripped tight in his right hand, though tremors still ran through his arm. "I don't think we'll need to worry about the woman. She and the old man seem to fight a lot. I think he might've broken a bone the last time they got into it."

Bear tried to answer, but he couldn't seem to get any words out. His ears rang and his vision tunneled, and his legs refused to move. In that moment, he knew he wasn't going to make it back to camp.

As if from a great distance, he heard Dragon asking if he was all right. He tried to tell Dragon how sorry he was with a look, but wasn't sure if it got across before the fever and blood loss caught up with him and he crumpled in an unconscious heap at Dragon's feet.

When Bear's eyes rolled back into his head and he slid to the ground, every impulse Dragon had screamed for him to scoop Bear up and run. To carry him back to the relative safety of their camp, stop the bleeding from the reopened wound in his leg—even Dragon could smell the metallic tang of blood, there was so much of it—and get some strong sage tea into him.

Dragon fought the urge and kept his gaze fixed on the figure in the doorway. If he didn't make a move in the next few seconds, Dragon would have to go after him. He couldn't risk having the man discover his balls *after* Dragon got Bear draped across his shoulders, when he was burdened with Bear's weight and unable to fight without risking further injury to him.

The old man edged forward a couple of paces, then retreated again. He licked his lips, clearly torn between fear and hunger.

Frustrated, Dragon knelt beside Bear, hiding his knife beside his thigh. Maybe if he pretended to ignore the man, it would draw him out. Dragon very much did not want to go back into that building, where there might be more people like the three who had captured him hiding. If he were caught again, there would be no more escapes. He would die in there, and Bear would either bleed to death here in the weeds or be taken inside and eaten himself.

The silence dragged on. A sidelong glance told Dragon the cannibal still lingered half in and half out of the doorway. Just when Dragon decided he'd have to pursue and kill the old man after all, he sprinted toward Dragon with surprising speed. The westering sun glinted off a metal blade clutched in his raised fist.

Finally. Dragon jumped up to meet him.

The man was no warrior. A single swipe of Dragon's knife sliced the tendons in the thick wrist. The old man let out an indignant squawk. His hand opened. The blade tumbled to the

145

grass in a shower of blood.

Dragon didn't wait to press his advantage. Tackling the old man to the ground, he thrust his knife under his foe's breastbone, turned it and cut sideways left, then right, severing the major blood vessels. The man didn't even have time to scream, never mind fight back. He died staring up at Dragon with an expression of shock frozen to his face.

Dragon sat back on his heels and looked around. The city was silent and empty as far as he could see. As he'd predicted, the woman hadn't come downstairs. He yanked his knife free of the dead man's body, wiped the blade as clean as possible on the skunk's hide around the man's thigh and replaced it in its sheath.

Pushing to his feet, Dragon trotted back to Bear's side and knelt beside him. He rested a palm on Bear's forehead. The skin felt dry and fiery hot. "Bear?"

No answer. Not even a twitch. Bear's breath came fast and short. His heartbeat, when Dragon laid a hand over his chest to check, galloped too fast to count and almost too faint to feel.

His worry rapidly turning to fear, Dragon wrestled Bear into a position where he could check his wound. Blood soaked the makeshift pant leg Dragon had sewn onto Bear's buckskins back in Lexin and pooled on the ground. When he looked back, Dragon saw a trail of blood from the building to the spot where Bear lay.

For a moment, Dragon wavered. He needed to get Bear out of here, *now*, before cohorts of the two they'd killed showed up. But Bear was losing blood fast. If Dragon waited until he got back to camp to try and stop it, would it be too late?

Maybe. Maybe not. He didn't *know*.

In the end, he wasn't willing to risk it. Keeping a sharp eye out for anything moving, Dragon rolled Bear's pant leg up over his wound, then pulled his own shirt off and tied it as tight as he dared over the folded buckskin. With an apology to Bear for the pain he was about to inflict—and a silent hope that it would wake him—he looped one arm around Bear's injured thigh to steady it and pressed the other hand as hard as he could against the wound. Bear moaned, but didn't wake.

Ages passed while Dragon sat there, trying to stop Bear from bleeding to death and half-expecting to be attacked any minute. A rat scurried through the vines and young trees nearby, but otherwise nothing moved. Not a sound cut the unnatural stillness.

By the time Dragon judged he'd kept pressure on the wound long enough, his nerves felt frayed to the breaking point. He moved his hand slowly, watching for any sign of renewed bleeding. It was hard to tell, since his shirt, Bear's pants and the skin below were all covered in blood, but after a couple minutes of close study he decided none of the bleeding was fresh.

Relieved, he glanced around one more time. A figure watched him from the shadows of a doorway about fifty paces away. As soon as he spotted it, the figure fled into the interior of the building.

A jolt of alarm went through him. He'd known there must be more of them, but to have them spot him was bad. If they followed him back to his and Bear's camp...

He gave himself a mental shake. There was no point in sitting here worrying over it. Securing their camp was already part of his plan for the night. So was staying awake to keep watch. The fact that he'd been seen and might be followed didn't make that much difference, really. A Pack Brother always assumed the enemy knew where he was, while trying to make sure they didn't.

Dragon levered Bear into a sitting position, took hold of his wrist and managed to get one shoulder wedged beneath his chest. From there, Dragon knelt on one knee with the other foot planted on the ground and maneuvered Bear's torso as carefully as he could across his shoulders. Dragon staggered to his feet, one hand tight around Bear's dangling arm and the other looped through the bend of his uninjured knee.

Hoping he had the strength to carry Bear as far as he needed to, Dragon shuffled off through the grass and knee-high weeds.

By the time Dragon kicked open the door to his and Bear's building and stumbled sideways through the aperture, the daylight had faded to a soft purple dusk. With any luck, none of the invisible watchers he'd felt staring at him would try to follow him in here before full dark.

The hallway to the back of the building where they'd set up camp was too narrow to carry Bear through. Dragon tried, but couldn't get through the cramped opening without knocking either Bear's head or his damaged leg against the frame.

"Dammit." Tired, frustrated and with night looming, Dragon lowered Bear carefully to the floor against one wall, as far from either door as possible. Bear let out a low, pained moan. Dragon bent to kiss his burning forehead. "I have to secure this room, then I need to go get our things. I'll be right back, okay?"

Bear didn't answer. Dragon hadn't really expected him to, but the knot in his gut twisted a little tighter anyway.

He couldn't figure out how to lock the outside door—it didn't work the same way as the back door, the one opening into the dirty little alley—so he blocked it as well as he could with a few large pieces of twisted metal dragged from the far side of the room. After wedging the hallway door open with another hunk of metal, he trotted down the hall in the near-blackness to the room he'd left so many hours ago. It remained empty, his and Bear's belongings undisturbed. He snatched up the bag, bow and arrows, blankets and water skins and hurried back to the front room.

He'd half-expected to find the place swarming with cannibals, even though he surely would've heard the screech of metal being shoved aside if someone had tried to get in. But the scrap he'd dragged in front of the door was still in place, and Bear lay unmolested exactly where he'd been left.

Some of the tension in Dragon's neck let go. Squatting on the ground beside Bear, he set down the water skins and blankets, opened the bag and dug out both coils of rope. He wanted to use part of it to help secure the door, if possible, but he needed to leave enough to make a litter to carry Bear out of the city tomorrow, since he obviously wasn't going to be able to walk.

And there was no question of whether they were leaving. They couldn't stay. Even if this place wasn't so much more dangerous than they'd first thought, Bear wouldn't survive much longer without more help than Dragon could provide.

He had to find Shenandoah. Soon.

Somehow.

For a moment, his task loomed larger than the mind-numbing structures outside. He covered his face with his hands. How was he to find Shenandoah in time to save Bear? He had no idea which way to go. All he knew was that the tribe supposedly lay deep in the mountains. He might wander for days yet—weeks, even—before finding it. By then, Bear would be dead.

The thought of Bear's bright spirit extinguished caused a dull ache deep in Dragon's chest. Dropping his hands, he bent low over Bear's still form, cradled Bear's fevered cheeks in his hands and rested his brow against Bear's.

"I don't know where it is, Bear. I don't know where to even start looking." He smoothed his thumbs over the corners of Bear's mouth. "But I'm not going to give up. I promise you that. Tomorrow, as soon as it's light, I'm taking you out of here, and we're going to find Shenandoah." *And Mother, I hope they can*

149

help you, because if they can't...

Dragon decided not to think about that.

After a few minutes he sat back with a sigh. To his surprise, Bear's eyes were open, watching him with the exhausted calm of the very ill.

A wide, relieved smile spread over Dragon's face. "Bear. How do you feel?"

Bear licked his chapped lips. "Weak. Sick. Leg hurts bad."

"Not surprising. That wound opened up, and you lost a lot of blood." Twisting around, Dragon picked up the skin he used for the herb tea. It was empty. He'd expected as much, but it was worth checking. He picked up a nearly full water skin instead, pulled the plug out of the mouth and set it aside. "Here, let me help you sit up a little bit so you can drink some water. I'm sorry there's no more tea. At least this'll rehydrate you, though."

If Bear had any complaints, he kept them to himself. He grasped at the skin with a shaking hand as Dragon slipped an arm beneath Bear's shoulders and lifted him up just enough so he could swallow. Bear drank, one sip at a time, until his breathing began to grow harsh. He hadn't had enough, in Dragon's opinion, but if he choked because he was too worn out to swallow properly, it would just make matters worse.

Dragon laid Bear back down as gently as he could, recorked the skin and set it on the floor. Picking up one of the blankets, he folded it and tucked it beneath Bear's head. He spread the other over Bear's shivering body. "Rest now. I'll give you some more in a little while. Do you want to try to eat some apple?"

Bear shook his head. "Not now."

His voice was rough, shaky and barely audible. Dragon hated hearing him sound so weak. "Okay. Maybe later. Try to sleep for a while." He leaned forward and kissed Bear's lips.

When he drew back and tried to stand, Bear's hand closed around his wrist with surprising strength. "I know where it is."

Dragon frowned. "What?"

"Sh-shenandoah. I know..." Bear stopped, breathing hard for a moment, then started again. "I know. Where it is."

Shocked, Dragon studied Bear, trying to determine how lucid he was. His cheeks burned with a deep red fever-flush, brilliant against his grayish-white pallor, but his eyes were clear. Still... "How can you know that? I mean, yes, we know *generally* where it is, but—"

"Been dreaming about it. For days now. And, and the Seer from Shenandoah came to me in a dream, earlier, after you left. This dream was...was different. She showed me. How to get there." Bear pinned Dragon with an intense stare. "I know you don't...don't really believe those things. But it's true. Trust me."

Mother, I hope he isn't seeing things after all. Peering into Bear's eyes, though, Dragon saw none of the vagueness and confusion that had plagued Bear lately. Hope rose in Dragon's heart, in spite of his lingering skepticism. Maybe Bear's dream had been just that—a simple dream—but what harm would it do to listen to him? At this point, one direction was as good as another.

And what if Bear was actually right?

Dragon nodded, as much for his own benefit as for Bear's. "Where? Which way do I go?"

"Follow this road until...'til it crosses another old road. Bigger one. Wider. Take that one west. When we pass the square, leave the road and...and head northwest. Toward the tallest peak. Don't worry. I'll guide you." Bear's fingers slipped from Dragon's wrist. His eyes closed. "Pack's coming. They'll find us."

Dragon twisted to look over his shoulder at the wall of the windows behind him before he could curb the impulse. Pack?

What Pack? Shenandoah's? Could they really get here so quickly? Were he and Dragon truly that close to the tribe they'd been trying to find all this time?

The thought was wonderful and terrifying in more or less equal amounts. Bear needed help, the sooner the better, and Shenandoah was his only chance of getting it. If their Pack really was on the way here, as Bear claimed, he'd get the help he needed sooner than Dragon had dared hope.

But. But, but...

He turned back to Bear, brow furrowed in thought. The Pack. Shenandoah's Pack. If what Bear had said was the truth and not just a fever dream, why would they come here? Why would Shenandoah's Mother and her council *send* them here? Did they send regular patrols to this place, for reasons of their own? Or was this one dispatched especially to fetch Bear and Dragon and bring them to the tribe?

And if that was the case, *why?* In Dragon's experience, tribes didn't go out of their way to help outcast members of other tribes' Packs, especially if helping those people put the tribe's own members in danger, as this rescue mission surely would. If Pack Brothers—or Sisters—were on the way here to bring Bear and Dragon to Shenandoah, there *must* be something in it for the tribe. If he could only work out what that motive might be...

Something hit the window. Startled, Dragon jumped to his feet, whipping out his knife as he moved. By the light of the half-moon outside, he saw a naked woman crouched in the tall grass about ten paces from the wall, staring at it as if she'd like to cut a hole in it with the power of her gaze. As he watched, she dug in the dirt at her feet, stood and whipped her arm at the building, then squatted in the weeds again. A rock bounced harmlessly off the transparent material.

Dragon shook off all his questions about Shenandoah, the Pack and what might happen if Bear was right. He'd deal with that when the time came. Right now, he and Bear still had to get through the night, and escape from this place in the morning.

Keeping one eye on the woman outside—and the equally naked man hunched on the ground beside her—Dragon stood, picked up a coil of rope and headed for the door. If there was any way to further secure it, he had to do that first. Once he'd strengthened the door as much as he could, he needed to clean and dress Bear's wound. Best to get as good a look as possible at the leg before the moon traveled west and he lost its direct light. After that, he needed to try to get Bear to drink some water, and to eat at least a little bit.

And you need to eat something yourself, he mentally amended as his empty stomach rumbled.

Another rock hit the wall. Outside, three more ragged, filthy people—two men and a woman—had joined the first two. The woman carried a long knife of black stone that gleamed in the moonlight. All three wore the tattered remains of buckskins similar to his own.

He watched with interest as the three new arrivals and the naked couple in the grass warily eyed one another. He had no idea how evolved the cannibal society had become here. For his and Bear's sake, he hoped the various groups had not gotten to the point of cooperating with each other while on the hunt. The more the people outside fought amongst themselves, the better chance Dragon had of getting himself and Bear out of here alive come morning.

After a couple of minutes, the two groups seemed to reach a silent accord. Ignoring the other two, the armed woman and her male companions approached the window-wall. The two men began running their hands over it, knocking on it here and there, while the woman stalked back and forth like a sentry, swinging her knife.

Heart in his throat, Dragon found a knob of protruding

metal in the wall a few paces from the door, tied one end of the rope to it and started winding the coil of strong, supple hemp through the piled metal scraps, around the door handle and across to the leg of what looked like a built-in table on the other side. It wasn't perfect, but it would have to do. After he'd taken care of Bear's wound, maybe he could use the blankets to drag him into a room that would lock.

And end up getting trapped in the interior of the building? No. If they find a way in, they'll just wait us out, or we'll both starve to death in there. Better stay out here, where we have at least a chance of getting away in the daylight. If it's only these five, I can take them anyway. Take out the woman with the knife first. The others will be easy.

His mind made up, Dragon went back to Bear and started setting out everything he'd need to clean and dress Bear's leg. He did his best to ignore the purposeful knocks and thumps along the outside of the building, and the hungry eyes that he knew couldn't see him.

Chapter Twelve

Clouds gathered as the hours passed. The moon eventually set behind a thick gray pall, bringing deep blackness with it. Dragon could no longer see the people gathered outside, but he heard their determined attempts to get in. He was fairly certain they couldn't, but still. The crowd had grown since sunset, and the noise of their explorations in the absolute darkness set his nerves on edge.

Toward morning, a gentle rain began to fall. The knocks, thumps and occasional rattle of the metal piled in front of the door never let up. In fact, the sounds became more desperate as the night wore away. Dragon sat facing the door, his knife at the ready, listening to the mingled noises of the people outside and Bear's incoherent mumblings and waiting for the dawn.

Just when Dragon began to wonder whether the night would ever end, movement caught his eye. He pushed to his feet and edged closer to the outside wall. Silhouettes stirred beyond the window, vague black shapes against a deep gray sky.

Morning. Finally.

Now if only the throng outside would give up and go away.

Dragon waited. As the darkness gave way to thin, colorless daylight, the figures slunk away one by one. The rain still fell, a steady patter on the walls and door, but that was okay. They had an oiled deerskin, taken from Lexin along with the other supplies. He could use it to protect Bear from the rain while they traveled. As warm as the weather had been, he himself wouldn't need any such protection.

Sheathing his knife, he turned away from the dreary outdoor view and returned to Bear's side. He crouched and brushed the sweat-soaked curls from Bear's brow. "Bear? It's morning. I need you to wake up now and take a little bit of food and water, then we have to leave here."

Bear's eyelids cracked open enough to reveal a bit of glittering amber. "Saw Rabbit last night. He's here." Bear paused, panting. Before Dragon could work out why the name sounded so familiar, Bear grasped at Dragon's forearm with a shaking hand. His eyes opened wide and stared at something only he could see. "Gotta find him, Lynx. I know we're not s'posed to go off into the city without permission, but..." His hand dropped to the floor. He frowned.

After a few silent moments Dragon laid a hand on Bear's cheek and gently turned his face toward the light. He looked exhausted and far too pale, but awareness had returned to his eyes. "Bear? You okay?"

"Yeah." Bear's brow creased. "What was I saying?"

The bewilderment in Bear's eyes broke Dragon's heart, but he made himself smile. "You were saying you wanted some water and something to eat before we leave."

Bear arched an eyebrow in obvious disbelief, but he let Dragon help him sit up and lean against the wall so he could drink from the water skin. He even ate an entire apple and some dried venison, much to Dragon's relief. He'd never managed to get any food into Bear last night, and he'd worried about what might happen if Bear went too long without eating. The return of his appetite this morning was encouraging.

Dragon wolfed down berries, meat and an apple while Bear was eating, then gulped some of the water from the other skin. When they'd both finished, Dragon tucked the water skins into the satchel and walked over to peer through the enormous window. Rain splashed into the puddles outside and turned the buildings across the way into sinister shadows, their tops lost in the clouds above. Of the mob that had spent the entire night trying to get to him and Bear, not a soul remained in sight.

Now or never. He went back to crouch beside Bear. "Okay. It's time we got going. I want to get as far away from here as possible before dark."

"Good idea." Bear looked around. "Where's my crutch?"

"You don't have it anymore. I used it to make a litter." Dragon gestured toward the makeshift litter, which sat against the wall a few paces away. "It isn't going to be very comfortable. But it ought to be strong enough. I used that hide I took from that last deer we killed and one of the blankets to put over the frame. You can cover up with the other blanket and the oilskin. It's raining out."

Bear blinked at him. "You're carrying me?"

"Well, yeah. You can't walk. And we can't stay here. We need to find Shenandoah. We need to get you some help."

There was no need to say anything more. They both knew what would happen if Bear didn't get help soon. Bear laid a damp, trembling hand on Dragon's cheek. Dragon leaned into the touch.

Slipping his fingers into Dragon's hair, Bear pulled him forward and kissed him. Bear's lips were hot and chapped. "Bring the litter over here. I can get on it."

"Okay." With one more quick kiss, Dragon let go of Bear and went to get the litter.

Bear scooted onto the padded frame mostly under his own power. Dragon helped him when his arms started to shake. Once he was settled, Dragon tucked a folded blanket beneath Bear's injured leg, set the satchel beside his other hip and covered him with another blanket and the oilskin. He used a length of rope to string the bow and quiver of arrows between

157

the two handles.

With that accomplished, there was only one thing left to do. Dragon drew his knife, cut the ropes away from the pile of metal in front of the door and moved it piece by piece, then used one of the metal scraps to block open the door.

He stood in the open doorway for a moment, poised in a fighting stance with his knife in his hand, gazing out into the rain and listening for even the slightest noise out of place.

Nothing moved. The only sound was the raindrops on the grass and the occasional distant rumble of thunder. Satisfied, Dragon returned to where Bear waited. "Okay, Bear. Here we go."

The oilskin moved, and Dragon knew Bear was drawing his knife. Bear nodded. Dragon lifted the litter by the handles he'd padded with pieces of his own buckskins and pulled. After a second's struggle, he got it moving. The bare wood squealed against the floor. He dragged the litter over the threshold and out into the rain.

Gooseflesh pebbled Dragon's arms as the cold water sluiced down his skin. He'd left his shirt in the satchel, since it was stiff with Bear's blood, so his upper body was left bare to the elements. Not that it mattered. The rain would've soaked through the material in no time. Dragon hunched his shoulders against the chill and kept moving. The physical labor would warm him up soon enough.

He turned north. He'd just dragged Bear's litter past the narrow alley between their building and the pile of weed-ridden stone next to it when a dark shape rushed at him from the shadows. Bear shouted a warning. Dragon caught a glimpse of bare breasts and a long, dark blade, and knew instantly what had happened. He dropped the litter, drawing his knife as he turned. The woman's blade missed its target and cut a painful but ultimately harmless slice high across the back of his left shoulder.

She didn't seem to know what to do after that, and Dragon didn't give her a chance to figure it out. He opened her throat from one side to the other with a single stroke of his knife. She dropped to the ground and thrashed in the mud for a moment before going still, her breath running out in a coarse, wet rattle.

Dragon cleaned his knife on the grass, then picked up the dead woman's abandoned blade. He examined it with a critical eye. It seemed to be carved from a single piece of something like dense black glass. He touched the edge with his thumb. Blood welled from a cut he hadn't even felt.

Sticking his thumb in his mouth to suck off the blood, he rounded the litter to where Bear lay waiting, helpless frustration radiating from him. Bear freed an arm from the oilskin to reach for him. "Dragon, you okay?"

"Yeah. I killed her." Dragon glanced around. He didn't see anyone else around. Which proved nothing, apparently, but maybe the woman's death would keep any further attacks at bay. He crouched beside Bear. "I took her knife. Here, take mine. I'm going to keep this one with me."

Bear took Dragon's knife and stuck it beneath the oilskin. "You're bleeding a lot." He touched Dragon's left arm.

Dragon looked down. To his surprise, blood ran from the wound and down the back of his arm to drip in a steady stream from his elbow. He frowned. "She cut me, but it wasn't that bad. It must be the rain making it bleed so much."

"Let me look at it."

"Bear, we don't—"

"We have time. If anyone else was going to attack, they'd be on us by now." Bear gave Dragon's knee a weak shove. "Turn around. Let me see."

The stubborn glint in Bear's eyes said he wasn't letting go of the subject. Pulling his braid over his shoulder, Dragon turned so Bear could see the wound on his back. He heard the oilskin rustle behind him, then Bear pressed gently around the edges of the cut. It stung more than Dragon would've expected. He grimaced.

"Not too deep. Bleeding a lot more than it should, though." More rustling as Bear's fingers fell away. His harsh breathing was loud enough to hear even over the rain. "Should bandage it."

"We really *don't* have time for *that*. Not right now." Dragon pivoted to face Bear again. He looked terrible, paler than ever and shaking beneath the oilskin. Worried, Dragon tucked Bear's arm beneath the cover again, then pushed to his feet. "I'll take care of it later."

Once I get you to someone who can help you. Dragon had no intention of stopping before then, unless the bleeding hampered his ability to pull Bear's litter.

Dragon resumed his spot at the front of the litter. He looked around. Nothing stirred along the ancient street, in the shadowed doorways or the alleys between the buildings, but he felt the eyes watching them.

He shoved the confiscated knife into his sheath. It didn't fit quite right, but it would have to do. He needed it within easy reach in case they were attacked again. Keeping a sharp eye out for any movement, he bent, lifted the litter's handles and started forward.

Bear could smell Dragon's blood.

The mingled scents of rain, mud and wet oilskin didn't mask it. Bear smelled it even over the ripe odor of dried blood, pus and damp bandages from his own wound. If he turned his head, he knew he would see a red river running down Dragon's back along with the water.

So much blood. Too much. They'd been on the move most of the morning, and the rain had tapered off to a light drizzle.

The sun burned behind the thinning cloud cover almost directly overhead. After all this time, Dragon's wound shouldn't still be bleeding like this.

Dragon stumbled, rocking the litter. It wasn't the first time. Bear craned his neck to catch a glimpse of his Brother's bowed head and straining back. "Dragon. Stop here. You need to rest."

Dragon shook his head. "Not yet. Need to get out of the city first."

Bear studied their surroundings. They'd turned onto the westward road hours ago. The buildings here were older, lower and set farther apart. Many had collapsed into piles of rubble so long ago that nothing was left but an occasional square stone block jutting from a green mound. It reminded him of the outskirts of Char.

Nothing moved. No people, no animals, no birds. Not even the drone of an insect broke the silence. It had been that way ever since they'd entered this Mother-forsaken place. The unnatural quiet made Bear's skin crawl. And when he remembered the dark, stinking little room where he'd found Dragon...

A hard shudder ran down Bear's spine. He wanted to get out of here. Yes. But not at the price of Dragon's life. Bear figured if they stopped here, he could take care of Dragon's wound—there was something *not right* about it and Bear wanted to puzzle out what—while they waited for the Shenandoah Pack to find them.

"If they're going to attack, they'll do it no matter what." Bear bit down on a hiss of pain when the litter bumped over a rock, jostling his leg. "I need to piss."

He didn't, not that badly anyway, but it worked. Dragon stopped moving and lowered the litter gently to the ground. "Hang on. I'll help you up."

Bear stopped him with a raised hand. "No. Don't think I

can stand up. Just sit for a minute, huh?"

It said a lot about how Dragon felt right then that he actually did it.

While he perched on the edge of the litter, rummaging in the satchel with one hand while scanning the surrounding ruins, Bear scooted as close to the edge as he could, rolled onto his side and threw off the oilskin. He used his knife handle to dig a shallow trench in the dirt, then unlaced his buckskins. The angle was awkward, but he managed to empty his bladder into the trench without peeing on himself. He shook off, tucked in and laced up.

It took every ounce of energy he had left to roll onto his back and return to the relatively comfortable spot in the center of the litter. He lay back, his heart racing. His injured leg hurt with a bone-deep agony that made him want to squirm away from it, but there was no place to go. He rubbed at his thigh with the heel of one hand, watching while Dragon shoved to his feet and staggered off into the weeds a few feet away to take a piss himself. Maybe he should tell Dragon how much he was hurting. If Dragon knew, he'd insist on brewing more herb tea to relieve Bear's pain, and that would mean building a fire, which would keep them here plenty long enough for the Shenandoah Pack to find them.

Bear dismissed the thought with a shake of his head. Judging by the slump of Dragon's shoulders and the stagger in his walk as he returned to the litter, he was in no shape to hunt up dry wood and build a fire. Blood soaked his left flank and the left leg of his buckskins, and his skin had taken on an ashen hue beneath its natural light brown.

An ugly suspicion began to form in Bear's mind. He'd seen things like this before, after a few nightfeeder attacks on long patrols. Wounds that didn't heal. Massive infections from the most minor lacerations. A Brother dying in fevered delirium nine days after a cut that should've healed without a trace in six. He'd never seen this sort of bleeding before, but that proved nothing. If this was the same sort of thing...

A cool, damp hand on his cheek brought him out of his thoughts. He blinked to clear the fog from his head. Dragon hovered over him, brow creased with worry. "Bear. Come on, stay with me, okay?"

Bear realized he must've drifted too far into his own thoughts. He wondered how long Dragon had been trying to get his attention. "Sorry. I'm okay. Just thinking."

Relief flooded Dragon's face. "What were you thinking about?" Sitting back on his heels, he held out a water skin and a hunk of venison. Bear hadn't even noticed him taking the things out of the satchel.

Bear wrestled himself to a sitting position, ignoring Dragon's protests. Pain thumped through his head with the change in position. His pulse hammered in his ears. He clung to Dragon's arms until he no longer felt like he was about to pass out, then propped himself up on one hand and took the skin with the other. He managed a few mouthfuls before his stomach protested. He couldn't even look at the venison, and Dragon put it back without argument.

Feeling a little better now that he could no longer smell the meat, Bear studied his Brother with a critical eye. Scabs and purple bruises circled his throat, the result of the same rope that had left Dragon's voice rough and raspy. The damage wasn't permanent, thank the Mother, but it had to be painful. Dragon didn't need this new injury on top of everything else. Especially when everything rested on his shoulders now.

He touched Dragon's knee. "Turn around. Let me see your back again."

The mix of anger, exhaustion and confusion on Dragon's face would've been funny under less serious circumstances. "What? Why?"

"I think there might've been some kind of poison on that knife blade. Something to make you keep bleeding."

Dragon glanced down at the long black knife now lying beside him on the litter. Without a word, he twisted around to present his back to Bear.

The instant Bear saw the wound, he knew he was right. The edges were raw, dark red and swollen. Blood flowed freely, with no sign of clotting. If the woman had stabbed Dragon as she'd probably meant to, he would have bled to death already.

Bear opened the satchel and searched through it. There wasn't much clean cheesecloth left, but it would have to do. He took it out of the bag.

Unfortunately, Dragon chose that moment to look over his shoulder. His eyes widened. "No. Put that back."

"This cut needs to be bandaged." Bear yanked the cloth out of the way when Dragon reached for it. "The Shenandoah Pack should be here soon. They'll take care of..."

A wave of dizziness hit Bear so suddenly he lost his balance and fell sideways. Dragon spun, caught him and lowered him carefully to the litter. He stroked Bear's face. "Just lie still, all right? And give me that cheesecloth."

Dragon's voice seemed to come from miles away. His face swam in Bear's vision. The motion made him want to throw up, so he shut his eyes, and Mother, it felt so much better when the world held still.

Everything was moving again. A jerky, start-and-stop motion that felt familiar, but not. He sniffed, to see what he could smell.

Dirt. Rain. Sickness. Sweat. Moldering ruins.

Blood. His own, old, and Dragon's, fresh.

His eyes flew open. *What happened?* he thought, but his tongue wouldn't form the words. He wished he could remember. The knowledge lurked right on the edge of his mind, but his head hurt and for some reason he kept thinking about Char and the day his patrol lost Rabbit in the depths of the ancient city, and the old memories held the newer ones down with both hands.

His eyelids drifted shut again, because the trees and the buildings and the mounds that used to be buildings all blurred together when he looked at them. In the dark, indistinct place that pretended to be Char in his mind, Rabbit stepped forward, unchanged from the day he'd vanished. From behind his back, he produced a long, shining black knife. *I found this, and I'm keeping it. But be careful, because it makes you bleed.* He flashed his familiar playful grin. *They're going to love this almost as much as they love your mind.*

Bear jolted to full consciousness with a start. "Rabbit?"

The movement stopped. He felt himself lowered to the ground. Tattered clouds flowed across the sky, letting hints of sunlight through. A face pinched with pain and full of concern appeared in his line of sight. "Bear. You've been out of it for..." The man swallowed. "Are you all right?"

It took Bear a second to attach the proper name to the obviously worn-out person kneeling above him. *Dragon. My Brother.* Bear's heart lurched. "Yeah. I saw my old Brother, Rabbit. I guess I was dreaming."

Dragon smiled, though his eyes remained clouded with worry. "I guess so."

A hazy memory floated to the front of Bear's brain. He grasped at it and held on tight. "You were hurt. That...that woman. Cut you." He frowned hard as all the events of the past day or so flooded back. "I was going to bandage your wound. You'd better let me go ahead and do that, before it gets any worse."

Dragon shook his head, though his relief that Bear remembered was clear as day. "The bleeding's already slowing down, especially since it stopped raining. It'll be fine until we can get you somewhere safe. Speaking of which, do you need anything before we move on?"

"I think we should wait here for the Shenandoah Pack." Bear didn't expect Dragon to listen to him, but he had to try.

Sure enough, Dragon's face became the stubborn mask Bear had come to expect and dread. "No. Not while we're still inside this city."

"Listen, they're on the way. They'll find us. They should be here any time." Bear touched Dragon's arm. "Dragon. Please."

Dragon's expression softened. Whether he would have relented or not, though, Bear would never know. His ears picked up the distinct creak of a wagon wheel, and he and Dragon both went silent.

In the weird stillness that plagued this place, the sounds of the wagon and the animal pulling it were unmistakable. When a breeze stirred from the west, the smells cemented it for Bear. Leather, hemp rope, treated wood, the musky unwashed stink of an ox, and—most tellingly—the mingled scents of at least seven different people.

Jumping up, Dragon grabbed the litter's handles and started dragging it toward the trees and tall weeds growing twenty paces or so from the old road. "You stay off the road. I'm going to find out who they are. If they're the Shenandoah Pack, fine. If not, then we move on."

Bear almost laughed. "Dragon—"

"We can cut across country. You say you know where to find the tribe, so you can tell me where to go. We can—"

"Dragon. Stop."

Maybe it was the command in Bear's voice, something he hadn't deliberately used in a long time, or maybe Dragon simply realized the futility of what he was doing. Whatever the reason, he did as Bear said. He stopped moving, lowered the litter with a sigh and stood there just out of sight. "What?"

He sounded so tired. So defeated. So afraid. Bear ached for him. He knew Dragon had no fear of death himself. All he wanted was to save Bear, and he didn't know how. Bear understood, because he felt the same way about Dragon.

Bear twisted until he could see the curve of Dragon's back. "Come here."

Once again, Dragon did as he was told. He walked over and sat beside Bear on the dirty oilskin, picking at his buckskins and staring at the ground. The black knife stuck out of the ill-fitting sheath.

Taking Dragon's hand, Bear laced their fingers together. "I know you don't believe it's really the Shenandoah Pack. I know you don't believe their Seer talked to me in a vision. You think I dreamed it. That's okay, I can't blame you. But, look, whether it's them or not, it doesn't matter. If it is, great, they can help us both. If it's not, either it's someone else who can help, or I'm going to die. Whoever's coming will kill me, or I'll die out there in the wilderness because we both know I won't live much longer unless we find someone who knows what to do about this Mother-damned infection."

Dragon said nothing. His throat worked.

Bear's chest felt tight. "You don't have to stay," he whispered, though he knew what Dragon would say.

Sure enough, Dragon's head shot up. His eyes burned with the stubborn fire that had drawn Bear to him right from the first. "I won't leave you."

His tone left no room for argument, so Bear didn't bother. He squeezed Dragon's hand.

They waited in silence. After a few minutes that felt more like years, Dragon tensed. "I see them," he whispered. "Coming around a bend up ahead."

Bear hoisted himself onto one elbow, but couldn't make it any farther than that. The muddy grass squelched beneath the litter and he slipped back down again. He growled in frustration. "Help me sit up."

For once, Dragon didn't argue. Winding an arm around Bear's rib cage, he hauled Bear into a sitting position and turned him around to recline in the V of Dragon's splayed legs, his back against Dragon's chest and his head on Dragon's shoulder. Dragon curved both arms around Bear's chest and rested his cheek against Bear's hair.

The deliberate defenselessness of Dragon's pose was not lost on Bear. He curled his hands around Dragon's arm, trying to convey with his touch how much Dragon's trust meant to him.

Meanwhile, the five men, two women and one medium-sized ox came closer. The ox drew a small wooden cart behind it. Even though Bear knew who they were, it took all his strength to resist the urge to draw his knife as the group stopped only a few paces away. He felt Dragon's body twitch with the same compulsion, born of years of Pack training.

A slight, wiry woman with deep brown skin and thick twists of dark hair tied together at her nape stepped forward. "You two. You're Bear and Dragon, right?"

Dragon's left arm tightened around Bear. His right hand slipped downward, toward the weapon at his side. Bear caught the wandering hand and held it. "I'm Bear. This is Dragon."

The woman smiled. "Excellent. I'm Sister Serafina. We've come to bring you back to Shenandoah."

Chapter Thirteen

It's real. Shenandoah is real.

Dragon's inner cynic wondered if he'd passed out at the last stop from the blood loss he shouldn't even be suffering and this was all a dream. His practical side, however, told him different. The burn where the Mother-cursed cut slashed across the back of his shoulder, Bear's solid weight against his chest, the smell of sour sweat and infection, the heat of the sun breaking through the clouds to dry his sodden, blood-sticky pants—it all anchored him firmly in reality. Therefore, Serafina and her fellow Pack members must be real also.

If they *were* all part of the same Pack. What sort of Pack combined male and female members? How in the Mother's name did they maintain the Pack bond without the threat of pregnancy hanging over them?

He shook off the thousand and one questions in his head. Now wasn't the time.

"He can't stand up," Dragon told the group, since no one made a move to come help. "We ran into some trouble in the city yesterday. He lost a lot of blood."

"We knew Bear was injured. Willow, our Seer, told us. But we didn't know about yesterday." Serafina walked over and knelt beside Bear and Dragon. "What happened?" She pressed gently on Bear's swollen thigh.

He tensed, but didn't otherwise let on how much it had to

hurt. "We were camped in an old building. Dragon went out to get water and firewood. He was captured by...by cannibals. They tied him and kept him there, I guess for later. I saw his knife on the ground, went in and cut him loose."

She eyed Dragon's throat. "Is that what happened to your neck?"

"Yeah. They hung me out the window until I passed out to subdue me." He stopped Serafina with a raised hand when she made a move to inspect his bruised throat more closely. "Look, it's fine. It's just a few bruises. Bear's the one who needs help here."

She frowned, but didn't argue. "You said he lost a lot of blood yesterday?"

"His wound had started to heal in some, but it opened up again when he had to kneel down to cut my feet free," Dragon explained. "It was just too much for him on top of the infection that had already set in." He frowned when one of the men walked over and started gathering the blankets and oilskin. "What're you doing?"

"This is Brother Lucian." Serafina gestured toward the tall man with the two long, fiery red braids. "He's going to get your things together while I have a look at Bear."

Lucian greeted them with a silent nod, big freckled hands busy folding blankets while his washed-out blue eyes swiveled this way and that. A jagged scar cut across his right cheek, forcing that corner of his mouth into a permanent half-smile. Other, smaller scars peppered his bare arms and the V of pale chest where his leather vest laced together.

Dragon found the man's battered appearance reassuring. Any Brother who had seen enough battle to gather those scars—not to mention that air of vigilance—would be more than a match for the city's cannibals. Not that there had been any sign of them since Dragon had killed the woman early this morning, but still. You never knew.

Serafina laid a palm on Bear's forehead. Her expression didn't change, but her jaw tightened in a way Dragon didn't like at all. "He has a high fever. What have you been giving him?"

Dragon fought down the urge to bristle at the implication that he hadn't been taking the best possible care of his Brother. After all, he probably hadn't. He did his best, but he was no Healer. "Willow-bark tea, mostly. I've used sage in it sometimes, and I was putting Valerian in it at night for a while, to help him sleep, but I ran out. I've been washing the wound with chamomile-infused water and using yarrow and sage poultices with the dressing changes. I couldn't make a fire last night, and I was out of yarrow and nearly out of clean cloth for dressings, so I couldn't wash it out or make a poultice, but I did change the dressing at least."

Her eyebrows rose. "You know something about healing. And you've been taught some field medicine, am I right?"

"As much as any Pack." Dragon glanced down into Bear's face. His eyes were shut, his breathing shallow and fast. "But it's not good enough. The infection's spreading, and nothing I do seems to help." He looked up, straight into Serafina's thoughtful brown eyes. "Can you help him?"

Please help him. Don't let him die. Please, please.

He didn't say it, but he knew she saw. It was right there on his face for anyone who cared to look.

Of course, saving Bear was the whole point, wasn't it? That's why Serafina and her group were here. They'd made the trek from their home specifically to bring Bear and Dragon back to Shenandoah, presumably alive.

Which begged the question, *why*?

It was the same question he'd set aside the night before because he had more urgent issues to deal with. He couldn't ignore it anymore. The situation was no longer part of the nebulous future. It was here, now, and he had to consider why the Shenandoah Tribe had sent a Pack patrol to rescue him and his Brother, at certain peril to Pack lives.

He'd have to keep his wits about him, and his eyes and ears open.

"You're injured."

Dragon swallowed a startled cry. He hadn't even seen the other man circle around behind him. *Mother, I must be more tired than I thought.* "It's just a scratch. I'm fine."

Serafina gave him a look that probably kept her entire Pack cowed, then tilted her head back to talk to the man behind Dragon. "Tell me, Valentine."

"It's shallow, but very inflamed, and it's obviously bled a lot. Still bleeding, in fact." The man—Valentine, presumably another Pack Brother—strode into Dragon's line of sight. He was short and slim, like Serafina, with a head full of golden braids that reminded Dragon of Bear's old Brother Lynx. "It looks like gang work. One of the poisons they put on their blades, maybe, only I've never seen one that makes the wound keep bleeding."

Serafina pursed her lips. "Dragon?"

He held her gaze. "A woman attacked me early this morning, just as we were leaving. She tried to stab me in the back, but I turned and the knife slid on my shoulder blade instead. It's been bleeding ever since."

Lucian stood, Dragon's satchel slung over one wide shoulder, and shot a glance toward the city center, where the ancient black towers rose against the sky. "Gangs were out in the daytime?"

"Just her," Dragon answered, guessing Lucian meant the cannibal packs they'd encountered yesterday. "She hid and waited for us. I saw her outside last night. There were a whole bunch of them out there all night long, trying to get in. She was the only one still there this morning, though."

Serafina nodded. "Ophelia! Ezekiel!"

The other woman and a man who looked like a male version of Serafina trotted over in response to her call. The woman bobbed her shorn head in a gesture of respect. "Yes, Sister?"

"It seems as though the gangs have discovered a new sort of poison for their weapons. One that causes prolonged bleeding, and possibly inflammation of the wound." Serafina cut her keen gaze back to Dragon. "Is there anything else?"

He shrugged. "It burns a lot more than a wound like this normally would. That's all I know. And she was definitely trying to do more damage than a simple scratch, so whatever it is, it must not be all that potent. Oh, and I have the weapon, for what it's worth." Shifting Bear's weight as carefully as he could, he drew the knife he'd taken from his attacker. The black blade glinted in the sunlight breaking through the clouds.

The entire group leaned close to examine it. No one tried to take it from him, which made him feel more secure than he had since the group arrived. He hated the feeling of helplessness that went with being unarmed.

"Okay, you two." Serafina pointed at Ophelia and Ezekiel. "Head back to Harrisonburg and see what you can learn about this new poison. If you can find the plant they're using, harvest some and bring it back. Return to Shenandoah within seven days whether you learn anything or not. Zeke, report to me nightly. Got it?"

"Got it." Ezekiel nudged Ophelia's side. "You grab a couple of bedrolls. I'll get us some rations."

The two hurried off. Dragon frowned. *How is he supposed to communicate with her when he's in that city—Harrisonburg— and she's back in Shenandoah?*

She shot him a sharp look, almost as if she knew what he was thinking. A hard chill ran up his spine.

Looking away, Serafina pushed to her feet and waved at the grizzled, stocky older man currently checking the ox's harness. "Llewelyn, bring the cart over here so we can lift Bear into the back."

The man nodded, grabbed the ox's halter and tugged. The animal plodded forward until the rear of the cart stood only two or three paces away. A slender, brown-skinned boy with straight black hair cut short around his ears sat in the back of the cart. He looked no older than sixteen or seventeen. Too young, in Dragon's opinion, to be included in a mission this dangerous.

"Brother Titus will be twenty-one in a few days." Serafina opened the gate at the back of the cart while Valentine, Lucian and Llewelyn hoisted Bear off Dragon's lap.

"I didn't say anything." Dragon pushed to his feet. His head swam. He clutched at the side of the cart.

She flashed him a wide smile. "You didn't have to. It was all over your face."

Titus leaned over to help lift Bear into the cart. "I get that a lot."

Dragon said nothing. He kept his expression impassive, as he knew damn well it had been all along. He knew better than to let strangers see what he thought of them. Also, unless Shenandoah was a truly enormous tribe, he doubted that Titus got that a lot. No tribe he'd ever seen or heard of was so large that its members didn't all know each other at least by nodding acquaintance.

He didn't wait to be invited into the wagon, but climbed up behind the three other men as they settled Bear onto a pile of furs. Lucian set Dragon's bag beside him. He and his Brothers jumped to the ground again. Serafina hoisted herself into the back and settled beside Bear. Titus clambered to the front to take up the ox's reins. There was a snap of leather and a creak of wood, and the cart began to move in a wide circle, turning

174

back toward Shenandoah.

Dragon watched as Serafina opened her own large leather bag and pulled out a little bottle half full of a milky solution and a small drinking glass scored along the side with markings at regular intervals, clearly meant to measure minute amounts of liquid. "What's that?"

"Opium. For pain."

"I don't know that one." Dragon studied the cloudy fluid. "What plant is it from? It *is* from a plant, right?"

"Yes. It's from the seed pod of certain poppies. It's *much* stronger than willow bark, chamomile or any of the other kitchen garden plants." Working with great care, she opened the bottle, poured up to the first line in the cup and closed the bottle again. "This will keep Bear comfortable on the trip, and keep it from hurting so much when I change his dressing. Help him sit up a little bit so he can swallow it."

Moving to Bear's head, Dragon bent to slide an arm beneath his shoulders. Bear's eyes opened when Dragon lifted his upper body. A faint smile curved his mouth. He fumbled for Dragon's free hand, found and held it. "Hi."

The lump that formed in Dragon's throat at the sound of that single soft, raspy word felt the size of a boulder. He pressed Bear's palm to his cheek. "Serafina has something for you, Bear. It'll help with the pain."

"It'll take a little while to work," she added. "But once it starts working, it's strong. You'll need it for when I clean and redress your wound."

Bear nodded. "Let me have it, then."

Dragon held Bear's head up while Serafina tilted the opium into his mouth. He wrinkled his nose but swallowed it.

Serafina tucked the cup back into her bag along with the medicine bottle. She dug around and came up with another one. The liquid in this one was clear. "One more."

Dragon eyed it with suspicion. "What's this one?"

"It's called penicillin. The healers make it from the mold that grows on bread." She poured some of the fluid into the measuring cup, resealed the bottle and dropped it back into the bag. "It kills the infection. The healers learned how to make it from books the ancients left. We found the books in Harrisonburg a few years ago. We've found a *lot* of things there, as a matter of fact, but healers' books have been the most useful."

"Oh." Dragon tried not to show how impressed he was. He watched Bear swallow the liquid. It must've tasted terrible, judging by the look on his face.

"Sorry." Serafina put the measuring cup in her bag. "I know it tastes bad."

"'S okay." Bear relaxed into Dragon's arms, panting.

"The opium will make you sleepy, but that's just as well. You need your rest." She pinned Bear with a strange, pointed stare.

Bear's body stiffened. His expression didn't change, but Dragon knew something was wrong.

"What is it?" he murmured in Bear's ear when Serafina turned to rummage through her bag again.

Bear shook his head. "Not sure. Maybe...just the fever."

This answer didn't entirely placate Dragon, but he decided to let it go, for now. He couldn't put his finger on the source of his discomfort with whatever had just passed—or not—between Bear and Serafina. Maybe it was nothing. Maybe he'd spent too long plagued by stress and worry of one sort or another. The Mother knew he couldn't even remember the last time he hadn't felt hunted. And Bear, well...it wouldn't be the first time Bear had seen, heard or otherwise imagined something that wasn't there in the past few days.

What nagged at Dragon's mind was, if it was only their

imagination, why were they both imagining it at the same time?

"Dragon?"

He started at the sound of Serafina's voice. He forced himself to focus on her face, far too close to his. "Yes?"

"I'd like to take a look at that wound on your back." Her brow creased. "I could give you some opium too, if you like. You look like you could use some sleep."

Nothing could have coaxed Dragon into letting his guard down long enough to sleep. Saying so wouldn't be in his or Bear's best interest at that point, though. So he forced as friendly a smile as he could manage and shook his head. "Thank you, but I'll pass. My body doesn't always react well to plant extracts. I have to be careful what I take." That was a bald-faced lie, but he didn't want her slipping a few drops into his food or water when he wasn't looking in a well-meaning attempt to make him rest.

Her expression was skeptical, but she simply nodded. "All right. Will you let me look at your wound?"

Dragon hesitated. Bear gave his hand a squeeze. "It needs to be cleaned and dressed, Dragon. Let her do it." He drew in a sharp breath, his fingers spasming around Dragon's. Before Dragon could say anything, Bear gave him a reassuring smile. "It's okay. I'm okay. And...and Serafina won't harm you. Or me." He stared hard into Dragon's eyes. *Trust me,* he mouthed.

With a tremendous effort, Dragon kept his growing alarm off his face. Bear would see, of course. He couldn't hide anything from Bear, even if he'd wanted to, and he never wanted to again. But he'd be damned if he'd let Serafina see how little he trusted her or any of the rest of them.

He held Bear's gaze long enough to tell him they'd be talking as soon as they got some time alone. "You're right. It *does* need looking at." He pressed a kiss to Bear's temple, then laid him back against the pile of furs. "All right, Sister. Do it."

She arched a dark eyebrow at him. "Thank you, Brother."

As he maneuvered himself into position for her to check his back, he got the distinct impression that she knew exactly what he'd been thinking.

They pushed on as fast as the ox, Daisy, could manage. Dragon volunteered to stand watch alongside Lucian and Valentine during their first brief stop, but Serafina wouldn't let him stand watch with her and Llewelyn on the second stop. She said he was too tired and needed to sleep.

As if he could even shut his eyes when Bear was barely conscious and incoherent with fever. After he ate and helped Serafina clean and redress Bear's wound, he stretched out beside his Brother in the cart, one hand resting over Bear's heart, and spent the long hours watching Bear's lips move in his dreams. Serafina shook her head and said nothing.

They reached Shenandoah around midmorning two days after Serafina and her fellow Pack members found Bear and Dragon in Harrisonburg. Bear had drifted into a restless half-consciousness long before the cart crossed the pass into the wide green valley which hid the city and its surrounding fields. He lay shivering beneath the blanket, alternately mumbling about Rabbit and Char and talking to someone named Willow, who Serafina said was Shenandoah's Seer. It was an eerie thing to hear, especially knowing that Willow was real and not just a figment of Bear's imagination.

As they passed through the gate, Dragon leaned down to kiss Bear's sweat-beaded brow. "We made it, Bear. We're in Shenandoah." He stroked the matted hair away from Bear's face. "Don't you want to wake up and look at it?"

Bear's eyelids fluttered open enough to reveal a quick glint of amber, but he didn't respond otherwise. Dragon straightened up, leaving his hand on Bear's forehead. "He's worse."

"We're taking him straight to the healers. I told you about those healing books we found in Harrisonburg, the ones the ancients left. Our healers have learned amazing things from them. Techniques you wouldn't believe." Serafina gave Dragon's shoulder a squeeze. "Courage, Brother. He'll be all right."

Dragon bit back the urge to tell her not to make promises she couldn't keep. During the journey to the city, she'd worked tirelessly to keep Bear's wound clean and make him as comfortable as possible. She and her Pack had earned Dragon's respect, if not his complete trust. The least he could do was be civil to them. He managed a nod and a grim smile, but couldn't force out any words.

According to Serafina, the healing center sat near Shenandoah's northern wall. To Dragon, the trip through the town's teeming lanes seemed to take forever. The place was huge. Larger than Carwin by a fair margin, and easily five times the size of Ashe. Men, women and children hurried up and down the wide, well-maintained roads and bustled in and out of the stalls of the busy central market. Neat cottages surrounded by flowering gardens fanned out in all directions from the market. A few people threaded through the crowd on horseback. Several ox-drawn carts rattled along, full of fruits, vegetables, animal skins and other wares.

Dragon had never even heard of a tribe this size, never mind seen one with his own eyes. It explained the number and proportions of the tilled fields beyond the walls. He wondered if they kept goats, chickens and cattle the way Bear said the Carwin Tribe did, or if they relied on hunting for meat. Maybe they combined the two. He couldn't imagine feeding a city this size with only one method or the other.

After what felt to Dragon like a lifetime, they approached a low, rambling building with many windows and an expansive garden full of fruit trees, flowers and little spots of shaded greenery. A sturdy overhang of logs and wooden shingles covered the circular drive where it ran in front of the door, shielding the sick and injured from the weather while they were taken inside for treatment. Three people wearing loose white fabric pants, fitted shirts and long vests with deep pockets waited outside the wide double doors. A litter padded with a thick layer of furs and blankets sat beside them.

Dragon turned to Serafina as the cart drew up level with the door. "How did they know we were coming?"

She shrugged. "They generally keep a lookout for new patients coming in. I suppose they saw us from the window."

Her tone was casual, but she wouldn't look Dragon in the eye. *She's lying,* he realized, studying the faint lines of tension between her eyes and around her mouth. *They knew we were coming, they knew we were coming* now, *and she knows* how *they knew we were coming.*

Why she would want to lie about such an unimportant thing, he couldn't imagine. But she had, and he didn't know why. Until he had at least some idea, he intended to keep his knowledge, his suspicions and his fears to himself.

Llewelyn opened the back of the cart. Serafina hopped to the ground and went to talk to one of the healers. Lucian, Titus and another healer climbed into the cart, bringing the litter with them. Dragon helped the other three ease Bear onto the litter, then jumped down and followed the two white-clad healers toward the hospital doors.

When he brushed past the third healer though, she stopped him with a hand on his arm. The two men carrying Bear stopped also when she gestured to them. "I'm sorry, Brother. You can't go in with him."

Instantly, every protective instinct Dragon had kicked in. He clenched his hands at his sides to stop himself from drawing the poisoned blade still stuffed into his sheath. His death at the hands of the Shenandoah Pack wouldn't help Bear.

He met the healer's stern gaze with as much calm as he could muster. "Why not? And who are you?"

"I'm Healer Aster. Your Brother is very ill, as I'm sure you're aware. The upcoming days will be quite difficult for him, and the next few hours in particular will be extremely tricky. I believe he is not beyond help, but it is essential that my assistants and I not be distracted while we treat him during this very delicate time." A gust of wind tugged a curl of graying reddish hair from the twist at her nape to fly across her fact. She tucked it behind her ear. Her expression softened into a sympathetic smile. "I understand that the Pack bonds are quite different where you come from than they are here, and thus you don't wish to be separated from your Brother right now. But I can promise you that we will care for Bear just as if he were one of our own from birth. This is our vow as healers, and our duty as human beings."

Her solemn tone did nothing to convince Dragon of her sincerity. Neither did the way she looked straight into his eyes. He'd had too many people lie right to his face without the slightest waver of their gaze or tremor in their voice. But something about the tilt of her chin and the open, relaxed line of her posture convinced him she was telling the truth. If he couldn't be certain of anything else in this tremendous, swarming, utterly strange place, he could at least be sure Bear was safe at last.

Safe. He's safe. They'll save him.

With that knowledge, all the endless days of worry, the lack of rest and the poisoned wound he'd suffered crashed through Dragon's mental barriers and pounced. He swayed on his feet.

"Brother, you really should go to your rest." Aster frowned. "Unless you need care yourself. You've obviously suffered your own injuries. Willow didn't inform me of this."

Willow. So that's how they knew we were coming. The temptation to let himself be treated just so he could get inside with Bear was strong, but Dragon resisted. He didn't trust them not to drug him against his will or take away his weapon. These people seemed trustworthy so far, but he couldn't afford to drop his guard until he knew for sure.

"I'm fine. The cut stopped bleeding two days ago, and there wasn't any real damage to my neck. Just some bruises." He rubbed a hand over his face. Unfortunately, his exhaustion wasn't fake. "I *am* tired, though."

"The council's prepared quarters for you. I'll take you there now." Stepping forward, Serafina took Dragon's arm. "Come on, Dragon. It isn't far."

He was so dazed that she actually got him a few steps toward the cart before he noticed what was happening. He shook her off. "No, wait."

She made an impatient sound. "Dragon—"

"I just want to..." He didn't finish, but spun and hurried off after the healers' assistants, who were taking Bear inside. "Wait!"

Sighing, Aster nodded to the two men. They stopped. Dragon stumbled over, bent and pressed a soft kiss to Bear's mouth. "I have to go," he whispered, stroking Bear's flushed cheeks. "The healers have to take care of you now, and they don't need me hanging around getting in the way. But I'll be back as soon as they'll let me, okay?"

Bear's eyes blinked open. His chapped lips curved into a faint smile. "Dragon. Love you, my Brother."

Dragon's throat went tight. He kissed Bear again, palms cupping his face. "I love you."

It felt like there were so many more things he wanted to say, but he couldn't pin them down and Bear didn't have the time for him to fumble with words, so he straightened up and let the healers carry his Brother into the hospital. He stood there with his arms around himself, staring at the doors and blinking away the sting behind his eyelids—who'd have thought there would be this much dust in the air so soon after a rain?—until Serafina looped a hand through his elbow and pulled him away.

Titus drove the cart down a narrow, winding lane that veered off the main road toward the west. A few minutes later, they came to a halt in front of a tiny cottage flanked by two tall sugar maples. Dragon caught a glimpse of a small garden behind the house.

"Here we are." Serafina jumped down when Llewelyn opened the back for her, then held out a hand for Dragon. "Come on."

Too shaky to manage alone and too tired to feel embarrassed by his weakness, Dragon took her hand to climb down from the wagon, but refused to let either of his companions help him into the house. He'd damn well walk unaided. He allowed Serafina and Lucian to flank him without argument, though. Titus snapped the reins, and Daisy clomped off down the lane with Llewelyn and Valentine perched in the cart.

Dragon looked around in astonishment as Serafina opened the front door, and he trailed her inside with Lucian at his heels. It wasn't a large house, but the single room felt spacious and the four windows—made of real glass—let in a flood of sunshine. The floor was made of wide pine planks scoured smooth and oiled to a shine. Two sturdy armchairs sat on a braided rug in the middle of the room. A simple wooden table with two kitchen chairs sat in the corner to the right of the door. A woodstove and several shelves took up the right-hand corner across from the table and most of the wall in between the two. To his left stood a hutch full of dishes, pots, pans and other necessities. The huge bed in the last corner, half-hidden by a standing screen, boasted what looked like a feather-tick mattress and four fat feather pillows. Just the sight of it made him want to sleep for a week.

He balked when Lucian nudged him toward one of the armchairs. "I can't be staying *here*."

"Yes, you are." Serafina pinned him with a cool look. "I'm sorry if it's not what you're used to, but it's the best we could do on short notice."

He laughed. Mother, had she ever gotten the wrong idea. "No, that's not what I meant. Back in the Ashe Tribe, our Mother didn't even have a house this nice. It's just... Are you sure I should be in here?"

Serafina turned away and started toward the hutch, but not before Dragon saw the pity on her face. For once, he couldn't summon the energy to resent it.

"We're lucky to have good building materials and some very talented artisans here. In Shenandoah, this is a very average house." She opened the hutch. "Sit."

He looked at the armchairs with their beautiful fabric-covered cushions, then at the blood and dirt covering his body. "I'm filthy. I don't want to get the chairs dirty."

She exchanged an exasperated glance with Lucian. He nodded, steered Dragon toward the table and deposited him in one of the kitchen chairs. "Good luck, Brother. I hope we'll see each other again soon."

"Yes." Dragon twisted around to clasp Lucian's scarred hand. "Thank you."

Lucian smiled and clapped him on the shoulder before heading for the door. "Serafina, I'm going to check in at Pack headquarters then head home. Iris and the kids'll be looking for me."

"Of course." Serafina walked back to the table, arms laden with what looked like bathing cloths, clean buckskins and a soft silk vest. "I'll see you tomorrow."

Dragon watched Lucian go, then sat in silence while Serafina crossed to the shelves between the stove and the table. He wished his mind wasn't so fuzzy, so he could find the words to shape the hundred half-formed questions bumping around in his brain.

"What did he mean?" he blurted finally, when Serafina set a plate with a wedge of cheese and a hunk of brown bread on the table.

She gave him a puzzled look. "What? Who?" She went back to the shelf and returned with a blue earthenware bottle and a matching goblet. Uncorking the bottle, she poured the goblet full of pale yellow wine. "Here. You need to eat and drink something, then you can wash up and sleep for a while. There's a barrel out back for bathing, next to the well, and there's soap on the shelf here."

"Thank you." Dragon took a sip of the wine. It tasted tart and crisp, better than anything he'd had in a long time. He held it on his tongue for several glorious seconds before swallowing. Picking up the cheese, he tore off a piece and bit into it. Mother, it was good, mild and sweet. He took a larger piece, along with a strip of bread. "I meant Lucian. He said he was going home. He said something about...about Iris. And kids. What did that mean? I thought he was Pack."

"He is."

"Then what was he talking about?"

"Willow said yours and Bear's Packs were different from ours, but..." She shook her head. "Iris is Lucian's bondmate. They have three children together. Our Pack, you might have noticed, is mixed male and female. We don't all live together, and we don't have a sexual bond together. Anyone in the tribe, including Pack, is allowed to bond with whoever we like, whether it's another Pack member or someone outside the Pack. There are a few group bonds in the tribe, but it's mostly one-on-one."

"Oh." All the things Dragon didn't understand about this place seemed to gang up on him at once. He dropped his head in his hands, fighting off exhaustion. "When can I see Bear again?"

"In the morning. Willow will be over early to get you." Serafina gave him an odd, sidelong glance.

Willow. The Seer. The one who visited Bear in his dreams. Dragon hated the thought of this Willow person sharing a level of intimacy with Bear that he himself could never hope to achieve. He hated even more that it bothered him at all, when he knew he and Bear were connected in ways only Pack Brothers could be. Ways the Seer could never truly understand.

Thinking of the Seer reminded him of other things he'd been wondering about. He took a deep gulp of wine. "Why did you do this?"

Serafina's eyebrows rose. "Feed you?"

"No. Why did your tribe send you and your Brothers and Sister out after us?" He stared hard into her eyes. "What do they want with us?"

Her face gave away nothing, no matter how much he wished it would. "It's not for me to say." She took a brown pitcher from a shelf and set it on the table. "Would you like me to get you some water from the well?"

So. No answers today. He bit back the urge to lash out. It wasn't Serafina's fault. "No thanks. I'll get some when I go to bathe."

"All right. Well, then, if you're going to be okay, I'll leave now. My bondmate's waiting for me." She leaned both hands on the table. Her gaze seemed to penetrate straight through his skull. Whatever she saw in his face, it didn't reassure her, because the worry line Dragon had already learned to recognize dug deep between her eyes. "Will you be all right?"

No. Not until I can be with Bear. The tension in Serafina's brow softened into something Dragon would've called sympathy if there'd been any reason for her to feel it. He forced a smile. "I'll be fine. Thanks for everything, Sister."

She smiled in return. "You're welcome, Brother." Pushing away from the table, she crossed to the front door. "I hope to see you again soon. Come by the Pack headquarters anytime. Anyone in town can tell you how to get there."

He nodded. With one more thoughtful look in his direction, she opened the door and walked outside.

Dragon waited until the door closed behind her to let his head slump down into his hands. After all the stress and worry of the long days since Bear's injury, he was finally in the hands of competent healers. It was always possible they wouldn't be able to save him, but Dragon refused to think about that. Healer Aster had seemed pretty confident in her ability to help Bear, and Dragon latched onto her confidence as if it were the only torch in an underground cave.

Bear was safe. They were both safe—truly safe, within tribal walls, well-fed and protected—for the first time in over a moon cycle. So why did he feel as if he were being watched, even though the cottage was empty but for himself? Why did his stomach roll with a vague sense of dread?

Why did he feel like the dream of perfection being offered would be yanked away the minute he reached for it?

He let out a harsh laugh. *This is what comes of growing up in the Ashe Tribe. Nothing can ever just be what it seems.*

Picking up the goblet, he drained half of it, then attacked the bread and cheese with an appetite that surprised him. He hadn't realized how hungry he was. It was nice to eat his fill of food that wasn't berries, wrinkled apples or dried venison, and wash it down with tart, delicious wine. It would be even nicer to scrub the caked grime from his body, crawl naked into that gorgeous bed and sleep to his heart's content, then wake up and put on clothes that weren't permeated with sweat and dirt and covered in bloodstains.

Even better than that would be the day when Bear could share all this with him.

The thought of Bear in the hospital building, alone among strangers and drifting in whatever strange dreams his fevers brought, hurt Dragon's heart. Closing his eyes, he reached out in thought to his Brother. *I wish I could be there with you, Bear. But I'm thinking of you, every minute.*

He wished Bear could hear him.

Chapter Fourteen

After Dragon left him, strangers carried Bear into a place so bright it hurt his eyes and gave him more of the bitter opium, and he drifted back into the twilight world that wasn't sleep, exactly, but wasn't waking either.

Not that he minded so much. At least in this weird in-between state, he didn't feel cold, weak and sick, and his leg didn't throb with an agony so intense he sometimes wished he could cut off the limb with his knife.

Willow waited for him in his fever dream, as she often did. He'd grown used to seeing her there between that first vision in Harrisonburg and now, whenever *now* was. His whole, healthy dream-self walked up to where she waited on a gentle green rise leading to an imposing structure that must be the council building, and greeted her with a smile. "Hi, Willow."

"Hello, Bear." She took his outstretched hand in both of hers. "Walk with me?"

"Of course."

He stood aside, and she led the way down the slope toward the road. They slipped through the crowd like a pair of ghosts. Bear studied his surroundings as he followed Willow's purple-clad form. Until now, he'd always met Willow at the city gate. This was the first time he'd been inside, and he wanted to see everything. Especially since his physical body had been unconscious when they arrived in the city.

It was a beautiful place. Bright, clean, full of life. The central market teemed with people, every home had a garden bursting with color, every face he passed glowed with health and prosperity. A dark, suspicious part of him couldn't help wondering if Willow was just showing him what he wanted to see.

She turned where a narrow, shaded lane wound away to the west from the main road and smiled at him. "When I am controlling your dreams, you can't see anything that isn't truly there. But our dreams are always colored by our beliefs, our experiences, and our expectations, and I have no power over those aspects of the dream world, or those parts of a person's mind. I can't see Shenandoah through your eyes, or I would at least tell you how close you are to the mark."

He didn't know what to say to that, so he chose to let it lie. Instead, he asked the questions that were uppermost in his mind. "Where is Dragon? Is he all right?"

Her smile widened. "Your Brother is well, though naturally worried about *you*." She started off down the curvy little lane. "It's funny you should ask me that, just now. Or perhaps not."

Bear wasn't sure what she meant, but he thought he could guess. The longing to see Dragon dug in hard enough to leave even his incorporeal form breathless. If he'd known how to find Dragon himself, he would have left Willow behind in his eagerness. But he didn't, so he followed the Seer along the road under the long evening shadows of hickory and maple trees, past several neat little houses with their vibrant gardens, until they reached one that didn't stand out in any way from all the others, except for the fact that Bear could *feel* his Brother here.

This time, he didn't wait for Willow. He ran up the rock-lined walkway and let his spirit form bleed right through the front wall.

It was a nice house. Light, airy, and so clean Bear automatically looked down to make sure he hadn't tracked dirt in, though he knew he wasn't even solid at the moment. He didn't see Dragon anywhere. Frantic, he glanced around. *Dragon? Where are you?*

Then he saw. The person-shaped lump under the covers of the big bed in the corner, the dark head on the pillow.

Throat tight, Bear walked to the bed and sat on the edge. He studied Dragon's sleeping face in the sunset light. Even now, the lines of care and worry hadn't entirely gone away. But at least he was asleep, which was something. Bear wasn't positive, since he himself had drifted in and out of consciousness ever since Harrisonburg, but he didn't think Dragon had slept at all for at least three nights and four days. Possibly longer. It would've been nice to talk to Dragon, but it was better to see him resting for a change.

"You couldn't have talked to him. Not here." Willow glided up to the foot of the bed and stood there gazing at Dragon with an expression Bear didn't know how to read. "He hasn't the mind of a Seer."

"I'm not a Seer either. But I guess my fever made it easier for me to be receptive." He reached out to touch Dragon's face, then changed his mind. Everything here seemed as real and solid as the waking world ever had, but he knew it wasn't. Not really. If he couldn't touch Dragon here, he didn't want to know. "Some people in Carwin used to take extracts to mimic fever so they could have spirit journeys. They said it opened their minds and made it easier to connect with the Great Mother."

Willow laughed. Something about the sound made Bear's dream-flesh crawl with a mix of apprehension and anticipation he didn't understand and liked even less. He peered at her with a newfound suspicion. "Willow? What aren't you telling me?"

"This isn't the time. Not yet."

A sharp thrill ran up his spine. He didn't know why, but he felt as if he stood on the edge of something wonderful and terrifying, and he wanted desperately to know what it was.

She shook her head, the sweet but unrevealing expression never leaving her face. "Not yet, Bear. As soon as you're well enough, we'll meet face to face in the daylight world, and I'll explain everything to you. Right now, though, it's time for you to go."

A stab of panic shot through Bear's insides. He stared at Dragon's face, at the curve of the jaw, the arch of the cheekbones, the sweep of the lower lip. This time, he gave in to his urge and cupped Dragon's cheek in his hand. Dragon felt warm and real and alive against his palm, and he wished with all his being that this wasn't just a dream.

Leaning forward, he kissed Dragon's slack mouth. He drew a deep breath, trying to catch Dragon's scent.

Nothing. He hated the reminder that none of this was real.

A sudden sharp pain in his leg drew Bear upright with a surprised hiss. He glanced down. Blood soaked through his buckskins and spread in a red puddle on the bed. Shocked, he looked at Willow. "What's happening?"

Her smile was sad this time. "Time to wake up, Bear."

Bear's stomach clenched. He dug both hands into the bedding, as if he could stay here just by holding on tight enough. But the pain in his leg exploded into a white radiance that tore the sky apart and left him blinking up at a kind, serious face illuminated by soft golden light.

"I'm sorry if we hurt you," the young woman said. "I'm afraid moving is going to be painful for a while." Her words sounded muffled like she was talking underwater. A dark head entered Bear's field of vision to his left. An arm slipped beneath his shoulders and the world spun around him as his torso was lifted and someone wedged something soft behind his back. The woman smiled at him. "Here. Drink this."

The dark blur to his left resolved into a boy who held a mug to Bear's lips. The rich scent of chicken broth rose around him.

He drank, one sip at a time, until his stomach rebelled against any more. After that came a cup of cold, clean water, followed by the now-familiar opium. He swallowed it without complaint, because his leg hurt with a gnawing, bone-deep ache and the opium helped, if only by sending him back into the twilight world where everything was beautiful and nothing hurt anymore.

He wondered if he'd be able to go back and see Dragon again in his dreams.

He thought about Dragon to distract himself from the pain while the woman and the boy eased him onto his side and rearranged the pillows to support his body in the new position. They extinguished all but one of the candles in the wall sconces before leaving the room. Bear lay gazing into the single flame until lethargy dragged his eyelids down and he slept once more.

This time, the city in his dream looked more like Char than Shenandoah, and Willow was nowhere to be seen. But the bright little cottage stood in the midst of the ruins like a beacon of hope in the dark, never mind that it shouldn't be there at all.

When Bear entered he found his Brother curled naked in one of the big chairs, his knees drawn up to his chest and his side pressed to the chair's back, staring into the darkness. Bear's heart lurched. He walked over, and even though he knew that none of this was actually happening, even though he knew Dragon was sleeping right now just as he himself was, he wedged himself into the space between Dragon's bare back and the chair arm and wrapped his arms around Dragon.

Dream-Dragon made a soft, surprised sound. He tensed, then relaxed in Bear's embrace. "Mother's sake, I'm imagining things now." Dragon rested his head on the back of the chair. Bear laid his cheek against Dragon's hair.

Eventually, Dragon's breathing became slow and even, and Bear realized he was asleep. Gathering Dragon carefully to his chest, Bear carried him to the bed, tucked him under the covers and, after a moment's consideration, climbed in beside him. Dragon rolled over and curled into Bear's arms just like he always had before Bear's injury changed everything.

Bear didn't question the logic of his Brother falling asleep within his dream. It didn't matter whether or not it made sense. He was grateful for the chance to feel his old strength run through his limbs again, to lie down beside Dragon and hold him while he slept. It comforted him, even if it wasn't real. He hoped it would comfort Dragon too, somehow.

Dragon woke at dawn feeling better than he had since before Lexin. He lay in bed with his eyes closed against the level rays of the rising sun, trying as hard as he could to hold on to his dream. He could practically feel the warmth of Bear's body against his. The pillows even smelled like Bear.

Wait.

Pillows. He was in bed.

Dragon opened his eyes and frowned at the ceiling. Hadn't he fallen asleep in the chair? Yes, he was sure he had. He'd woken from his earlier nap in the dark, feeling melancholy and alone, gotten up and gone to sit in the chair to think for a while. He'd felt...something. Almost like a soothing embrace. Whatever it was, it had eased him to sleep in spite of his troubled mind, right there in the big armchair.

So why wasn't he still there?

A knock sounded on the front door. His pulse sped up when he realized it must be Willow, the tribal Seer, coming to take him to Bear.

Throwing the covers off, he slid out of bed. "Just a minute!"

He found the clothes Serafina had left for him the day before and pulled on the buckskins. His unusual bout of sleepwalking didn't matter. Only two things mattered right now—seeing for himself that Bear was all right, and getting some answers about why he and his Brother had been led to this city.

After he got his pants laced, he dug through his bag to find the knife he'd carried since leaving Carwin, put it back where it belonged in its sheath—he didn't much want to carry the strange black blade anymore—and secured the sheath belt around his hips. Once he had the bottom of the sheath secured to his thigh, he crossed the room and opened the door.

A tall woman with long, dark hair and a serene expression stood on the other side. She smiled. "Good morning, Brother Dragon. My name is Willow. I've come to escort you to the hospital to see Bear."

"Yeah, hi. Serafina said you'd be coming by this morning." He raked a hand through his tangled hair, feeling self-conscious. "Sorry, I just got up. Come on in, let me finish getting dressed and we can go."

He caught a glimpse of Willow's brow furrowing as he turned to go back inside. "I'm sorry," she said, following him through the door. "I didn't mean to wake you."

"No, you didn't. I'd already woken up when you knocked, just hadn't gotten out of bed yet." Dragon grabbed the vest from the back of the chair and slipped it on. He wondered if there were any moccasins here. Walking to the hutch, he opened it. A pair of moccasins that looked like they'd been made to fit him sat on the second shelf. He took them and slipped them on, then went to the table and gulped the rest of the water from the cup he'd left sitting there last night after his bath. "Okay, I'm ready to go."

Willow gave him a look that reminded him of the one his mother once used when he'd done something wrong yet amusing as a child. "You should eat something first. We have time."

Dragon fought back his impatience with an effort. "I'm not

195

hungry. I want to see Bear."

To his relief, she merely nodded. "Very well."

They left the house and followed the lane back toward the main road. As they walked, a cool breeze rustled through the leaves overhead. Dragon drew a deep breath scented with grass, apples and flowering herbs. A flock of geese cut a wedge across a hazy blue sky that spoke of more rain by nightfall. It was nice to know he and Bear would both have a roof over their heads when the rain came, even if they weren't under the *same* roof.

Willow never spoke during the short walk down the lane to the main road. An ox-drawn cart passed them at one point, heading back the way they'd come. The man at the reins nodded in greeting. Willow waved to him. Dragon returned the man's nod and made himself smile. He ignored the stranger's curious look. Of course people were going to wonder who he was and where he came from. That was only to be expected.

In the gathering morning crowd on the main road, Willow drew closer to Dragon and hooked her hand through his elbow. "Bear should be awake when we arrive at the hospital. He should also be much more lucid than he was yesterday. You'll be able to speak with him, and the healers have assured me that the two of you will be able to spend some time together."

"Good. Thanks." He tried to think of a polite way to make her let go of his arm, but nothing came to mind. "I've been really worried about him."

"I know." One corner of her mouth lifted in a wry half-smile. She let her hand drop away from his arm.

Dragon shot her a sidelong glance, trying not to look like he was staring. Being around her made him feel naked. It was a hazard of dealing with Seers. He had never learned to be comfortable around them.

Then again, she was the best chance he had of getting his questions answered.

He stepped over a pile of dung in his path. "Do you think you and I might get a chance to talk later, Willow?"

"Yes, certainly." She looked at him without a trace of surprise on her face. "You have many questions for me, I believe."

"That's right." He stared at her without bothering to hide it this time. "Are you reading me?"

She laughed. "Only the surface of your mind. I wouldn't be much of a Seer if I didn't do at least *that* much to protect my tribe. But any reasonable person would expect you to have questions. I wouldn't need to read you to know that."

"Oh." They rounded a bend in the road and the hospital came into view ahead. "So, when can we talk? I've got nothing but time after I see Bear."

"I will need to speak with Bear myself at some point today. After that, you and I can talk and you may ask me all the questions you wish. Will that do?"

He nodded. "That'll be great. Thanks."

"I'll look forward to it." An elderly woman passed by, a basket full of flowers on her back. Willow greeted her with a smile and waited until she was out of earshot before speaking again. "Dragon, I realize that you're suspicious of me, and of this tribe. You suspect our motives in bringing you and your brother here."

A lifetime of habit kept his expression neutral. He supposed it didn't matter, though. She'd know what he thought anyway. Never mind that a Seer shouldn't delve deeper than purely surface emotions without either a person's permission or a council order. The Ashe Tribe Seer had always played fast and loose with that rule. Why shouldn't Willow?

"You protect your tribe. I protect my Brother." The healing center was close now. Morning sunshine picked out shades of gold and red in the wooden shutters flung open beside the windows. Dragon wondered if Bear was gazing out one of the windows right now, watching him. The thought sped up his heartbeat and his footsteps.

On impulse, he stopped about twenty paces short of the building. Maybe a direct question would give him the answers he wanted. "What *are* your motives?"

Her eyebrows rose. "Must we have one other than saving fellow human beings from the clutches of the degraded?"

"No. But I know you do." He crossed his arms and held her gaze. "My old tribe ran on secrets, lies and games. I'm done with that. Tell me the truth."

She smiled. "You're a very direct person, Brother. I like that. But you must realize that I can't simply divulge certain things to you before I've discussed them with the person who they affect the most."

"Meaning Bear's the one you want." *He's trapped in there. I've taken him straight into a trap. The Mother only knows what they're going to do to him.* Dragon's right hand twitched toward his knife. He laced his fingers behind his back and blanked his mind as best he could before the urge to cut through everyone in his path and get Bear out of here could take readable shape in his mind. "Why?"

Willow didn't answer, but swiveled on one booted heel and strode toward the hospital, leaving Dragon to follow her. She didn't speak until they reached the covered doors. He'd given up and was trying to think of a way to reintroduce the topic later, when she grasped him by the wrist. Startled, he stared at her. She stared back, her mild expression in stark contrast to her painfully strong grip.

"Your Brother is a very special man. He is safe here, with us. That is all you need know for now." She let go, smiling. "I meant what I said before. I will answer all of your questions fully, to the best of my ability. But only after I speak with Bear. I'm sorry if that does not meet your needs, but it's the best I can do."

He nodded. "That'll be fine. Thanks." He did his best to make the thought uppermost in his mind as well. Judging by the barely perceptible tightening of Willow's lips, he wasn't sure he succeeded.

Willow tugged on a rope hanging outside the door. Dragon heard the deep clang of a bell inside. A moment later, a young girl in a white dress opened the door and beckoned them in. She seemed to be expecting them. They followed her down a wide hallway lined with doors.

She stopped outside one that looked exactly like all the others. "Healer Aster's with him. She'll be right out, then you can go in."

Willow smiled at the girl. "Thank you. Dragon and I will wait here. You may go about your duties."

The girl dipped her head in a gesture of respect then hurried off down the hall to another room.

Dragon stood shuffling from foot to foot and staring at the closed door between himself and his Brother. He wondered how much the healer would mind if he just went on in. The need to see Bear was a physical ache inside him.

"Wait, Brother."

He clenched his jaw. *Stop reading me, Seer.*

Willow gave him a cool look. "One needn't be a Seer to know what you were thinking. Wait."

Before he could say a word, the door swung open and Healer Aster emerged. She greeted them with a brisk nod. "Good morning. Dragon, I know you're anxious to see Bear. You may go in now."

Dragon's heart turned over. He took a couple of steps and stopped. "How long can I stay?"

"As long as Bear feels up to it. He's doing much better this morning, so he should be able to tolerate visiting with you for long enough to satisfy both of you. But if he tires or needs to be medicated for pain, you'll have to leave. Do you understand?" Dragon nodded, and Aster smiled at him. "Very well." She laid a hand on Willow's arm. "Seer, Councilor Laurel is here. I'll take you to her."

"Thank you." Willow followed Healer Aster down the hallway, giving Dragon an unreadable look as she passed.

Dragon ignored the mental image of invisible fingers sifting through his brain. Even if it wasn't his imagination, there was nothing he could do about it, and he had more important things to think about right now. Like Bear. He slipped through the open door into his Brother's room.

Bear lay in a narrow bed with a simple wooden frame, his back propped against a couple of fat pillows. He still looked tired and far too pale, but his eyes were clear. His face broke into a smile when he saw Dragon. "Hi."

"Hi." Dragon crossed to the bed and sat on the edge. He took Bear's hand in his. "How are you feeling?"

"Much better. The leg still hurts, but not as bad. And my fever's down." Bear squeezed Dragon's hand. "What about you? You okay? How's that cut?"

"I'm fine." Dragon rolled the injured shoulder. It barely twinged anymore. "The cut's nearly healed. It doesn't even need a dressing now."

"Good. I'm glad you're okay. I was worried about you."

Dragon laughed. "*You* were worried about *me*?"

"Well, yeah. I didn't like being away from you, and I know you didn't like being away from me either." Bear slid his free hand around the back of Dragon's neck. A familiar hunger burned in his eyes. "Come here and kiss me, Brother."

Relief, desire and lingering worry lumped together in the back of Dragon's throat. Scooting forward, he let go of Bear's hand to cup his face in both palms, leaned down and kissed his lips. His mouth opened, and Dragon groaned as Bear's tongue slid against his. Mother, it felt so *good*. Lately he'd wondered if he'd ever feel Bear kiss him like this again.

When Bear's hand dropped from his neck and wormed down the back of his pants instead, Dragon broke the kiss. No matter how much he wanted it—and Great Mother he did, it had been far too long since he'd felt Bear's hands on him—this wasn't the place for it, and Bear wasn't yet well enough for even the gentlest sex.

"Not now." Dragon carded a hand through Bear's hair. "You have to rest. Healer Aster would throw me out and never let me back in if she found out I came in here and wore out her patient with sex."

I can't leave him here. I have to get him out.

Before he's even healed? That's insane, and you know it. He'd die if you took him back into the wilderness now. Wait. Watch. Try to gain the tribe's trust. When Bear's well enough, get him out of here before they can do whatever it is they want to do with him.

Dragon managed a smile to hide his fear and confusion. Bear didn't need the stress of knowing about all this right now.

Bear's expression remained solemn. "I dreamed about you last night."

A strange sensation fluttered in the pit of Dragon's stomach. "Did you?"

"You were in a little house, sitting in a chair in the dark. I knew you couldn't see me, because I knew I wasn't really there, but I went and sat with you and held you, and you fell asleep in my arms. I carried you to the bed and stayed there with you the rest of the night. It seemed so real." Taking his hand out of Dragon's pants, Bear laid his palm on Dragon's cheek. Bear's skin still felt too warm, but no longer fiery hot like before. "I don't know what I'm trying to say. I know I can't fuck you right now like I want to. I just need to touch you. Something's...*different* about me, since the fever, and I need you to remind me of what's real."

Dragon had no idea what to say to that. Especially since Bear's dream meshed a little too well with his own memories. The brush of Bear's presence in his mind, Bear's scent on the pillows. Sleep only coming once he let himself imagine Bear's big body curled around him.

What if it was real?

If Bear was looking for reassurance, he wouldn't find it. But Dragon would give him the truth, as far as he knew it. He owed his Brother nothing less.

"The house is real, Bear. That's where I stayed last night. And...I felt you there." Dragon kissed the furrow that formed between Bear's brows in an attempt to soothe his obvious distress. "Listen. Maybe the Great Mother sent us both the same dream to comfort us. I couldn't sleep any more until I felt you there with me, so for me, at least, it worked. That's real enough for me. And *this* is real. You and me, in Shenandoah. We're here, and we're safe." *Maybe. Maybe not.* "And you're going to be okay. *That's* real." He drew back enough to look into Bear's troubled eyes. "If there's one thing I've learned from you, it's that something doesn't have to be literally, physically *there* to be a true thing. Whatever happened last night, we both felt it, so it must be real. I can't find anything wrong with that."

One corner of Bear's mouth hitched up in a half-hearted attempt at a smile. "Good point."

Something told Dragon that wasn't the end of the story. "But?"

"But, last night wasn't my only..." Bear made a helpless gesture. "Dream. Vision. Whatever it is. You know about the one I had in Harrisonburg, the day you were captured. There've been more since then, where I've talked to Willow. She showed me the city in the last one we shared. I never had these dream-visions before the fever, and even after that, I never had them without Willow. I mean, I'd have occasional little flashes before. Small things, for most of my life, and I've had dreams where I saw Shenandoah ever since we left Char. But never anything like the dream-visions I've had since the fever. And the one last night, with you...I thought that was just a regular dream, until you said you felt it too. And now I know it wasn't a regular dream at all, it was a dream-vision just like when I meet Willow, only I did it by myself, without her guiding me, and that's..." He shook his head. "It's *crazy*. I shouldn't have been able to do that. It's not *normal* for someone like me who's not a Seer."

So he wasn't just dreaming about *Willow these last couple of days. He was really, truly talking to her. Oh, Mother.* Dragon ignored the automatic surge of possessive jealousy at the thought of all the time Willow had spent with Bear in dreams and how close they must have become and forced himself to think of the implications of what Bear had just told him. Especially in light of his recent conversation with Willow. "It's unusual, sure. But lots of things about this tribe are unusual. What do you think is going to happen if anyone finds out?"

Bear shook his head. "I don't know."

He *did* know. Dragon saw it in the frown lines around his mouth and the tightness in his jaw.

Death. Slavery. Banishment. The fear of all those punishments and as yet unknown ones showed on Bear's face.

For his own part, Dragon couldn't decide if Bear's newly discovered talent eased his suspicions of the Shenandoah Tribe or sharpened them. Either way, he thought he knew why they'd sought Bear out. The question was, now that they had him, what did they mean to *do* with him?

Dragon couldn't imagine. But he intended to find out.

The hours Dragon spent at his bedside passed far too

quickly for Bear, even though Dragon seemed on edge for reasons Bear couldn't pin down. When Healer Aster entered with a tray of bread, cheese and broth, he glanced out the window in surprise. "Is it time for lunch already?"

Aster nodded. "It's midday. You must eat. And I'm afraid you need to take some opium, whether you think you need it or not, so that we can check your bandage. I want to make sure the maggots are still in place."

Dragon stared. "Maggots?"

"Yes. It's one of the techniques we learned from books the ancients left in Harrisonburg. They taught us how to grow maggots in special cultures and use them to clean wounds. They only eat dead or infected tissue and leave the healthy tissue alone." She set the tray on the small bedside table. "It's also time to take your penicillin."

Bear made a face. The stuff tasted awful, even worse than the opium, but it seemed to be curing the infection that had spread through his body so he couldn't really complain.

The healer smiled as if she knew what he was thinking. "I'm sorry to have to end your visit, Bear. But Willow wants to talk to you after you eat, then you really need to rest."

Reaching for Dragon's hand was automatic. Bear didn't want him to leave. Not even for a little while. "I'm not really tired. I feel fine. Can't he stay?"

"I can help him with his lunch." Dragon stroked the back of Bear's hand with his thumb. He kept his gaze on their joined fingers and didn't look up. "I'll clear out after that. I don't want to be in the way, or hold up Bear's treatment. I want him to get better."

Aster's expression softened with sympathy. At that moment, the healer's assistant walked in, carrying a basket Bear knew contained the opium and penicillin, as well as fresh bandages in case they were needed. Aster gestured for her to set the basket beside the lunch tray, then turned back to Dragon. "Very well. You may stay and help Bear with his meal. Then perhaps you'd like to look around our city while Bear rests. You'll be able to see him again either this evening or tomorrow, depending on how he's feeling."

"Okay." Dragon lifted his head and smiled at her. "Thanks."

"Of course." Aster touched her assistant's shoulder. "We'll be back soon."

As soon as the two women had left the room, Dragon rose and crossed to the other side of the bed. Bear watched with grief weighing on his heart. Dragon had seemed tense ever since Bear confessed his fears about his newfound abilities and what might come of them. After all they'd suffered to find this place, it killed Bear to know he'd put his Brother in danger all over again, even though it was purely accidental.

"I'm sorry," Bear said as Dragon helped him sit up and wedged the pillows behind his back. "I didn't mean to be able to do this. I won't use it anymore. If I don't use it, maybe they'll never find out. Maybe it'll even go away and we won't have to worry about it."

Dragon looked confused for a second, then shook his head when understanding dawned on his face. "Bear, no. You have nothing to be sorry about. You haven't done anything wrong. And if the Great Mother gives you a gift, you shouldn't have to pretend you don't have it." Taking a hunk of cheese from the tray, he folded a slice of bread around it and handed it to Bear. He leaned close, his voice lowered to a whisper. "I won't let anyone hurt you. Never again. I swear it. Leave everything to me."

Bear studied the tight lines of Dragon's face and hard gleam in his eyes, and believed him. Clasping his free hand around the back of Dragon's skull, Bear hauled him forward into a hard kiss that said all the complicated things he didn't have the words for.

Dragon kissed back, just as hungry for it as Bear was, but ended it after only a few seconds. Bear smiled at Dragon's stern order to "stop trying to get into my pants and just eat". Dragon had always been the practical one.

Whatever happened next, Bear needed his full strength to face it, and a man didn't recover his strength on an empty stomach. He did as he was told.

True to his word, Dragon left when Healer Aster and her assistant returned. Bear didn't quite know what to make of the penetrating stare Dragon gave him when he kissed him goodbye, or the way he squeezed Bear's hand as if trying to convey a secret message through touch alone. But he returned the pressure of Dragon's fingers anyway, smiled at him and sent him on his way with a silent promise of trust. He had no idea what—if anything—Dragon was planning, but he *did* trust Dragon, with his whole being. With his very life. Whatever else Dragon might be, he wasn't rash or impulsive. He wouldn't risk both their lives by saying or doing anything to bring suspicion down on either of them.

After Healer Aster and her assistant gave Bear his medications and changed the top layer of cloth on his bandage, they made sure he was comfortable then left him alone. He wasn't sure how much time passed after that, but he'd begun to doze when someone tapped on the door.

He jerked awake. "Yes?"

Willow walked into the room and stood just inside, one hand on the doorframe. "Bear? Do you feel up to talking for a while?"

He didn't, really. His leg ached and even though he wouldn't trade the hours he'd spent with Dragon for anything, the visit had left him worn out. As tired as he felt right now, he wasn't sure he could hide the knowledge of what he'd done last night from Willow.

He smiled, allowing his exhaustion to show while keeping his mind blank. "Actually, I'm pretty tired. I'd like to rest, if you don't mind."

Willow's usual calm yet unrevealing expression turned sorrowful. Shutting the door, she hurried over, perched on the edge of his mattress and took his hand. "Bear, please don't be afraid. Not of your gift, and certainly not of us."

Adrenaline shot through Bear's blood. He fought to keep it off his face. "I don't know what you mean."

"You had a dream last night. One that frightened you, because it shouldn't have been possible. Am I right?"

A strange mix of excitement and pity lit her face. Bear swallowed, his throat dry. He wanted to look away, but couldn't. His heart galloped so fast it made him sick. "I...I don't—"

A faint tremor ran through Willow's fingers where she gripped Bear's hand. "You're a Seer, Bear. You have the gift. And the Shenandoah Tribe needs it."

Chapter Fifteen

Bear stared, shocked to his core. Not so much by the revelation that he was evidently a Seer. Hadn't he known it, deep in his heart, when Dragon confirmed that what they'd both experienced last night was real? No, what surprised him was the part where Willow said the Shenandoah Tribe *needed* his gift.

He shook his head. "I don't understand. How...? And why would anyone need *my* gift? It's...it shouldn't have happened!"

Willow nodded, and Bear felt instantly better. He didn't know why, but he trusted her to grasp exactly what he was trying to ask. *Of course, my mind's an open book to her.*

He tried not to think too hard about that. He'd never spent this much time with a Seer before, and he found it more than a little nerve-wracking to feel this bare. The idea of being a Seer himself, of making other people this uncomfortable around him, depressed him.

Willow's lips curved into a wry smile. "You must have had the gift all along. I've found that one is either born with it, or not. The fever probably triggered it, but it must have been inside you all your life, lying dormant. Serafina is blessed with a less potent form. You may have noticed, yes?"

Bear frowned. The memory was vague, like many of his memories from Harrisonburg, but if he concentrated he could "hear" Serafina's voice in his mind. Yes. "I remember her speaking to me, mind to mind. It was...strange. I wasn't sure at the time if it was just a hallucination, or what. But it convinced me that she and her Pack were friends." A thought struck him. "Wait, she told Ezekiel to report to her from Harrisonburg nightly. So Ezekiel has the gift too, doesn't he?"

"Yes, but he is only able to communicate mind to mind with Serafina. No one else. We think it's because they are twins and thus shared a womb. That communication is invaluable when the Pack needs to split up. The fact that Serafina can communicate with me via her gift is equally invaluable. It has made the Pack and our tribe much safer over the years."

Comprehension struck. "So you've learned to find people who have the gift and lead them here."

"I have, yes. We've found a few of the gifted that way, and it's been a good thing both for them and for us." She gazed into Bear's eyes with a seriousness he found both thrilling and a little scary. "But that isn't why you've been led here."

"It isn't?"

"No."

Confused, he shook his head. "Then I don't understand. Why does the tribe need my gift?"

"You aren't simply one of the gifted. As I said before, you're a Seer. A true Seer, like me. With a bit of time and training, you have the potential to become far stronger than I am."

Bear's stomach rolled. He wasn't sure he liked where this was going. "Willow—"

"Please, hear me out." Willow squared her shoulders, as if getting ready to pass on unpleasant news. "I'm dying, Bear. There's a sickness inside me that the healers can't cure. I'm not sure how long I have to live, but I doubt very much that I will see another summer. Shenandoah needs a new Seer. Someone strong in the gift, strong in themselves, with love in their heart and a passion for doing the right thing for their tribe. You have all of these qualities, and so many more." She held Bear's gaze, her eyes wide and all her hopes and fears raw on her face. "You've journeyed long and far to seek this tribe. Will you help us, Brother?"

Bear felt as if a ball of ice had lodged in the center of his chest. He forced out the question he had to ask anyway. "Do I have a choice?"

She looked stunned, as if it had never occurred to her that he might think such a thing. "Of course. Shenandoah is your home now, whether you choose to become Seer or not. If you doubt it, I invite you freely inside my mind to see for yourself. I won't fight it, or hide anything from you."

He wasn't so sure her mind was really as open to him as she said, even if he'd had the slightest idea how to go about reading her. But it didn't matter. The truth of his ability to freely choose came through loud and clear, and for him that was the deciding factor. "In that case, I'd be proud and honored to become Shenandoah's new Seer."

Relief flowed over her features. She beamed at him. "Thank you, Bear. For myself and all of the Shenandoah Tribe, thank you."

He returned her smile, his heart light.

Someone tapped on the door. "Come in," Bear called. He wasn't expecting anyone, not even the healer, but that was okay. In his current mood, he didn't mind another visitor.

The door swung open. The healer's assistant edged into the room and bobbed her head at them. "Seer Willow, you're wanted at Council."

Willow's eyebrows rose. "Very well." She patted Bear's hand, then let go and rose to her feet. "We'll talk again later. Your training won't begin until you're fully healed and Healer Aster has given you leave to work. In the meantime, feel free to explore the limits of your gift on your own, if you like." She flashed a wide smile. "Just don't tire yourself. All right?"

"I promise I won't."

"Good." She touched his shoulder. "Take care, Brother. Until we meet again."

She turned and followed the young assistant out of the room, closing the door behind her.

Bear relaxed against the pillows, his mind at peace for the first time in ages. He felt light as air, buoyed by the certainty that he was doing the right thing. For himself, for his Brother, for a whole city full of people he didn't yet know but hoped to soon. It was a good feeling.

As his eyes drifted shut, his last conscious thought was, *I can't wait to tell Dragon.*

After he left Bear, Dragon found a small door hidden at the end of a side hall and wandered out into the healing center's expansive gardens. He wasn't sure what to do with himself. With no idea how long he'd need to wait before Willow came to talk to him, he didn't know if he should stay nearby or if he had time to look around the town.

Not that he felt much like exploring. His instincts told him to grab Bear and run. To kill every man and woman who tried to stop him, if he had to, but to get Bear out at all costs. Every nerve, every muscle twitched with the need for action. Fighting it took all his energy, but he had no choice. Escape from Shenandoah wasn't physically possible right now because of Bear's injury. Even if Bear was up to running away, Dragon couldn't be sure whether or not fleeing was even a good idea. Not yet. Not until he knew more about what the tribal council had planned for Bear.

Dragon left the gardens after a few minutes of aimless walking and struck out toward the midst of the city. Willow would find him, wherever he went, he had no doubt. Meanwhile, he would poke around. Talk to people. Learn as much as possible about this place from its ordinary citizens. Maybe they could shed some light on the situation in which he and Bear now found themselves.

Even if it turned out to be a waste of time, it would keep him occupied. Dragon figured that was as good a goal as any at the moment.

A short walk down the main road brought him to the teeming market in the town's center. Clouds scudded overhead in a freshening breeze, creating an endlessly changing pattern of sunlight and shade. Men, women and children browsed the various stalls, smiling and shouting greetings to one another over the noise of oxen and carts and vendors calling the virtues of their wares. Looking around, Dragon saw a wealth of merchandise available for trade. Clothes, wine, freshly baked bread, cheese wheels. One stall boasted a row of beautiful glass bottles filled with various oils. The scents of food, flowers and animals floated on the wind.

Dragon paced through the crowd, smiling in spite of the sense of apprehension hanging over him. Shenandoah seemed such a rich, lively place. After all he and Bear had gone through to find it, he didn't want to be forced to leave again.

He hoped he was just letting his suspicious nature get the better of him and the council's motives were more benign than he thought. After all, he didn't really *know* what they wanted with Bear's newly discovered talent. This wasn't the Ashe Tribe, corrupt to the core, every action driven by a dozen equally sinister reasons. This was Shenandoah, the tribe he and Bear had sought out with the intent of starting over together. Maybe he should give them a chance.

But it's Bear's life at stake here. What if I'm wrong? What if he doesn't want to do whatever it is they want from him and they try to make him do it anyway? What if he's right and they decide this thing he can do means he can't be allowed to live?

Dragon drew a deep breath to steady himself. Bear was safe, for now. Dragon would just have to figure out the Shenandoah Council's plan for Bear by the time he healed enough to be of real use to them.

How he was to do that, he had no idea.

"Dragon!"

Startled, Dragon whirled toward the sound of his name. Lucian and Valentine strode toward him through the throng. It was a relief to see the two familiar faces in a sea of strangers. Dragon smiled. "Brother Lucian. Brother Valentine. It's good to see you."

The two shared an uncomfortable look. An ugly feeling curled in the pit of Dragon's stomach. He backed up a couple of paces before good sense took over and he stopped. It took every ounce of willpower he had to keep from reaching for his knife.

Valentine stopped a few paces away. Lucian walked closer, his expression grim. "Brother Dragon. By order of Councilor Laurel, head of the Shenandoah Tribal Council and leader of the Shenandoah Tribe, you're to be brought before the council immediately."

The council. Not good. Dragon kept his voice calm and his stance non-threatening with an effort. "Why?"

Lucian met Dragon's gaze, his expression regretful. "Suspicion of murderous intent toward innocents."

Chapter Sixteen

Dragon stared, rooted to the ground with shock. Cold fear lodged in his chest. Mother, first the Ashe Tribe, now here. "I haven't hurt anyone, Lucian. I have done *nothing* wrong."

"For what it's worth, I believe you. All of us who traveled with you believe you. You're Pack, and a warrior. You'd never harm an innocent, and we all know it. In fact, Serafina's with the council right now, arguing for your honor, and your freedom. But our orders were to bring you in, so we have to do it." Lucian gestured to Valentine, who moved behind Dragon. A length of hemp rope dangled from his hand. He shot Dragon an apologetic glance as he brushed past him. Lucian grasped Dragon's shoulder. "I'm sorry, Brother."

Dragon said nothing. He wanted to believe Serafina's intervention would help. Maybe it would. But right now, with the stares of the curious and the disgusted all around, he found it hard to hope.

Behind him, Valentine cinched the rope snug around his wrists. Panic raced through his veins.

Run. Lucian and Valentine like you, and that makes them careless. You could take them both down with a couple of kicks and disappear in this crowd in no time. Just do it. Don't let them take you. Don't let the Shenandoah Council execute you. Or worse, banish you like the Ashe Council did.

An innate sense of fairness made him hesitate—in a city full of strangers, why betray two of the very few friends he had?—but what stopped him was Bear. What would Bear think if he learned that Dragon had run? Or been killed by the Shenandoah Pack while *trying* to run?

No. Running wasn't an option. He owed it to Bear to stay. If that meant proving his innocence on a charge of murderous intent—what in the Mother's name did that even *mean?*—then so be it.

With his arms restrained, Valentine took his left elbow and Lucian his right. They led him through the market, past knots of townsfolk whispering behind their hands or outright staring. Dragon kept his chin up and his gaze fixed on the horizon. Whatever happened, he refused to look guilty when he'd done nothing wrong.

They walked for what seemed like ages in the shade of spreading maples before reaching the foot of a grassy slope dotted with daisies, buttercups and the occasional bright orange tiger lily. A hay-strewn path wound up the hill to a peak-roofed structure built of heavy logs. Pack stood at attention at each corner of the building and flanked either side of the wide double doors.

Lucian stopped at the foot of the path and looked down at Dragon with a faint frown tugging down the corners of his mouth. "I need to take your weapon before we approach the council."

Dragon forced down the instinctive urge to fight. It wouldn't do any good. He nodded. "Do what you have to."

Lucian reached down to loosen the tie holding Dragon's sheath to his thigh, then undid the leather belt around his hips. He took belt, sheath and knife, rolled them together and stuffed them into a bag hanging at his own belt. Dragon noted with reluctant admiration that he made sure to stay out of easy range of Dragon's feet while working, and kept the bag out of

Dragon's reach.

With Dragon's knife stowed where he could no longer get it, he and his guards started up the hill. Each step felt like it took him closer to his doom. He stopped when Lucian and Valentine stopped and stood there in front of the doors with his heart racing and his pulse pounding in his ears, trying not to look as terrified as he felt.

"Good day, Sister, Brother," Lucian greeted the guards. "We've brought the newcomer, Brother Dragon, to the council as ordered."

The man to the left of the door pinned him with an ice-cold stare. "We should call a murderer of innocents Brother now?"

Lucian glared. "He's murdered no one. He only stands accused of murderous *intent*, and his guilt is unproven. Which is why he is here, and you know it. Besides, he's Pack. Any Pack has the right to the title. Something else you ought to know."

Valentine stepped forward, his expression matching the angry growl in his voice perfectly. "Now. Will you let us pass, or not? Councilor Laurel herself sent for Brother Dragon, and you know she doesn't like to be kept waiting."

"You may pass." The woman took hold of her side of the door, set her shoulder to it and pushed until it swung inward. Her glare suggested her Brother do the same, or else. "Good day to you, Brothers."

Grumbling, the man heaved his door open as well. Lucian and Valentine led Dragon inside.

A long table sat to the right. A group of men and women gathered around it. The council, Dragon assumed. He couldn't see their faces. Sunlight streamed through narrow windows set high in the walls, but after the bright afternoon outdoors the interior seemed dim.

A small but sturdy woman with copper skin and sharp

black eyes rose from the head of the table. A single black braid liberally streaked with white hung over her right shoulder. "Brother Lucian. Brother Valentine. You've brought him?"

Dragon saw Lucian's jaw tighten. "Yes, Councilor Laurel. This is Brother Dragon."

"Good, thank you." She turned to her left. "Willow?"

A tall figure rose from the chair beside Councilor Laurel's, and Dragon's stomach dropped into his feet. His eyes had adjusted enough by that time to recognize the tribe's Seer. If anyone here could twist the truth enough to make him look as bad as possible, it was her. She'd been inside his head. Further inside than he'd wanted her to be, he was fairly certain. Not that it would've taken much for a Seer of her strength to learn things the council wouldn't like. If she'd delved as deeply as he knew she was capable of doing, she would know he'd realized that the council wanted Bear, even though he hadn't yet known *why* at the time. She also would have surely seen the desperate thought he hadn't been able to help—the need to *get Bear out.*

Get him out. Whatever it took. Whoever he had to go through to do it.

Great Mother.

If she'd seen that in his mind, if she'd told the council...

He fought off a surge of overwhelming despair. *Don't ever let the bastards know they scare ya.* Another of his old Sarge's sayings. He'd learned it well. He squared his shoulders and made himself stare straight into Willow's eyes.

To his surprise, she looked as distressed as he felt. She held his gaze for only a second, not nearly long enough to answer all the questions he tried to ask without words. She whirled to face Laurel. "Councilor, please. I don't believe this is necessary."

The Councilor laid a hand on Willow's arm without looking away from Dragon's face. "Calm yourself, Seer. Nothing has been decided yet."

"There's no need to bring him here restrained like a common criminal." Willow glanced at him, her eyes wide and her face pinched. She turned away quickly. "Councilor. Laurel, please, don't do this."

In a flash of insight, Dragon recognized the way Willow's shoulders hunched and the cringing tone in her voice. She felt guilty. Guilty, because her ill-gotten knowledge of his mind was now being used against him.

He hoped she choked on it. What in the Great Mother's name did she think the council would do with what she told them?

A man two chairs down to Laurel's right pointed a long, pale finger at Willow. "If this man has entertained thoughts of murdering our healers in order to remove his Brother from their care—our *healers,* my fellow councilors, let us remember that— then he *is* a common criminal."

"This man is *not* a criminal. How can you bring a man to trial based on nothing but a *thought?* One, I might add, that came solely from a desire to protect someone he loves."

With a jolt of relief, Dragon recognized Serafina's voice. He watched her face down the unknown man from across the table, anger in every line of her body. She had spent two days traveling with him. Maybe she could convince the council he was innocent.

The faintest shadow of a long-suffering expression crossed Laurel's features as she turned toward Serafina. "Sister, the council and I do thank you for presenting us with your thorough and...lengthy viewpoint. Your unique knowledge and opinions in this case are appreciated."

Serafina glowered. "With respect, Councilor—"

It seemed Councilor Laurel was at the end of her patience, because she cut Serafina off mid-sentence. "Sister Serafina. I understand that you have spent time with Brother Dragon, and you feel a kinship with him as a person and as a fellow Pack member. But you must understand the position the council and I are in. When we learn that there is a potential danger to this tribe, we cannot let that go without investigation. And I will remind you both..." she shot stern looks at Serafina and Willow, "...that at this time we are not merely investigating the possibility that Brother Dragon contemplated the murder of innocent healers. If it is indeed true that he thought this, *for whatever reason*, then we as a council must consider whether his potential for violence is a danger to this tribe. This council is not in the business of punishing potential crimes, but we are charged with the solemn duty of ensuring this tribe's safety. Brother Dragon is a stranger to us. If anyone here knows of a way to evaluate him fairly and impartially other than bringing him here in restrained custody for an official investigation, I invite you to share it with the council."

Silence fell while Laurel stared down Willow, Serafina and each council member in turn. When she seemed satisfied that everyone had gotten her point, Laurel nodded, stepped away from the table and walked up to Dragon. Her gaze never once wavered from his eyes, and he began to understand why she was the city's leader.

She stopped a bare two to three paces from him. "Brother Dragon, I'm truly sorry that our meeting couldn't be under better circumstances. Seer Willow insists that the dark thoughts you harbor stem merely from your loyalty toward your Brother Bear, rather than any innate desire to harm anyone in this tribe. I hope and believe that is so. However, my duty to my people compels me to be certain. I hope you understand."

He understood, all right. They wanted to keep Bear so badly that even Dragon's private thoughts of protecting his Brother from some sort of forced usage were enough to get him labeled as a potential murderer, restrained and hauled up before the council.

It did nothing at all to make him think more charitably toward them.

Across the room, Willow shot him a look full of misery, and he knew she'd picked up on his fear, his rage and his sense of betrayal. He knew none of it showed outwardly—he'd had a lifetime to learn how to hide his emotions—but it all boiled just beneath the surface. Even the weakest of Seers would feel it, and Willow was hardly weak.

"I understand, Councilor." His voice sounded calm, controlled. "Thank you for giving me the chance to prove my innocence."

Her expression didn't change at all. "Believe me when I say, the council and I would be very pleased to find you innocent of all charges. It would give us no pleasure to take your freedom, or your life."

He wasn't sure how to answer that without sounding disrespectful—something he couldn't afford to be—so he bit his tongue and dipped his head instead.

One corner of the Councilor's mouth twitched upward, as if she knew how hard he held himself in check and was amused by it. Dragon could have cheerfully spit in her eye. He stared resolutely over her left shoulder instead.

"Seer," she called without turning around. "Please come forward."

Willow walked up to him, her face expressionless. He was glad she'd regained her equilibrium. For reasons he couldn't define, the idea of her rummaging through his thoughts while still radiating guilt like a bonfire made him furious. If he had to endure a mind-fuck, he'd just as soon have it as quick, efficient and painless as possible.

She stared into his eyes. "I know you already know this, Brother, but it's easier if you don't fight it."

He smiled, and hoped it looked as cold as it felt. "Funny thing, a man from my old tribe said that same thing to seven little girls before he raped them."

Willow's eyes narrowed. Dragon shut up before he could do himself any more damage. He wasn't helping his case, and he knew it.

At least he hadn't told them how he and two of his Brothers had hunted down the filthy excuse for a man and cut his throat in front of the council building, with the families of all seven children as witnesses. He didn't think Willow would appreciate the connection right now. He knew for a fact that Councilor Laurel wouldn't like knowing what he was capable of doing when he chose.

"Seer Willow. If you please."

The Councilor's calm voice broke the tension between Dragon and the Seer. Visibly gathering herself, Willow drew a slow, deep breath. Blew it out...

...And just like that, Dragon felt her in his head. Sifting through his thoughts, his feelings, his memories. She slipped like fog around the curves and corners of his psyche, swift and insubstantial, leaving a vague, comforting warmth behind.

It was completely unlike the torturous intrusions he'd suffered from the Ashe Tribe Seer. He wondered if he would've noticed, if he hadn't known she was about to do it.

When she withdrew, he blinked at her in surprise. "You... That's it?"

"Yes." She touched his shoulder, just for a moment, then let her hand fall. "Your Seer in the Ashe Tribe has a strong gift, but her control is poor, and her technique is... Well. Perhaps she was badly taught. It should *never* hurt like that. I'm sorry."

Dragon's eyes stung. He stared at the floor, not knowing what to say. He wanted to ask what she had *seen*, and what it meant for his future, but he didn't know how. Where he came from, questions from the prisoner were frowned on.

Willow let out a soft laugh. "Laurel, I can say with no hesitation whatsoever that Brother Dragon harbors no ill will, and in particular no violent thoughts, toward this council, or this tribe. He is angry at having been brought here under suspicion of plotting the murder of innocents, but I think that's understandable. A deeper reading confirms what I told you before—that all of his fear, all of his anger, stems only from love for and loyalty to his Brother. He would do anything to protect Bear." Her voice dropped low. "Wouldn't any of us do the same for those we love?"

Her tone sounded sad. Wistful. Dragon looked up. She gave him a faint smile.

Councilor Laurel nodded. "Of course. My concern, as you know, is Brother Dragon's obviously violent nature and tendency to jump to the wrong conclusion."

Dragon swallowed the retort that wanted to come out. It wouldn't help.

"The council should discuss the case," said one of the women who'd remained silent at the table up until now. "We have Willow's and Serafina's testimony. We should hold Brother Dragon in the guardhouse while we talk over his case and decide what to do with him."

"I don't think there's anything to discuss." Serafina leaned both hands on the table. "Councilor, unless Dragon is allowed to remain here as a free member of this tribe, Bear will never agree to serve as our Seer. Where one goes, the other goes also."

Dragon had to fight to hide his surprise. He'd figured out that the council wanted Bear for his abilities, but he'd never dreamed they wanted Bear as the tribe's Seer. Why would they need another Seer when they already an extremely powerful one? He cut a questioning look to Willow.

Willow held his gaze for a moment, but her expression told

him nothing. She turned to Councilor Laurel. "Serafina's right. We need Bear. If that's going to happen, Councilor, you have to allow Dragon to go free."

The room stilled. Councilor Laurel searched Dragon's face. She stared so hard and deep that for a few seconds he wondered if she was a Seer herself. When she finally swiveled on her heel and returned to the table, he felt wrung out.

"I believe you're both right." The Councilor took her seat, facing Dragon. Sympathy showed in the tilt of her chin, but her expression remained hard, and Dragon knew he wouldn't go free today. Her next words confirmed his gut feeling. "However, I cannot in good conscience allow him to walk free without first considering what we already know and gathering as much other evidence as we can."

Serafina opened her mouth as if to protest, but subsided when the Councilor glanced her way. She met Dragon's gaze. *Sorry*, she mouthed. He gave her a tiny smile in return. He could hardly blame Serafina for his predicament. She'd done everything she could.

"Brother Lucian, Brother Valentine, please take Brother Dragon to the guardhouse. Leave him there under other guard, then return here with Brothers Titus and Llewelyn." Laurel looked over at Serafina. "Sister Serafina, you will remain here."

The three Pack members exchanged relieved looks. Lucian nodded toward the council table, a smile on his lips. "Yes, Councilor."

She pinned Dragon with a penetrating gaze. "Brother Dragon, if you are indeed innocent as you claim, you will be as free as any other citizen before the day is out. It is my sincere hope that this is indeed the case. Good luck to you."

Fuck you. "Thank you, Councilor."

Lucian and Valentine led him to the door. Valentine knocked, the door swung open and the three of them walked outside. Dragon looked around at the green grass, the blue sky, the nodding orange lilies. As they walked down the hill, he couldn't help wondering if this was the last time he'd walk under the blue sky and sunshine, and feel the cool breeze on his face.

More importantly, he wondered if he'd ever see Bear again. The thought of being executed without ever again touching his Brother made him feel sick.

At the foot of the hill, Lucian laid a hand on Dragon's shoulder as they continued down the path. "Don't worry, Brother. Everything will be fine."

"I don't know what makes you think so." Dragon glared at a pair of women who'd stopped in their tracks to stare at him. They hurried on their way, whispering. "Things don't look so fine from where I'm sitting."

Valentine grinned. "Councilor Laurel asked us to come back and Serafina to stay because she's going to have Willow look into our minds, to find out what we know about you."

Dragon scowled, remembering how a session with the Ashe Tribe Seer had always left him feeling as though someone had buried a large knife in his brain. Willow's mental touch hadn't felt anything like that, but still. He couldn't imagine submitting to such a thing as if it were nothing. "How is that a good thing?"

"Because she'll see that you're no danger to the tribe." Lucian led the way down a narrow path that wound through the stand of trees behind the market. "Beyond that, she'll see what an asset you could be to our Pack." He glanced at Dragon. "Only if you'd like to join us, of course. We'd be honored to have you."

Dragon had no idea what to say to that. Not only were these people willing to go through a Seer's examination to clear his name, they wanted him in their Pack. Such faith from relative strangers was completely beyond his experience. It humbled him.

He met Lucian's gaze. "Brother, if I go free, I would love to join the Shenandoah Pack. It would be a privilege."

Lucian smiled. "You'll go free."

"He's right." Valentine nodded his agreement. "You will."

Great Mother, he wanted them to be right. He wondered if it was some sort of a sign that no matter how hard he tried, he couldn't kill the hope that flared to life inside him.

In spite of Councilor Laurel's promise, she didn't return with the council's decision until the following morning. By then, the hope Dragon had felt the previous day was gone. He watched from the pallet on the floor, his gut on fire with a simmering fury, as Calista, the Sister guarding his cell, opened the door to allow the Head Councilor in.

Laurel gave him a brief nod. "Good morning, Brother."

His hand dropped to his side automatically before he remembered that his weapon had been taken from him the day before. The irony of his instinctive action, considering why he'd been detained, made him laugh. "Is it?"

If she thought it was strange to hear him laugh, she didn't show it. Her expression remained as unrevealing as ever. "I hope you'll think so, when you hear what I have to say."

And there it was again. Hope.

He really wished he could get his emotions under control.

"We'll see." He held the Councilor's gaze, keeping his own face as blank as hers. "What do you have to tell me?"

"The council has reviewed your case, and we have come to the conclusion that you pose no danger to the Shenandoah Tribe. You are free to go." She held out a sheathed knife with a belt wrapped around it. "Your weapon."

He stared. After the shock of his trial, after the endless,

sleepless hours wondering if he'd live to see another day, it felt like she should have something more to say to him. But she apparently didn't, and he had no idea why that made him so fucking angry.

Rising to his feet, he took his knife, buckled the belt around his hips and tied the sheath to his thigh. The solid weight of it centered him. Made him feel normal again.

Part of him wanted to let loose all the venom inside him on her head, but he didn't. She'd done what she had to do. It was over, and he had to put it behind him. He bowed his head in a gesture of respect. "Thank you."

"I'm truly glad it worked out this way." She smiled. It made her look younger, though not much less intimidating. "I hope we'll meet again soon, under better circumstances. Good day, Brother."

She turned on her heel and walked out of the dark little room.

Dragon stood there, staring at the open door. After a few minutes, Sister Calista stuck her head in to see what was keeping him. Shaking off the strange spell that had come over him, he slipped his shoes on and strode out the door, giving Calista a nod and a smile on his way out.

Outside in the cool morning air he realized he had no idea where to go. He supposed the cottage was still his to use, if he wanted. But it wasn't where he wanted to be right now.

What he wanted was Bear. He wanted to lie down next to him, hold on as tight as he could and never let go. It was still early. Bear might still be sleeping, which meant the healers would try to keep Dragon out, but he wouldn't let that stop him. Not now. He needed to be close to his Brother, and he knew Bear needed him close as well.

Dragon headed up the road toward the healing center. By the time he reached the outskirts of the market, the day's crowds had already begun to gather. It didn't take him long to figure out that word of his trial had spread. He kept going, his head down and his gaze fixed on the ground in front of him. He wished he knew of a way to avoid the market. The accusing looks, the whispers, the people drawing away from him in poorly concealed alarm—Mother, it was depressing.

In spite of all his doubts going in, he'd hoped he and Bear could start a new life together here in Shenandoah. That they'd live out the rest of their days here in peace, in a place that accepted them. Apparently that wasn't to be his fate.

It could be Bear's. If you left him to it.

The thought shook Dragon to his core. He stopped in his tracks. Could he? *Should* he? Bear would mourn his loss, but he'd move on. After all, the two of them hadn't even known each other that long. Everyone Bear met loved him. Maybe he would find a bondmate to share his life with. He would be taken in by the Pack, if nothing else.

In his mind's eye, Dragon saw Bear's fever-flushed face smiling up at him from the healers' litter, amber eyes bright. *Love you, my Brother.*

The memory made Dragon's decision for him. No matter how deep his humiliation, no matter how crippling the blow to his pride, he couldn't leave. It would wound Bear in ways no healer could fix. Nothing on the Mother's earth could make him hurt Bear.

Dragon tilted his head back. Sunlight filtered through the leaves overhead to dapple the road gold and green. A breeze brought the scents of grass, flowers and fresh-baked bread from the market, mixed with the musk of oxen and goats.

It was a beautiful day. He was alive. Bear was on the mend. Surely that counted for something.

Straightening his spine, Dragon strode down the path toward the healing center and his Brother.

Bear drifted out of troubled dreams and hovered just below full wakefulness. He felt a familiar fiery presence nearby and knew his Brother was with him again.

Something wasn't right, though. Dragon's mind felt confused. Miserable. A little angry. His jumbled thoughts and emotions fractured the peace of Bear's in-between state. Bear let himself sink deeper into Dragon's head. He didn't consider whether he ought to, or worry about whether he had the skill to pull it off. He just let it happen.

It didn't take him long to figure out that something had happened while he slept. Something to shake Dragon deep down. Bear couldn't see the event, but whatever it was, it had come close to driving Dragon out of Shenandoah.

He'd almost left. He'd actually thought, however briefly, that Bear would have a better chance at happiness without him. Which was ridiculous. Mother, he'd even wondered if going back into the wilderness alone would be better than staying here and facing...what?

Wake up. Find out.

Bear opened his eyes. Dragon lay stretched out on the bed, lying on his left side with his head pillowed on his folded arm, watching Bear. The corners of his mouth curved up when he saw Bear wake, but the troubled crease between his eyes stayed put. "Did I wake you?"

"No. I feel like all I do is sleep lately anyway." Bear stroked Dragon's cheek. Raked his fingers through Dragon's hair. "What happened? You never came back yesterday. I was worried."

Dragon squirmed close enough to slip an arm around Bear's waist. "You're a Seer. You were in my head just now. I felt you."

So he knew. Bear nodded. "Yes." He debated telling Dragon

about Willow's offer, but decided now wasn't the time. First, he needed to find out what was troubling Dragon. "I couldn't see exactly what happened to you, though. Just that it hurt you, and it scared you. So much that you almost left me here alone."

Dragon closed his eyes. "I didn't, though. I couldn't. I would never do that to you."

The unhappiness in Dragon's voice made Bear ache for him. Rolling carefully onto his side, Bear wound an arm around Dragon and pulled him close. "Please tell me what happened."

Silence. Dragon rested his forehead against Bear's. Bear held him and waited.

"The council accused me of murderous intent toward innocents," Dragon said finally. "They sent Lucian and Valentine to bring me to trial."

Whatever Bear thought he'd hear, it wasn't that. He stared in shock. "Murderous intent toward... What? I don't understand."

"Willow looked into my mind and the council didn't like the things I was willing to do to protect you from being used by them." Dragon let out a bitter laugh. "Willow and Serafina both spoke for me, but in the end the only reason I went free was you. Because the council wants you, and they realized they couldn't have you without me."

Memories, images and feelings rolled from Dragon's mind. This time it all made more sense. Bear clenched a handful of Dragon's silk vest in his fist. "Mother-damn bastards."

"Yeah, well. At least I wasn't banished this time. That would've been a new record, I'm sure. Banished after one day in the tribe."

Bear heard the attempt at a joke, but he wasn't falling for it. He drew back enough to look into Dragon's eyes. "We'll go. As soon as I'm well enough, we'll leave. They won't try to stop us. We'll go and find somewhere else."

Dragon's eyes widened. "You can't be serious."

"I am." Bear hadn't known it before this moment, but even as he spoke he realized it was true. He'd gladly give up Shenandoah and everything about it in exchange for Dragon's happiness. Bear figured he himself could be happy anywhere Dragon was. "When my leg's healed, we'll leave here and find a place to call ours. Make our own home. Just us."

Dragon's fingers wound into the blanket bunched around Bear's hips. The pulse jumped hard and fast in his throat, right above the spot that always made him shiver when Bear kissed it. Bear gazed into his Brother's eyes and waited. Whatever Dragon decided, he'd take it and be content. Dragon meant home to him, wherever they happened to lay their heads. He'd decided that when it first dawned on him that he might not live to see Shenandoah.

Eventually, the feel of Dragon's mind softened. Lightened. Changed. He unfolded the arm under his head and laid his hand on Bear's cheek. "We worked too hard to get here, Bear. I won't let you throw all that away because of me. We're staying."

Stay. Bear couldn't help hoping. Still... "I want you to be happy."

Dragon traced Bear's cheekbone with his thumb. "Things won't be perfect. But I'll forgive them, I'll meet them halfway, if they'll give me a chance." His eyes searched Bear's face as if memorizing every line, angle and curve. "Whatever happens, I'll be happy as long as I'm with you."

Warmth blossomed in Bear's chest. He pulled Dragon close and kissed him, enjoying the soft, needy sound he made when their tongues slid together. It wouldn't be easy for Dragon to make a place for himself here after what had happened yesterday. Bear realized that. He had to trust his Brother to do it, though. It had taken time and hardship, but the roots of the trust between them went deep now.

When the kiss broke, Dragon rested his cheek against Bear's. "Well. That's it, then. We're home."

Bear buried his face in Dragon's hair. *Home is wherever you are, Brother.*

Somehow, he thought Dragon understood.

Epilogue

Bear loved the apple grove in spring. Loved the rustle of the leaves, the scent of the flowers, the way the light reflected off the mass of white blossoms.

Mostly, though, he loved that the grove lay outside Shenandoah's city gates. It meant he'd be the first to greet Dragon and the Pack patrol when they returned home.

He'd taken to waiting here the first time Dragon went out with the Pack on a long patrol. It was winter that time, and the snow had settled like apple blossoms on the bare branches. Since then, he'd come here every time Dragon was due home from patrol. Spring, summer, fall, another winter, now spring again. Each time, he left the city walls and waited out here until his Brother came back to him.

He didn't even mind anymore that he could no longer go on patrol himself, because of the limp that restricted him to a halting walk. The Pack had accepted him as one of their own, just as they'd accepted Dragon. No one seemed to care that he was the tribe's Seer as well.

It was one of the countless things he loved about his adopted home.

When he spotted the four figures moving down the road from the west, Bear made his way through the trees to the edge of the orchard. He stood and waited in his usual spot, his heart beating fast with anticipation. Dragon had been gone for twelve days this time. It felt like forever. Even though Bear had visited him every night in their mutual dreams, nothing took the place of having Dragon's body real and solid against his.

Finally, Dragon and his companions halted at the place where the road passed close to the trees. Lucian waved. "Good evening, Seer!"

"Good evening, Brother." Bear limped forward, grinning. "How did the patrol go? Did you find anything this time?"

"Oh, we found things all right." Dragon dropped his satchel on the ground and threw himself into Bear's arms, his face alight with an enthusiasm that wasn't entirely about coming home. "Kiss me and I'll tell you about it."

Ever since the patrol had found the ruins of an ancient town full of old-world artifacts high in the western mountains six moon-cycles ago, they'd made new discoveries every time they went back. Exciting discoveries that had changed their views of the old world and taught them things that promised to revolutionize tribal life. They didn't know the original purpose of the place, though survival seemed likely to be the primary reason it was built. Its construction differed in significant ways from other towns and cities of the ancients, with a closely grouped huddle of stone buildings inside a high, thick stone wall clearly built to withstand siege from the outside. However, judging from the sheer amount of information gathered in the place—in buildings, in metal boxes, in underground rooms that had collapsed and needed to be dug out—the town had also served as an archive of human knowledge.

In any case, it had yielded a wealth of information for Shenandoah. Bear was always as eager as the rest of the tribe to hear about whatever new discoveries the patrols made.

Laughing, Bear wound one arm around Dragon's waist and buried the other hand in his hair. "You don't need to bribe me into kissing you." He tilted his head downward and met Dragon in a hungry, open-mouthed kiss. His eyes closed, the better to take in the sweat-and-earth scent of Dragon's body, the taste of his mouth, the warmth of him pressed close.

When the kiss broke, Bear opened his eyes to look into Dragon's smiling face. Dragon snaked a hand down to squeeze his ass. "You know the electricity the ancients had to run their machines?" Bear nodded, and Dragon grinned. "We found plans for a device we think we can actually build to make it. To *make electricity*, Bear. Using water. Can you imagine what we could *do* with that?"

He couldn't, not really. He wasn't sure what they would do with electricity that they couldn't do without it. But he loved the way the idea made his Brother lean forward and bounce on his toes as if he wanted to chase after it right then and there. "That's an amazing find. The council's going to love it."

"Brothers, we should go." Sister Calista lifted the hand not linked with Brother Titus's and pointed toward the city gate. "The people will be waiting."

Dragon grimaced. Bear leaned down to kiss the worry line that automatically formed in the center of his forehead at any mention of the Shenandoah citizenry. By now, most people no longer whispered behind his back like they had in the beginning, and the steady flow of petitions to the council to banish or execute him had slowed to a trickle ages ago. But a steadfast minority of townspeople still shunned him. If it weren't for the Pack, who'd remained unwavering in their support, Bear wasn't sure he and Dragon would have stayed here after all.

Which made it particularly interesting that Dragon was now a people's hero of sorts for discovering the town in the western mountains, and thus all of the interesting and useful things inside.

"Why do they have to wait for us every time we come back?" Dragon drew out of Bear's arms, picked up his satchel and slung it over his shoulder. "They didn't used to do that."

"We didn't used to bring back such great things every time we came home," Titus pointed out. "We didn't even get as much good stuff from Harrisonburg as we've gotten from that town."

Taking Dragon's hand, Bear started toward the city. "Tell me what else you found."

Lucian outlined their finds—with frequent interruptions from his Brothers and Sister—while the group covered the short distance between the apple orchard and the city walls. The book detailing how to generate electricity using a water wheel was by far the most important discovery, but they'd also uncovered a few other relics of the long-lost past. Photographs. Two books. A bag made of some nearly indestructible substance and swirled with unnaturally bright colors. A flat, palm-sized black metal rectangle with a glass front whose purpose no one could figure out. Nothing happened when Bear pressed the indented spot on the front, though he felt it click.

Yes, the council would love these finds, as would the townspeople. Most of this city was every bit as curious about the old world as Bear.

Another reason he loved it here.

The road rounded a tremendous boulder, veered sharply to the left beneath a tulip tree older than Shenandoah and came within sight of the city walls less than a hundred paces away. A cheer rose from the crowds gathered at the gate and along the road just outside the city. Bear grinned as he handed the black rectangle back to Lucian. "I think you've been spotted."

"It would seem so, yes." He slapped Dragon's back. "Prepare yourself, Brother."

Bear smiled at the scowl on his Brother's face. Dragon still hadn't gotten used to being greeted with applause, cheers and flowers tossed in his path. Not to mention the occasional young lady expressing a desire to bear his children.

As they approached, the crowd grew louder. Titus and

Calista waved to the crowd, grasped hands and kissed cheeks. Lucian strode along greeting friends by name and nodding to everyone else. Dragon clung to Bear's hand, flashed the throng a fixed smile and walked as quickly as Bear's leg would let him.

Lucian broke from the group when they reached the southern edge of the market and hurried over to where his bondmate and their three children waited. Iris greeted him with a kiss and waved to the rest of the group. Lucian swung his youngest onto his hip, called good night to his Brothers and Sister and headed off with his family down a narrow side lane toward their house. Titus and Calista decided to stop and lift a mug or two of beer with friends before heading home, and Bear and Dragon continued on alone.

When they reached the flower stall, Dragon traded a bit of polished rose quartz for a bundle of white daisies and blood-red day lilies with a silk ribbon tied around the stems. He and Bear stopped at the young willow tree planted at the crossroads on the north side of the market. Dragon laid the bunch of flowers at the tree's base.

He followed the same routine after every patrol. Willow had died while he was out on long patrol with the Pack last spring. Though they'd grown to respect each other, he and Willow had never gotten past the wall Dragon's trial had put between them. She'd never shaken off her guilt, and Dragon had never been able to truly forgive her. Though he didn't say so out loud, Bear knew it bothered him that she'd died before the two of them could make their peace with one another. So he honored her memory after each patrol with flowers and a moment's silent contemplation.

After their stop at the willow tree, Bear and Dragon took the westward road leading to their house. The setting sun cast the trees' elongated shadows across the houses and gardens to either side of their path. The drone of bees passing from flower to flower, nearly constant in the middle of the afternoon, had quieted now in the cool of the evening. Somewhere nearby a goat bleated from behind someone's cottage. Bear caught the rank smell of it winding through the scents of grass, flowers and springtime herbs.

At the door of their bright little house, Dragon turned and wound both arms around Bear's waist. "I'm glad to be home, Bear. I missed you."

Bear gazed into Dragon's shining eyes, and his heart swelled. "I missed you too." He pulled Dragon close and grabbed a double handful of firm ass. He slipped a leg between Dragon's thighs. "Let's go inside, and I'll *show* you how much I missed you."

Predictably, Dragon's cheeks flushed. His cock filled and hardened against Bear's leg. He answered by fisting both hands in Bear's hair and kissing him brutally hard.

Bear fumbled for the door handle, found it and got them both inside without breaking the kiss. Dragon dropped his satchel and tore at the laces of Bear's buckskins. His fingers shook, his breath coming harsh and fast through his nose.

Before Bear's lust-hazed brain could coordinate his hands well enough to untie Dragon's pants, Dragon dropped to his knees, taking Bear's buckskins down as he went, and swallowed Bear's cock to the root.

"Oh, fuck." Bear fought to stay upright. Great Mother, but Dragon knew how to use his mouth. Bear gave his hair a tug. "Dragon. Wait. I want to fuck you."

Dragon pulled back enough to swirl his tongue around the head of Bear's prick, then slid his length back into his throat once more before pulling off of him. Sitting back on his heels, Dragon tilted his head sideways and gave Bear a wide-eyed look. "But I'm filthy."

Bear glared, and Dragon grinned. Bear liked to fuck him right after a patrol, with the sweat and dirt of the trail still on him. It reminded Bear of the time they'd spent in the wilderness together, searching for Shenandoah. A time when they'd had no one but each other. He didn't want to go back to that time, but he clung to a certain nostalgia for it anyway. Dragon knew it, and humored him even though he didn't understand it any more than Bear himself did.

Just because Dragon indulged his quirk, though, didn't mean he never teased him about it.

Bear stepped out of his moccasins and pants and kicked them aside. Bending down, he hooked his hands beneath Dragon's arms and hauled him to his feet. He ignored Dragon's indignant squawk. He'd felt the brush of arousal from his Brother's mind enough times to know that Dragon didn't hate being manhandled nearly as much as he pretended to.

Clenching Dragon's hair in one hand, Bear kissed him. He tasted faintly salty this time, the flavor of Bear's skin lingering on his lips. Bear stroked his tongue deep, and Dragon opened wide for him. *Mother, yes.* He loved that this man, one of the fiercest warriors Bear had ever known, surrendered his body so completely, so willingly, to Bear.

His mouth still latched to Dragon's, Bear snaked his free hand around Dragon's waist, lifted him right off his feet, and carried him to the shelves beside the woodstove. Dragon clung to Bear with both arms around his neck. Needy whimpers bled from his mouth to Bear's.

Setting Dragon on his feet in front of the shelves, Bear disentangled his hand from Dragon's hair and plucked the little bottle of oil from the shelf without even looking. He walked them sideways the two or three paces to the table.

It took him several attempts to put the bottle on the table right side up. By the time he managed, Dragon's shoulders shook with silent laughter and Bear was grinning so hard it was impossible to hold on to their kiss.

Deciding enough was enough, he pulled away and started

unlacing Dragon's shirt. "Not a word. I'm undressing you. Then you're bending over that table, and I'm having my way with you."

Dragon's eyes went heavy-lidded with a familiar desire, though amusement still showed in the curve of his lips. "You better *believe* you are."

Shaking his head, Bear laid a hand over Dragon's mouth before he could say anything else. "Hush. Shirt off."

Dragon obediently shucked his stained shirt. Bear took a moment to run both hands over Dragon's bare chest and belly, admiring the ridges of lean muscle, the hard brown nipples, the inevitable scars that shaped the story of a Pack Brother's life. Dirt streaked Dragon's skin. Bear leaned close, though he didn't need to, and sniffed. The smell of sweat and sun-warmed skin flooded his senses. His hips moved of their own accord, rutting against Dragon's belly.

The hard ache in his groin told him if he didn't act soon, he'd come right here, right now, like this, and he didn't want to. Taking hold of Dragon's shoulders, Bear turned him and pushed him face down across the table. "Stay."

Dragon stayed, his hands curled into loose fists on the tabletop. His chest rose and fell with quick, panting breaths. Bear bent to kiss the dark, puckered scar where the poisoned blade had cut Dragon's back. From there, he licked a trail to the sensitive spot at the back of Dragon's neck, moved the braid out of the way and bit down.

Dragon's back arched. "Oh. Bear."

Bear sucked hard. The skin in his mouth tasted hot and briny from hard work and a long day's walk in the sun. He let go and dragged the flat of his tongue over the purpling mark he'd left, over and over until he tasted nothing but his own saliva. Dragon moaned and squirmed beneath him. He gave Dragon's ass a sharp smack by way of telling him to be still. It didn't work, not that Bear had expected anything else.

Leaning sideways, Bear untied the knife sheath from Dragon's thigh, undid the belt around his hips and let belt, sheath and knife all drop unheeded to the floor. With the belt out of the way, it was only a moment's work to open the laces of Dragon's buckskins and shove them down his thighs.

Dragon let out a cry when Bear breached him with a single saliva-slicked finger. "Oh, fuck. Bear. Fuck me."

"Not yet."

Dragon wrapped both hands around the back of his head in obvious frustration. "*Bear...*"

"You've been gone twelve days, Dragon. Twelve days." Bear rubbed the pad of his finger over the spot inside Dragon that made him shudder and rock his hips. "You know I can't go that long without tasting you inside."

A violent tremor ran the length of Dragon's back. His hole clamped down hard on Bear's finger. "Yes." His voice came out in a hoarse whisper.

Pulling his finger out, Bear lowered himself carefully to his good knee, keeping the bad leg bent up. He yanked Dragon's buckskins down to his ankles. Dragon kicked off his moccasins, shook free of the pants and slid his feet apart just enough to put his ass at the perfect angle. The fact that he could do it without conscious thought made Bear grin. Evidently they used the table a lot.

Bear spread Dragon wide, buried his face in the damp crease and drew a deep breath. Mother, Dragon smelled good— dark and earthy, the musk of sex so strong it made Bear's head spin. He dug his thumbs in to force the dusky little hole open and plunged his tongue deep, savoring the bitter-salt flavor.

"Fuck! Fuck. Mother, oh." Dragon swayed backward. His left leg shook where it touched Bear's raised knee. "Bear. *Please.*"

Bear understood his Brother's desperation—he felt it

himself, his balls tight and aching between his legs—but he wasn't ready to stop. Not yet. He stroked one hand along the solid length of Dragon's shaft, drew the foreskin down, caressed the soft skin at the head of his prick with his fingertips. Cursing, Dragon reached back to grab a handful of Bear's hair, holding him in place. Not that Bear minded.

Once Dragon's pleas became incoherent and his hips rocked constantly between Bear's tongue and his hand, Bear pried Dragon's fingers loose of his hair and pushed to his feet. It only took a moment to open the oil, slick his cock and slide himself past the loosened ring of muscle into Dragon's body.

As always, the hot grip of Dragon's insides threatened to destroy Bear's control. He leaned over Dragon's back, one hand around his cock and the other planted on the table, nuzzling Dragon's hair while he fought to keep from coming.

Dragon didn't let him wait for long. He pressed backward in a clear signal to move. "Move," he growled, evidently thinking Bear wouldn't get the hint.

That single word killed the last of Bear's restraint. Bracing himself on the table, he slammed into Dragon as hard as he could, over and over and over again. He jerked Dragon's cock in the closest approximation to a rhythm he could manage while teetering on the edge of release.

"Oh, Mother, *fuck!*" Dragon's back bowed and he let loose a shout as he came, his seed flowing over Bear's hand.

Much as he'd like to make it last, Bear couldn't hold out against the rippling clutch of Dragon's ass around his prick. He came with his face buried in Dragon's hair and his fingers still curled around Dragon's cock.

Eventually, Dragon twisted around until he could kiss Bear's chin. "Fantastic."

"Mm. Agreed." Bear let go of Dragon's softened cock to stroke his hip. "I wish I could stay inside you forever."

Dragon laughed, forcing Bear partway out of him. "The council might not appreciate us walking around town like that."

"True. And I have enough trouble walking around already, some days." Bear straightened up and pulled out of Dragon's body. His seed trickled from Dragon's stretched hole. Bear caught some with his finger and sucked it off.

Pushing himself upright, Dragon turned and slipped his arms around Bear's waist. "Are you all right? Has your leg been giving you trouble?"

"No more than usual." Bear kissed the worry line between Dragon's eyes. "Dragon, come on. Still?"

Dragon's gaze cut sideways. "I can't help it."

Bear shook his head in fond exasperation. A lot of things had come out after they settled here. One of those things was Dragon's continued sense of guilt over Bear's injury. Every time Bear thought he'd gotten rid of it, he found he hadn't.

He cupped Dragon's jaw, forcing him to look Bear in the eye. "I was hunting. I would've gone hunting even if we hadn't fought. I've told you that so many times I've lost count."

"I know."

"But you don't believe it."

"I do. But if you hadn't been distracted—"

That was all Bear could take. He stopped Dragon with a hand to his lips. "Listen to me. What happened, happened. It's in the past. The reasons don't matter anymore. We can't change anything. And even if I could, I wouldn't."

Dragon stared. "For the Mother's sake, Bear, why not? You nearly *died*."

"Nearly. But I *didn't*. And because of that injury, and that infection afterward, this tribe found us, sought us out, and took us in. We might never have gotten here if it wasn't for that." Bear cradled his Brother's face between his palms. "I don't regret anything, Dragon. Not one minute of our life together.

Not even the bad times."

There were so many more things Bear wanted to say, but he couldn't quite put them into words. Like how he counted himself the luckiest man in the world when Dragon curled into his arms at night. How he loved Dragon's suspicious nature even though it frustrated him. Or how this tribe, this city, this neat little cottage, wouldn't feel like home without Dragon in it.

For several long seconds, Dragon's gaze searched Bear's face. Then his brow smoothed out. He rose onto his toes and kissed Bear's lips. "Thank you."

Bear held Dragon close in the fading light, his heart full and his mind at peace now that his Brother understood at last.

About the Author

Ally Blue is acknowledged by the world at large (or at least by her heroes, who tend to suffer a lot) as the Popess of Gay Angst. She has a great big penis hat and rides in a bullet-proof Plexiglas bubble in Christmas parades. Her harem of manwhores does double duty as bodyguards and inspirational entertainment. Her favorite band is Radiohead, her favorite color is lime green and her favorite way to waste a perfectly good Saturday is to watch all three extended version LOTR movies in a row. Her ultimate dream is to one day ditch the evil day job and support the family on manlove alone. She is not a hippie or a brain surgeon, no matter what her kids' friends say.

To learn more about Ally Blue, please visit www.allyblue.com/. Send an email to Ally at ally@allyblue.com, or join her Yahoo! group to join in the fun with other readers as well as Ally! http://groups.yahoo.com/group/loveisblue/.

Watch that first step. It could turn your life upside down.

Life, Over Easy
© 2010 K.A. Mitchell
Fragments, Book 1

Until a fall ended his Olympic diving career, John Andrews lived for the seconds he spent in the air. Now he's adrift on a college campus, grounded by paralyzing vertigo and double vision. Worse, he sees shimmering colors over everyone's heads.

The last is hardest to ignore, and impossible when it comes to Mason. While sex with the hot, moody computer major gives John a rush as heady as diving, Mason's the only person John's ever seen surrounded by *two* distinct colors.

Mason feels like a stranger in his own life. His lover is dead, and he drowns his guilt in bourbon and sex—until John's innocence reawakens the man he used to be. After Mason gives the young virgin a proper introduction to sex, he plans to send him on his way. But John sees too much to make things that easy.

For John, their connection is more than just sizzling sex, it's something worth fighting for. The more he learns about the colors, though, the more he realizes the free-spirited Mason isn't free at all. John doesn't take second place to anyone—even the dead.

Warning: Anyone wishing to read this title should be an adult, free from any condition that might be aggravated by the presence of a not-too-scary haunting, sizzling sexual chemistry, and angsty young men having mildly kinky sex. Other restrictions may apply. No additional equipment needed—unless you like that sort of thing.

Available now in ebook and print from Samhain Publishing.

Truth. Lies. A century-old mystery. What a tangled web…

Love, Like Ghosts
© *2009 Ally Blue*
A Bay City Paranormal Investigations story.

At age eleven, Adrian Broussard accidentally used his mind to open a portal to another dimension. Now, ten years later, he's successfully harnessed his strong psychokinetic abilities. In the process, he's learned the lessons which have become the guiding principles of his life. Absolute truth. Absolute control. Always.

Sticking to his personal code of ethics has never been a problem, until two chance meetings—one with a hundred-year-old ghost, one with a handsome, very-much-alive man—turn his orderly existence upside down.

Having grown up in a family of paranormal investigators, Adrian is intrigued by the spirit of Lyndon Groome and determined to solve the mystery of his death. Greg Woodhall, however, affects Adrian in unpredictable ways. Not only does his every touch challenge Adrian's hard-won control over his abilities, his company quickly becomes a light in Adrian's lonely life.

As the mystery surrounding Lyndon's death turns sinister, Adrian's relationship with Greg deepens into something serious. Something Adrian wants to keep. But intimacy isn't as easy as honesty, and when the heart's involved, the line between right and wrong can blur.

Warning: This book contains a gory ghost, a haunted castle, nerdy college parties and gay sex enhanced by psychic powers.

Available now in ebook and print from Samhain Publishing.

HOT STUFF

9 781609 281793